Not since Robin Cook's COMA has a suspense novel so vividly captured the drama—and dangers—of the medical profession . . .

## PRACTICE TO DECEIVE

"TAKES OFF LIKE A ROLLER COASTER! . . . TIMOTHY MILLER CREATES SOME REMARKABLE CHARACTERS, A STUNNING PLOT AND A BOOK THAT IS EXTRAORDINARILY HARD TO PUT DOWN."
—Baltimore Daily Record

"SHARP SURGICAL DETAIL . . . ENRICHED BY MILLER'S FIRSTHAND KNOWLEDGE OF HIS SUBJECT."
—Kirkus

"PRACTICE TO DECEIVE IS THE KIND OF NOVEL THAT GRIPS AND WON'T LET GO UNTIL THE VERY LAST LINE OF THE VERY LAST PAGE!"
—Wisconsin Bookwatch

"CHILLING!"—Orlando Sentinel

"ONE OF THOSE GREAT MEDICAL THRILLERS THAT HAS DEEPER SLICES THAN A SURGEON'S SCALPEL!"
—Ocala Star-Banner

"A CHILLER OF THE FIRST ORDER! . . . YOU CAN'T PUT IT DOWN."
—Inland Empire [CA]

# PRACTICE TO DECEIVE

## TIMOTHY MILLER

BERKLEY BOOKS, NEW YORK

PRACTICE TO DECEIVE

A Berkley Book / published by arrangement with
Donald I. Fine

PRINTING HISTORY
Donald I. Fine edition / April 1991
Published simultaneously in Canada by
General Publishing Company Limited
Berkley edition / March 1992

All rights reserved.
Copyright © 1991 by Timothy Miller.
This book may not be reproduced in whole or in part,
by mimeograph or any other means, without permission.
For information address: Donald I. Fine, Inc.,
19 West 21st Street, New York, New York 10010.

ISBN: 0-425-13206-4

A BERKLEY BOOK ® TM 757,375
Berkley Books are published by The Berkley Publishing Group,
200 Madison Avenue, New York, New York 10016.
The name "BERKLEY" and the "B" logo
are trademarks belonging to Berkley Publishing Corporation.

PRINTED IN THE UNITED STATES OF AMERICA

10  9  8  7  6  5  4  3  2  1

*Dedicated to*
*Matthew Christopher and Florence Algena*
*and to*
*surgeons who have devoted themselves to the*
*training and practice*
*of the art and science of plastic surgery*

This novel took many years to write, and during that time several individuals were very helpful.

Thanks first must go to Mabel J. Hendricks, who was there when it started, always supportive. George Diskant, Gene Wilder, K. Wilde and Loretta Barrett were honest critics. There are others to whom I owe a great deal. Special thanks to Shaye Areheart for her persistence and encouragement and to Lisa Eskow—a very perceptive and skillful editor.

"Oh, what a tangled web we weave
When first we practice to deceive!"

—Sir Walter Scott,
*Marmion VI*


"If anything is sacred the human body
is sacred."

—Walt Whitman,
*Leaves of Grass*
"I Sing the body electric"


"It is the divine right of man to appear human."

—Author Unknown,
Inscribed on an Italian
Cathedral, circa 1400

*1*

THE PATIENT WAS on the operating table, already covered by sterile sheets with the exception of her breasts, which were perfectly framed by sterile towels. Illuminated brightly by a pair of dish-shaped ceiling lamps, her breasts appeared level and quite flat, a precise rectangle of flesh adrift in a sea of green.

"How are we doing, sweetheart?"

"Sweetheart," a blonde twenty-year-old Pan Am stewardess, was heavily sedated. She mumbled incoherently from beneath the tent that shielded her face.

Morrie Gold, M.D., director, The Gold Institute of Surgical Rejuvenation/South America, injected a local anesthetic, first in the fold beneath each breast then, with the long needle, penetrating the skin deeply over both sides of the chest. From Sweetheart there was only a deep, pharmacologically induced sigh. Oblivion from pain. Morrie liked that. Control over pain was at the very core of what it meant to be a physician. What could be more satisfying? He knew the answer to that too: the ability to give someone a new body. A new sense of self.

And then there was the money.

Morrie waited impatiently for his dark-skinned surgical nurse to hand him the scalpel. "Señora!" All the while, his eyes were focused on his operative field, specifically on the fold of skin beneath each breast where he would make the incisions. He waited for the skin to blanch as the

1

adrenaline within the anesthetic squeezed the blood from the capillaries.

The nurse, of mixed white and Indian descent, still lived in one of the villages in the hills around Bogotá. She placed the scalpel gently in his palm. Morrie looked up angrily. Mestizas! He missed the smart, sharp slap with which Mrs. Evans back home in Los Angeles (The Gold Institute of Surgical Rejuvenation/North America) handed him a scalpel. "Señora," he said, firmly grabbing her wrist. The woman's black eyes widened. He opened her gloved palm and slapped the scalpel into it with a loud pop.

"Sweetheart," he said to his patient, "you just wouldn't believe how dumb they are down here. Poverty. It rots the brain."

Morrie cleared his throat and made the incision, a line about three inches long. The skin separated with very little bleeding. He continued talking to Sweetheart, although with the heavy sedation she heard essentially nothing.

"Perfect!"

Without a word, the nurse took the knife and replaced it with a pair of blunt-nosed scissors. Morrie cut into the fatty, now bloodless tissue until the rust red of the pectoralis major muscle appeared in the depth of the small wound. "Beautiful!" He inserted his index finger into the opening and with violent, probing motions forcefully separated the breast tissue from the muscle, creating a space between them. The surgical task was accomplished in a matter of minutes.

Then he glanced over at the implants on the green draped Mayo stand behind him. The opaque white hemispheres were the size of a softball cut in half. Morrie had warned the mestiza never to touch them, squelching her curiosity with a tone in his voice that told her she was not good enough to touch them.

Morrie reached for an implant, holding it in his hand as though weighing it. He nodded, speaking to the nurse. "And now I'm going to change this young woman's whole life. Until now she would never run naked on the beach the way you can. Or make love in the sunlight. It has nothing to do with what color you are, my dear. Or how much money you have. It all comes down to this." Smiling triumphantly, he held up the implant. "All right, sweetheart," Morrie said to his patient before pushing the implant into the pocket he had just created. "One pair of gorgeous knockers coming up!"

# 2

THE PILOT CIRCLED the makeshift landing strip and two flashing lights signaled that it was safe to land. The altimeter read 12,500 feet above sea level.

In the first minutes of morning, the sun reflected only the softest shades of pink and gray from the severe mountainous landscape below. The thin air that swept across the Cordilleras was barely sufficient to keep the twin-engine Cessna in control as it began to descend. The engine's roar became a high-pitched whine, straining to propel the plane to a small field carved out of the forest. The pilot shook his head. He should have asked for more money.

Not that he wasn't experienced in unusual landings. He rarely landed at airports that had names. Indeed, he rarely landed at airports of any kind. But this one was pushing it. As the plane descended rapidly, the pilot saw an Indian in a bowler hat waiting next to three llamas whose elegant necks were roped together in a line. Their shoulders were covered with brightly embroidered packs.

The plane landed with a jolt severe enough to startle the llamas, but the man in the bowler didn't flinch. The pilot taxied to the other end of the field, then doubled back so he could take off into the wind. At the end of the strip of dirt, a tiny house made of sticks was the only evidence that anyone had even set foot on this barren plain high in the northern limits of the Andes. As he opened the cockpit door, the icy air knifed through his thick windbreaker. Swept up from the valley below, the gusts were strong and sudden, coming like a series of explosions. It would make the takeoff that much more difficult.

"I should have asked for more money," the pilot mumbled again, as his breath made puffs of steam. The dark small man in the bowler led the reluctant llamas toward the plane. Without exchanging a word, the pilot gave the Indian a legal-sized envelope. The Indian walked over to the lead llama and unstrapped a small suitcase wrapped by rope fashioned into handles. He lifted it with great effort, and it took the two of them to carry it to the plane. Both men were breathing heavily in the thin air, exhaling small white clouds. They did not speak. The only sound was that of the wind that swept upward, harsh and icy.

The pilot, wondering how much the Indian was being paid, turned back to the plane. But he took no more than two steps before he stopped. He heard something. It didn't matter what: any sound was a threat. He bolted for the cockpit, started the engines and headed straight into the gusting wind. As he approached the end of the field, he saw four men pointing rifles at him. A fifth man, wearing mirrored sunglasses, smoked a cigarette and watched.

The engines sputtered into a smooth hum as the pilot realized they were shooting at him. He felt a familiar wave of nausea. Despite the cold that surrounded him, his hands were suddenly wet. The plane gathered speed. The gusts of wind seemed to grab at the wings and the pilot felt the reassuring lift off the ground. In a comparatively long career of fast exits, this was as close as he had ever come. The pilot promised himself that this was the last time.

A moment after the plane took off, the left engine stopped turning the propeller. The right engine cried out, unable to keep the plane aloft. Bullets had penetrated the engine casing. The pilot had only enough time to look out the window and see the man in the mirrored sunglasses wave goodbye as the Cessna lunged suddenly in the direction of the now-silent engine. The pilot's last thought was that he should have asked for more money.

# 3

LUISA OBREGON HAD been prima ballerina with the Ballet de America Latina. She performed *Giselle* and *Swan Lake*, receiving standing ovations at opera houses throughout the Americas and Europe before retiring at the height of her career to dance off with coffee king Antonio Obregon. For nearly five years, the Obregons traveled from royal weddings and Hollywood funerals to charity balls and Broadway opening nights. There had been Windsors and Kennedys; then there were the Obregons.

In the six months since her husband's death, Luisa Obregon withdrew from the international charities that had previously benefited from her imprimatur. The coming-out had been a typically flamboyant affair, superbly orchestrated, culminating in the announcement that it was now time for charity to begin at home. There was a vague reference to the tarnished reputation of her country, a plea for nationalism that gracefully slid into a gentle moral statement recorded photographically and journalistically in all the important magazines and papers. Luisa cut the ribbon for her newest project, the Gold Institute of Surgical Rejuvenation/S.A., which offered indigent Colombians the means to correct the disfiguring birth defects of their children, reconstruct burn deformities or repair whatever might be the consequence of living in an impoverished place. Luisa, with her world-famous face, angular and brooding, a face that depended upon the olive complexion and radiant black hair of her Indian heritage rather than the slightest hint of cosmetics, was the ideal champion for this celebrated cause.

Luisa's car screeched to a halt in front of the Gold Institute. She ran from her white Mercedes SL560, ignoring the vehicle's irate beep that signaled she had left the door open. She effortlessly bounded three steps at a stride and opened the door as if she were throwing a discus in the Olympics. The hurried motions were exquisitely graceful and powerful, as much Odette-Odile as the widow recently out of mourning of one of the richest men in South America.

Without pausing to return the guard's greeting, she hurried through a door marked *SE PROHIBE LA EN-TRADA*.

The click of her heels on the tile floor echoed the anxious pumping of her heart. She turned the corner, not stopping to acknowledge the smile from a little girl with a bandage covering half her face. Luisa keyed in the entry code on the unmarked door in front of her. It slid open and she rushed into the marble foyer, breaking into a run as she headed down the hallway, shouting, "Morris!"

But Morrie Gold couldn't hear her. He was in the shower. He was in the shower with his surgical nurse. Luisa opened the door to find the mestiza on her knees, rubbing soap onto Morrie's legs.

Luisa reached in and grabbed hold of the nurse's arm. *"Pare! Es suficiente! Salga!"* She threw the nurse a towel and pointed her out of the room. Morrie began to laugh. Slowly, Luisa turned off the water. She glared at Morrie for a moment. Before he could respond she said coldly, "I told you it was stupid. When will you listen to me? The Indian is dead." She slapped his face and stormed back down the corridor.

# 4

LIONEL STERN LOOKED more like a linebacker than a plastic surgeon. Large and muscular, his rough facial features stretched the definition of handsome. Unlike most plastic surgeons in Los Angeles he saw his patients at University Hospital, a huge red-brick monolith where all types of medicine and surgery were taught, practiced and flourished. It was a very busy place with a defined hierarchy. The residents wore white uniforms, the medical students short white coats. After four years of medical school, two years in the army, four years of general surgery training and two years of plastic surgery residency, Stern wore a long white laboratory coat that signified he was a member of the surgical faculty. The coat was always neatly pressed, the back wrinkleless, testimony that he had not sat down since he had put it on at five-thirty that morning. His shoulders completely filled the usually loose-fitting coat.

A man in his late thirties, Stern trusted few people except himself. He had few friends, even fewer enemies. There was little that he allowed to show that could cause anyone to dislike him. He did his best to avoid socializing with other faculty. Since his divorce he rarely socialized with any group larger than two or three.

Lionel didn't belong to a country club or play tennis or golf on Wednesdays; he operated on Wednesdays. He operated just about every day of the week. Most of his time both day and night was spent surrounded by the green tile of an operating room. He rarely wore street clothes except early in the morning before he changed into the green scrub suit he wore for the remainder of the day and quite often into the night.

After giving a lecture to the third-year medical students, Lionel walked briskly to his office, noticing that the two gurneys outside had been in the sixth-floor corridor since the day before. His secretary greeted him with a smile, a steaming cup of coffee and an apology. "I spoke to them about the gurneys. Twice."

He smiled and slowly shook his head. "Would you mind making it three? Don't I have a patient to see before surgery? They're going to think they're in Beirut."

He walked across the light brown carpet, past the sand-colored sofas, rust textured walls and the aquarium. A large neon yellow fish was chasing a small blue one. The small blue one was much quicker. Must be younger. Stern stopped and proudly adjusted the bright geometric print on the wall. "Art Institutionale" he whispered. Like the aquarium, it had been put in the waiting room after countless phone calls and several threatening letters to the hospital administrator. The geometric had replaced mustard-colored chrysanthemums.

Lionel sank down heavily into his desk chair, and it responded with a high-pitched squeak, as if injured by the impact. He picked up the messages that had accumulated on his desk and dealt them like playing cards. *Medical School admissions committee meeting 6 P.M. tomorrow.* That meant sitting around a table for hours with stale sandwiches while a bunch of long-winded socialist basic scientists who hadn't taken care of a patient in years decided whom to educate and train to take the Hippocratic Oath. Have to show up for that one, he thought, or else they'll fill the next class with sandal-wearing do-gooders who want everybody to be happy but can't spell their names. *Time* magazine. *Telephone interview about "What Plastic Surgery Will Be Like in Fifty Years."* Better set some time aside for that one. *Mme. Germont, wife of the finance minister, Brussels, would like a private consultation at her home. Can you fly over for the day?* Stern printed "No" on the message and sailed it into the out box. *Jason Smiley. Real Estate investment. Limited partnership. Substantial write-off due to leverage structure of the financing.* Wrong plastic surgeon, Jason. If you want, call my ex-wife, he sighed. The paper twirled down into the trash. *Dr. Stoltman. Bakersfield. Wants to refer 45 y/o man with extensive basal cell CA of nose.* "OK," he wrote. Must be a really large tumor for Stoltman to call. Lionel glanced at his watch, put down the messages and reached for the phone. He dialed Casey's private line.

"Dr. Crawford," she answered briskly with her husky voice. Casey's voice was more powerful than five cups of coffee.

"Alone at last."

A short pause. "I've been meaning to call you."

"And here I thought only housewives had midmorning sexual fantasies."

"Lion, about the reception tonight . . ."

"I don't think I'll be out of the operating room until at least eight . . ."

"Eight means nine. I need you at six."

"Oh, come on, Casey. Even if I got through early, you know how I feel about cocktail parties."

"Oh, come on, Lion. You know how *I* feel about cocktail parties. This is business for me. Important business. We're meeting with the people in the attorney general's office and the director of the BMQA will be there. I'm making a pitch for some more staff. I can't do my job with so few people. We have two hundred complaints a month from patients and I just can't keep up. I've written letters, but they didn't do any good. Tonight I can twist a few arms."

"Can't you twist them without me? What am I supposed to do—hold them down while you do?"

There was no response. He could only imagine her expression on the other end of the phone.

Dr. Casey Crawford was chief investigator for the Los Angeles district of the Board of Medical Quality Assurance. The daughter of Ellsworth Crawford, Lionel's advisor and mentor throughout medical school, Casey had met Lionel when she was a college freshman and he was married to Ginny. She was as stubborn then as she was now.

"Lion, I told you last night, I'm not going to another of these receptions alone. I don't know what to do to make myself understood."

Lionel and Casey were back at square one, a place they found themselves all too frequently of late. Lionel blamed it all on parents—this time, Casey's. When Casey was in college, her mother had divorced Ellsworth to find a new life that didn't include emergencies and a twenty-four-hour involvement with surgery. Medicine had allowed them no time to be together. To please her father, Casey finished medical school but, to please her mother, never went into practice. Instead she channeled her respect for the medical profession into a nine to five job in which all loose ends could be tied up by the end of the day or put on hold until morning. She was determined to normalize her life and have a real relationship. Casey vowed never to marry a doctor. Then she met Lionel.

"But you don't understand," he began. "When I'm done I'll take you to a romantic restaurant." Lionel had tried to conceal, at first to himself, that he had fallen very deeply in love, perhaps further into what he perceived to be quicksand than he could control. And control had become a very important issue indeed.

Half laughing, Casey quipped, "What the hell would you do in a romantic restaurant?"

"What kind of crack is that?"

"It's a compliment." She paused. Her voice changed tone. "I've been sitting here checking the staff's performance ratings and I couldn't get you out of mind."

He hunched forward. "How do I rate?"

Her voice grew soft. "After last night, they should make you surgeon general."

"Then it's settled," he said.

"Yes. I'll be ready for you at six."

"I can't!"

"You won't."

"I'll be in the operating room! Casey, why don't you go, and then sneak out and meet me at about nine?"

"I told you. I don't want to. I will not go alone."

Lionel paused. He considered the unfamiliar reality that part of him said "go" to a cocktail party where he wouldn't know anyone. But that wasn't what was in his mind. Casey Crawford was in his head. It was unfamiliar territory, attractive and intimidating all wrapped up together. "So where does that leave us?"

"Maybe it's about time I find someone who can show up before the wee hours of the morning."

His voice quickly had an edge. "How the hell do you think it makes me feel? Especially after last night?"

"That's the whole point, Lion. How do you think it makes *me* feel? Especially after last night."

"I'm afraid this conversation is too Zen." He paused, unfamiliar territory indeed.

"Sorry, Lion, I have another call. Can I put you on hold?" Without waiting for an answer, Casey pressed the button.

Lionel, knowing that he was speaking only to himself, said, "No." Then he hung up. It had become a battle. No, it was now a war. Again it was parents. And it was control. Worse yet, so far as Lionel was concerned, it could be much more serious than that.

His secretary knocked on the door and opened it. She looked hesitant and apologetic. "Mrs. McWaters? She said, when she called, that it was an emergency. That's why I put her in so early. I'm sorry, Dr. Stern, but I'm afraid . . ."

"I'll take care of it." Lionel nodded and took the file from her. He stepped into the waiting room. "Mrs. McWaters?"

Elizabeth McWaters was in her late forties. A prototype of the west Los Angeles matron, she was neatly attractive, round full face, blonde hair helped by sunlight and a judicious use of bleach. Slightly overweight, stocky, girlish, she wore a conservative dark blue suit and a white silk cravat carefully tucked upward so that it covered most of her very full and very wrinkled neck. Her plump, well-tanned cheeks made her face look much heavier than the rest of her thick but athletic figure. At hearing Lionel's voice, she turned her head to the side, looking at him from the corner of her eyes, her body language suggesting that she deferred to men. Elizabeth McWaters wore no makeup.

"Doctor." There was a definite tone of relief in her voice, as if she had reached an aid station after weeks in the jungle.

Lionel smiled, waited for her to enter his office and closed the door.

"How can I help you, Mrs. McWaters?" It was Lionel's standard opening. Professionally or otherwise, small talk was a foreign language.

She smiled nervously. "According to Dr. Simmons, there's nothing you can't do."

You could ask Casey Crawford about that, the thought flashed. Lionel was about to compliment Simmons, who had made the referral, but noticed his patient hesitating. He waited for her to continue.

The confession came out in a rush. "I didn't wear any makeup and if you think it didn't take guts to walk out of my house looking like this. My house? My bedroom! But I wanted you to see me the way I really am. The painful truth."

"What about your face concerns you?" he asked gently.

"Well, you're the doctor!" There was a long moment of silence between them. "What do you think?" she asked with a certain desperation.

"I usually let the patient tell me."

"Maybe it's too late. Have I waited too long? Am I beyond salvage?"

"Salvage?" Lionel smiled thinly.

"I look like an overweight chipmunk. With wrinkles. I look tired, a hell of a lot worse than I feel." She sighed in resignation. "Gravity finally won the war. But, Doctor, I want you to know I gave it one hell of a fight. I've tried every face cream in every magazine and every fad diet the 'Tonight Show' has to recommend. But it seems to be growing obvious, they're no match for genetics." Her mouth tightened, then she whispered, "I look just like my mother."

"How old is your mother?"

"Seventy-two." Then she smiled. "I know. I don't look a day over sixty."

"You're a very attractive woman, Mrs. McWaters."

"Maybe I was once upon a time. But not now. I *must* get rid of this." She grasped her throat, pulling the redundant skin defiantly in Stern's direction. "Can you do it, Doctor?"

"I think so. It would involve a face-lift. Tightening the facial skin. I make an incision in the hair of the temple and down in front and inside the ear to hide the scars as much as possible."

"Scars?" she exclaimed with uncamouflaged horror. "I don't want any scars. I have enough wrong with my skin."

"I'm afraid it's a reality neither of us can avoid. If you make an incision, and that's what you do in surgery, you create a scar. But where you place the incisions and how they're sutured can make a big difference."

"But can't you use a laser?"

"Not for a face-lift."

"But . . . I read about lasers being used in plastic surgery . . . so there won't be any scars."

Stern paused and shook his head slightly. "I'm afraid you can't believe everything you read these days, particularly when it deals with plastic surgery."

"I'm disappointed. I hadn't planned on scars." She fumbled with the cravat, asking, "What about this new suction method? I thought that doesn't leave scars."

"It does, but they're very small. The problem is you have a good deal of extra skin in your neck and your cheeks, and while the liposuction removes the subcutaneous fat, it doesn't do anything about the redundant skin."

Libby McWaters's eyes grew very moist, then tears formed and came down from the corners. She reached for her purse and opened it. Then she looked up. "My husband was a lifeguard when I met him." She sat in the chair as though it were a witness stand. From her purse, she took out an envelope and handed Lionel the evidence.

It was an old photo of her and her husband, a worrisome symbol of an expectation and hope that could never be realized. "None of us can go backward in time, even with the best plastic surgery," he said softly.

Her voice grew tense. "Well, I'll tell you, he hasn't aged a day in the past twenty-five years." She reached for a handkerchief. "It isn't fair. Why does it only happen to men? That ability to age and become even more attractive?"

This patient wanted more than plastic surgery. "Your husband?"

"He looks better than ever, and I'm going downhill on roller skates. These wrinkles. This fat turkey neck. I scare myself when I look in the mirror. Why shouldn't I scare him?" She began to cry. "He left me two days ago. What I'm afraid of, Doctor, is that I won't be able to get him back."

Lionel waited a moment and touched her arm gently. "Mrs. McWaters, do you believe that your husband left you because of some wrinkles?"

"He didn't stick around long enough to give me an explanation. He just left. Now he's living with his floozy secretary. From what I hear." She reached for his hand and held it tight. "Dr. Stern, my doctor told me you were the best. If anyone can get him back for me, you can."

"I can't do that. Plastic surgery is not a cure for marital problems. I'm afraid no surgeon can give you what you're asking for." Over the years Lionel had begun to develop an odd, but very real appreciation for vanity—that primitive, but reasonably predictable urge that made people simply want to look good for themselves. It was much easier to deal with when it did not involve expectations of achieving some secondary goal, another person, a change in career. He tried to withdraw his hand, but she held on.

"Doctor, you're married, aren't you?"

"No."

She was surprised. "No?"

"Divorced."

"Wouldn't you know. I walked right into the enemy camp."

"I did not divorce my wife. She left me." He cleared his throat. "And that's really beside the point. Mrs. McWaters, I'm no expert, but I don't think men leave their wives because of wrinkles."

She sat back in the chair and took a deep breath, her head nodding slowly. "You're right, of course." She looked up as if she suddenly understood what it was all about. "I should have my eyes done, too. Doctor, you don't understand. I need surgery and I need it now! I need the bags under my eyes to go. I need to get rid of my turkey neck, my sagging breasts, my flabby thighs, my lardy hips, and I want a flat stomach too. I want you to put one of those vacuum cleaners inside me and suck out everything from nineteen sixty-five on. I'm in a hurry, Doctor. That's why I told your secretary it was an emergency. It is! He's out there, somewhere in the Valley with this, this woman, and I don't know how much time I have left."

Elizabeth McWaters had long before crossed the point of no return with Lionel Stern—that moment when it became clear that desperation had taken over for common sense, when medicine crossed over to a trivial fashion choice or a quick solution for some problem a surgeon, no matter how skilled, could never touch with a scalpel. Lionel considered himself more than anything a reconstructive surgeon. He rebuilt the body in all its various locations with a scalpel and suture in an operating room. He repaired cleft lips and softened burn scars, and he never backed away or apologized for the indisputable fact that what he did made people *look* better. And that very much included cosmetic surgery too—something he did often and without apology to the doctors who made locker room remarks about his "going to the beauty parlor" while on route to do what they did *inside* their patients' bodies, away from what was immediately visible. Elizabeth McWaters was the kind of patient that Lionel had, for the most part, avoided, not intentionally, by locating his office within the confines of the hospital. No parking validation, party invitations, cappuccino, or international editions of *Vogue* stacked neatly in the waiting room. There was no question about it, he knew that he would not—no, he could not operate on this sad woman.

"Well, I want everything, and I mean everything, done."

"You've outlined a rather extensive program."

"Oh, don't worry. I can afford it."

"I wasn't referring to money. Frankly, I'm concerned about your expectations."

She held up the photo. "This is what I want. It's me, not someone else. Just me. That's all."

Lionel got up and sat on the edge of his desk. "With or without your husband?"

"Doctor Stern, you do your part, and I'll do mine."

"Mrs. McWaters, I can't make you into a twenty-five-year-old woman."

"That's not what they say on television. None of the ads I see . . ."

"That's not all they don't tell you." Stern spoke as gently as he could. "I don't think . . . I would feel comfortable doing surgery." He hesitated as he saw the devastation on her face. "You might want . . . to discuss this with your doctor."

"He told me to come here!"

"I'm glad he did." He reached out for her hand. "Mrs. McWaters, I'm not certain this is the best time for you to have the surgery. I understand how upset you are, but what we're talking about is a matter of elective surgery and I've always interpreted that as being elective for the surgeon as well as the patient. I would urge you to get a second opinion, from someone Dr. Simmons recommends."

"You expect me to listen to that quack after he sent me here?" She stood up indignantly, her voice now an octave higher. "What the hell is the matter with you? You only do movie stars or something? My money isn't good enough?" Her eyes were once again growing moist.

"I don't think cosmetic surgery will bring your husband

back," he said softly. "You've got to want to do this for yourself, not because it will change your life or solve your problems. It rarely does. I would be happy to give you the name of a good marriage counselor."

Libby McWaters stared at him for several long moments, then stood up and walked out the door.

# 5

THE OPERATING ROOMS were located at the very bottom of University Hospital. Placed below ground for maximum protection against earthquakes, the labyrinth of twenty green-tiled rooms was an isolated place, accessible only through two locked doors controlled by an intercom and a video camera. Inside, the air was chilled. Most of the fixtures and furniture were made of metal. They were cold to the touch.

Lionel approached the operating-room door that led to the locker room as John Maltry, chief resident in plastic surgery, was coming out. A slender man with black hair and large black glasses, Maltry winked. "Thought I'd get the jump on you for a change."

"You'll have to do more than get here early."

"Felix's X rays are up on the view box. Anesthesia is trying to get their act together. Christ, those guys are slow. Even Sweeny moves like an old lady." Maltry put on the yellow cotton wraparound gown required for anyone wearing a surgical scrub suit outside of the operating room. "Got to run down to the ER. Somebody was sober enough to use his garage opener but too damn drunk to find the brake pedal."

"His face?"

"The ER docs are looking for the rest of it." Maltry tied his gown with a one-handed surgeon's knot. "I may have to add him on after Felix." Maltry groaned. "Bet you a week's salary this is going to be a very long day."

Lionel smiled. "Don't kid yourself, John. You don't make a week's salary."

Maltry nodded toward the coffee room. "Someone's waiting for you. He put on greens like he knows what he's doing. Except he looks nervous as a cat. Downright scared."

"He is," Lionel replied. "That's why he's here."

Maltry waited for an explanation.

"Dr. Dalway is going to observe. I may even have him scrub in."

"Visiting plastic surgeon?"

"He's a urologist." Lionel saw the expression change on Maltry's face, the curve of his mouth asking why a urologist would scrub in on a craniofacial surgical procedure. But if Stern wanted him here, there must be a good reason, although try as he might, Maltry couldn't think of one.

"See you later, John," Lionel said, not offering an explanation. He was annoyed with Peter Dalway for not covering his nervousness better. But, of course, if Peter could have handled things better, he wouldn't be here in the first place.

Lionel walked down the corridor with a graceful, athletic precision. It was a very subtle strut that contained just a hint of narcissism. Both in and out of the operating room, his methodical, soft-spoken manner almost camouflaged an intense physical power that he held under conscious control.

Halfway to the coffee room, Lionel turned and went downstairs to the observation dome over OR 9, one of the four ORs designed to allow medical students and physicians to view surgical procedures. He looked down and saw the enormous frame of Norma Schultz dressed in scrubs that had to be specially made for her. She was laying out instruments with her usual casual ease. Lionel tapped the glass with his knuckle. Norma looked up and gave him the finger. It was a favorable sign. She was in a good mood.

When he had asked Norma to be his circulating nurse, her gruff, pain-in-the-ass agreement almost covered her appreciation of the implied flattery. Norma intuitively understood sick people and what surgery could do for them. She knew how to find special instruments and how to deal with the varied but substantial egos of the individuals who held the scalpels. She had the rare ability to make things happen in an arena where any number of details could fuse into a formidable obstacle. With Norma around, Lionel could afford to ignore some of them.

He smiled, enjoying the way people, glistening instruments and machines came together, the OR's sterile personality redefined by the type of surgery performed and the people who made it run. Lionel had arrived early because he knew that the pace established in that first hour was crucial. Insignificant delays—the orderly picking up the patient a few minutes late, the anesthesiologist having trouble starting the IV, the file clerk not finding the X rays, the nurse not being able to read the handwriting on the scheduling slip and picking the wrong instruments—those crucial minutes could add hours to the time when he would finally close the incision that evening.

Lionel walked into the coffee room. Peter Dalway was sitting at one of the empty tables, watching the closing minutes of Captain Kangaroo on the wall-mounted television set. In front of him were three empty milk cartons and two untouched cups of coffee whose surfaces were covered with half-smoked cigarettes.

"Looks like you're off to an early start, Peter."

"Looks can be deceiving," he responded without looking up.

Lionel stared at him. Although Peter was still in his late thirties, his boyish good looks had rapidly begun to age. California-handsome, his face devoid of wrinkles, Peter was blond, tan and had the build of a surfer. But there was the slightest yellow hue to his skin and a sluggish quality about his eye movements.

"Okay, Doc. Up and ugly," Lionel said with forced enthusiasm. "Time to get the show on the road." Sipping his coffee, Lionel walked to the dressing room, with Peter trailing close behind.

As Lionel opened his locker, Peter pointed to the surgical

journals on the shelf inside. "If you don't know where to put the chisels by now, better cancel the case."

Lionel took off his lab coat, shirt and tie. "Easy for you plumbers to say. Either the water doesn't run or the faucet is stuck. Ream it out or make it go in some other direction." Lionel grunted as he reached for a set of sea green scrubs from the stack marked Large. "And, if that doesn't work, just put a catheter in it. Not much to it, is there?"

Peter didn't laugh. He was staring at Lionel's chest. The shrapnel wound just below his right clavicle had contracted to a shiny stellate scar half the size of a silver dollar. It curved around his right chest and had faded so that it was barely visible. Peter turned away and lit a cigarette. "So. What's it to be? Another of your FLKs?"

"My man Felix isn't going to be a funny-looking kid much longer. Not when I get done with him," Lionel said, putting on his scrub pants. "He's going to look like a nine-year-old Tom Selleck."

Peter raised his hand dramatically. "For God's sake, Lion, leave off the mustache!"

But Lionel didn't laugh. "So, how come you're up and at 'em so early this morning?"

"Never went to sleep."

"Nervous?"

Peter shrugged. "Not that I noticed." He dropped his cigarette into a cup. It went out with a hiss. "Maybe. I was a little edgy about this morning."

"Some woman?"

"Two actually."

"Two? What do you mean, two?"

"As in, one plus one equals two." Peter flashed a smile that had a gleeful, contagious energy, but Lionel's face was impassive. "You know the tall nurse in the recovery room?"

"The slinky one? Irene?" The pitch of Lionel's voice moved up.

"Well, she has a roommate. That's how I arrived at number two."

"My god."

"I'm a little nervous about this whole thing. Haven't slept

well for months. I needed some company last night, that's all. Working in these community ERs you get so that you don't know day from night. Hell, they're not even ERs really. Sore throats and runny noses. Rewriting a Valium prescription is as close as you come to an emergency."

"How are you feeling?" Lionel asked, pulling on what looked like a pajama top.

"A little tired."

"I mean about the operating room," Lionel said with visible irritation.

"So far, so good, I guess. Feels pretty good to be back," Peter said, taking a deep drag from another cigarette. "But I don't know really. We're not there yet."

Lionel finished his coffee in a single gulp. It was his sixth cup. "Time to get you out of these doc-in-the-box places and back where you belong."

"Wish it were that easy. Believe me, I've tried. Give me credit—you haven't seen me on television, plugging bulimia." He blew a perfect smoke ring. "Tough to make people forget."

"Other people can forget. I just wonder if you can, Peter. Leave the past where it belongs. You've had some rough times," Lionel said firmly.

"Yeah, and the Elephant Man had a little touch of puffy eyelids," Peter replied.

Lionel went back into the coffee room and poured more coffee. When he was not in the operating room, his left hand always held a cup.

"That stuff is terrible. You're going to drop dead one of these days from an overdose of that shit. It'll kill you, sure as hell. Burn a hole right down the center of your stomach." Peter sighed, watching Lionel finish the coffee. "Do you know how many urologists are on the west side of Los Angeles? Have any idea? Too many!" Peter exclaimed. "Before long, they're going to start operating on themselves. Too much competition out there."

"From the way you look this morning, it's possible you could try a little harder to get a practice together. You know, that old hard-work ethic—the early bird. That sort of thing." Almost as if on cue, Lionel felt a burning in his stomach, reached into his pocket and popped two Maalox tablets into his mouth.

"Sounds good when you say it, but I've tried it, believe me. I've gone to all the medical staff conferences at every hospital on this side of town I can think of. Hell, last few weeks I've hung around doctors' dining rooms trying to get a referral until they thought I was one of the busboys." Another cloud of smoke. "Sometimes I don't even know if I want to be a urologist anymore. Everyone figures you open up prostates and treat VD." Peter blew a very large smoke ring. "Now, plastic surgery! That's what's happening out there," he exclaimed. "Tell someone you're a urologist and they smile. Polite kind of smile. But tell them you're a plastic surgeon and they'll talk your arm off. Take a crowbar to get away."

"You figuring a change in careers?" An affirmative answer would not have come as a great surprise. At this point, with Peter, anything was possible.

"No, that's just about the only thing I haven't considered." Peter sighed and thought for a moment. "It wouldn't be that easy. The competition out there is a killer, *particularly* in plastic surgery. You don't hang out your shingle and rake it into a large wheelbarrow and trot to the bank. It's a different world out there, Lionel. But you wouldn't know about that."

"About what?" Lionel replied quickly with a bit of irritation.

"The outside world!" Peter lit another cigarette, oblivious to the other one, which lay smoking on the wooden bench.

"I know enough to know not to burn down the place," Lionel said as he extinguished the cigarette.

"Lion, look at the kind of surgery you're doing, for Chrissake! Taking some funny-looking kid's face apart piece by piece and putting it back together like Humpty Dumpty. How many plastic surgeons in Los Angeles are doing surgery like that? Nobody, that's who."

"So?"

"So, outside of this ivory tower they call University Hospital it's a different game. Plastic surgery isn't fixing funny-looking kids. It's face-lifts, boob jobs and taking bumps off noses. *Patients* are business. And cosmetic surgery is the biggest of them, all, particularly here in tinsel town. Around Southern California you've got to look good. Christ, everybody looks good."

"Surgery is surgery. You still do it with a knife."

"Yeah, but first you have to have someone to operate on," Peter said, dragging so deeply that the end of his cigarette became orange. "Have you seen this month's issue of *Los Angeles Magazine*? Twenty-two advertisements for cosmetic surgery clinics. Count 'em, twenty-two. With your reputation and your looks, you wouldn't have a problem in Beverly Hills, or any other place for that matter. But some other plastic surgeon just getting a practice together would have to advertise to get things going."

"Never."

"It's the only way. The medical schools are turning out more and more docs, and they're setting up shop faster than there is demand. You see it in the specialties that have something to sell to healthy patients—weight reduction, sports medicine, cataracts. I wasn't kidding about bulimia." Peter blew three perfect rings of smoke.

"You get patients if you're good and you work hard. Leave the advertising to the toothpaste salesmen."

"Times have changed, Lion. Working around this place with the residents and medical students, you just haven't noticed. Ten years ago the courts said it was okay to advertise. It's here, and Madison Avenue is going to take over. Whoever has the best pitch will end up on top. Take guys like Morrie Gold—he just saw what was coming and made his move before anyone else."

"*You* take Morrie Gold!" Stern had never met Gold but, like most everyone in Los Angeles, had seen him many times. In fact, it was impossible for anyone who watched television not to see Morrie Gold—perhaps several times in a single day. His commercials for the Gold Institute could be seen during late-night movies and at regular intervals throughout the weekend. In the art of selling, he was a master. "Maybe, Peter, if you try hard enough, you can develop a reputation as good as Morrie's."

"Reputation, my ass," Peter said. "I'm trying to make a living! At least Morrie Gold has some patients to operate on. That's more than I can say."

"That yo-yo isn't a plastic surgeon. He barely finished medical school! I don't know him and I don't want to, but I do know he's a fake and it offends me that you, of all people, would want to be like him in any way."

"Don't get me wrong," Peter said apologetically. "You're a much better surgeon than Morrie Gold. There's no comparison. *I* know that. *You* sure as hell know that. Most every physician in Los Angeles knows that. But do you think the suckers that read his advertisements and see him on TV know that? As far as they're concerned, Morrie's a name they know. Lionel Stern is a name they don't. Most people also don't know that he's not a plastic surgeon. What they know is what they read in Morrie's ads."

"He's nothing more than a cheap businessman hustling business."

"He's a very *rich* businessman," Peter said, lighting another cigarette. "He's doing something right. You always see his picture in the paper at all these charity balls. And that girlfriend of his!" Peter said with a whistle, as he paced back and forth. "You ever see her?"

"Can't say that I have. That's one part of the newspaper I don't pay much attention to," Lionel said out of the side of his mouth.

"The way you read the paper, I'm surprised you haven't seen them. He's always with the same one. Some honey from Colombia. And let me tell you, she does not need plastic surgery of any kind. She's the most beautiful creature I've ever seen." Peter's voice was reverent.

Lionel had seen the photographs but did not want to admit it. Morrie Gold's advertising campaign had been so massive and successful, it had escalated him to celebrity status in a city where public visibility was at a premium. His photograph seemed to be everywhere, eternally smiling. At political events, fund-raisers for charities, restaurant open-ings. At most of the affairs, recently, he was accompanied by a dark-haired, exotic woman whose face emitted a sensuous beauty and whose skin made you want to ask what kind of soap she used. Lionel had noticed indeed. It was impossible not to. Tall and elegant, she was a striking contrast to the round, soft and happy features of her companion. Her beauty was another form of advertisement. Gold never missed a trick.

Lionel noticed that Peter's pacing had become much more rapid. "You sure you're okay?"

"Maybe I'm not in the best of shape this morning." Peter shrugged with an artificial casualness. "I'm scared. I'm really scared that maybe I'll fuck up again."

"We're all scared. There's not a surgeon worth anything who goes into the OR and isn't. The people you have to worry about are the ones who aren't."

"Yeah." Peter blew another smoke ring. "Lion, I want you to know how much I appreciate . . ."

Lionel took the cigarette from Peter and put it out. Then he put his hand on Peter's shoulder and gave it a squeeze. "Let's go downstairs."

They put on their paper caps and masks. The brow of Peter's cap instantly became a darker shade of blue as it absorbed the moisture from his forehead.

Once in the scrub room, there was no conversation between the two men as they performed the methodical ritual of brushing the four sides of each finger and both surfaces of the hand repeatedly for ten minutes. Lionel mentally reviewed the steps of the lengthy surgery he was about to perform. He usually described it to medical students as "precise, but not necessarily delicate."

# 6

MORRIE GOLD WAS a fanatic about the magazines. Every morning when he unlocked the door and walked into his office, even before turning on the purposely unflattering overhead lights, his eyes went immediately to the magazines, and every morning he became angry. He had left strict instructions: only current issues, no frayed covers and all magazines at right angles. But the girls were so anxious to close up at night that they never checked. He knew that. They blamed the cleaning lady. Not that she could be trusted either.

After straightening the magazines, he checked the photographs on the grey ultrasuede walls. Overhead track lights illuminated pictures of Morrie with famous movie stars. At parties. Premieres. Benefits. Restaurants. That kind of photo was never difficult to get. The rest of the wall had glossies of Liza Minnelli, Sigourney Weaver, Joan Rivers—the implication being that they had been his patients. It was easier with dead celebrities: Christina Onassis, Rock Hudson, Natalie Wood. He had carefully scribbled words of appreciation in the lower right corners that they weren't around to deny.

Morrie had leaned over to straighten a picture he had taken with Liberace when the phone rang. It was NBC.

"Dr. Gold?"

"Speaking."

"Hi. This is the Geraldo show. My name is Judy Horn. I got your name from an agent, Danny Arnold."

28

"Yes?"

"Well, the problem is that we're taping a segment for New York and one of our guests just developed an allergic reaction to our makeup. I hate to bother you, but we've only got forty minutes and Danny said—"

"Of course. I'll be right there."

# 7

LIONEL PUSHED THE swinging doors aside as he and Peter stepped into OR 9. The room was filled with the heavy rhythmic beat of music. Flo the Flash glanced sideways and quickly turned down the volume on her cassette player with a long surgical forcep so she would not contaminate her sterile gloves. Without any other acknowledgment, she returned to arranging the shiny steel instruments in neat rows on her three green-sheet-covered tables. When they were not scrubbed, the personnel of the operating room wore name tags. It was one of the helpful regulations made by the University Hospital bureaucracy and neatly posted on the coffee room bulletin board. Some thought it was designed to give all who wore the identical shade of sea green scrubs an identity. So everyone in the OR wore a name tag. Everyone except Flo.

Very few people knew Flo's last name. Even fewer knew Flo at all. Flo had worked in the OR for a year but remained a mystery. In itself, no small accomplishment. She had applied for her job just after completing training at the county hospital across town. Flo was remarkable because she was black, much younger than most of the other nurses, and somehow managed to remain entirely apart from the rest of the operating room. And she didn't talk—any more than was absolutely essential. During her first week, one of the nurse supervisors concluded that Flo was a Black Muslim, at best a sullen malcontent. But it took Flo only a very short time to establish a solid reputation for *movement,* as if she were driven to prove something. She declined relief for the morning coffee break. Blasphemy! In the formica lunchroom, where conversation was infinitely more important than food, Flo ate, alone. But downstairs, she grabbed hold of the operating room as if the forty-square-foot parcel of territory belonged to her. And no one waited for Flo. In gown and gloves, she moved the shiny metal surgical tools around like a Las Vegas blackjack dealer handling a deck of cards.

In the middle of OR 9, a nine-year-old boy was lying on the operating table. Felix Enriquez did not look like other boys his age. The bones of his cheeks had failed to develop normally, and the recession made him look as though his face had been compressed from the front.

As Lionel approached, Felix raised an eyebrow somewhat sluggishly and extended his right arm, fist tightly clenched, over his head. It was a triumphant gesture the boy used whenever he greeted his surgeon. Felix had come to the hospital on several occasions before his surgery to have X rays and CAT scans that allowed precise measurements of the bony relationships of his face; he had seen the dentists; he had his own blood drawn so that it could be given back to him during surgery, thus avoiding a transfusion.

Felix's face could not be described as forgettable. His eyes exploded from an otherwise featureless face, and the overall effect could reasonably raise the possibility that the boy had come from another planet. But rather than instilling fear, his facade, along with his personality, had its own unique attraction. As soon as he was admitted to the hospital, Felix began making rounds with the residents and greeted visitors as they got off the elevator. The staff nurses started referring to him as "the frog," but the name was not used in a derogatory fashion. It was spoken with genuine affection. In fact, when the gurney arrived to take Felix to the operating room, two of the nurses whispered their concern that the plastic surgeons shouldn't change something that cute.

Felix's eyes slowly scanned OR 9. "Needed reinforcements, huh?" he said, motioning toward Peter.

"You've been telling me what a tough guy you are, Felix. I didn't have any choice. I had to bring in Dr. Dalway to help me." Lionel brushed the boy's jaw with his fist.

"Felix, you're going to get very sleepy now." Sweeny, the anesthesiologist, pushed the barrel of a syringe and sodium pentothal flowed into the IV.

Lionel reviewed the process: he would make an incision from ear to ear and lift the scalp and forehead away from the skull, folding it forward over the face. Four shallow holes in the skull would be drilled, outlining a square piece of bone that would be lifted off after sawing the intervening bone with a rough, diamond-covered wire. The frontal lobes of the brain would then be exposed. From that vantage point, looking down into the open dome of the encasement of the brain, the bony framework that formed the shape of the face would be accessible from the inside. Using stainless steel chisels struck by leather-covered mallets, Lionel would divide the attachments of the recessed facial bones from the skull. He would then make an incision slightly longer and three inches below the usual appendectomy scar and remove several cubes of bone from the boy's hip. These grafts of living bone would be wired into the new space created between the now mobile cheekbones and the more solid framework of the skull. By this forward advancement, the round rim of bone that encircled each eye, the prominence of the cheek and the brow would be reconstructed. Felix's eyes would then be surrounded by projecting bone that would more closely resemble the eyes of the people who so frequently stared at him.

Lionel made the incision five minutes before the time printed on the operating schedule. Flo was in high gear, juggling the four hundred instruments effortlessly and producing the correct rabbit from the hat and putting it in Lionel's hand without being asked. In the early part of the procedure, Lionel, intent on establishing a fast pace, said nothing, and the room fell silent except for the soft hissing of the respirator, which was now breathing for Felix after Sweeny had set it on automatic.

Peter seemed comfortable and assisted in applying Raney

clips, the removable semicircular plastic clamps that compressed the cut edge of the scalp to control the brisk bleeding. When bleeding vessels were tied, Peter cut the suture just above the knot. Lionel noticed that his hands were steady.

With a hand drill similar to those used by carpenters, Lionel made four holes through the skull, exposing small circular windows over the tough dural membrane that encases the brain. He passed the diamond wire saw from one drill hole to another using a small thin spatula. Like connecting dots in a child's drawing, the rectangle of bone was outlined and cut with the to and fro action of the saw in Lionel's hands. He lifted up the piece of bone gently, teasing the dura away from its attachments to the undersurface. It became free quite easily on each side, but in the middle remained adhered.

Lionel carefully reinserted the spatula. Suddenly, the entire wound was filled with blood that flowed over all sides of the rectangular outline like small red waterfalls. He had never seen so much blood appear so quickly. The very depth of Stern's stomach felt cold, and the sensation swept down to his legs, making them feel as if they might not support his weight. With the bone still adhered, it was impossible for him to identify the source of the bleeding.

"Norma, we're going to need those two split units and we're going to need 'em fast," Lionel said. She was already out the swinging doors. "I've run into some bleeding, Ed," Lionel said, his voice deceptively calm. "Felix is losing it fast. Better give him some volume until I can get it under control." *If* I get it under control, he thought, ignoring the sinking feeling.

One thing was clear. Without removing the bone, stopping the hemorrhage was impossible. "Let me have a periosteal elevator." No sooner had the words hit the air than Flo slapped the instrument firmly into his hand.

The elevator disappeared underneath the bone. Lionel made several sweeping motions to separate whatever was still attached. The piece of bone came away, but beneath it all that could be seen was blood welling up from the top of Felix's brain.

"His pressure is down to sixty, Lionel," Sweeny said from behind the sterile sheet that separated them. "I'm pushing everything I've got. Already given him two-fifty of albumen. We'll need more than his own split units," he said as Norma returned with the autotransfusion units, each one half the size of an adult donation.

"Ed, put his head down quick. It's a tear in a vein and it's a big one. I hope it's not what I think it is." Sweeny inclined the operating table so that Felix's head was the lowest part of his body. The risk was that with an opening in the low-pressure venous system, it was entirely possible that air could enter the circulation and embolize anywhere in the body, acting like a blood clot.

Lionel continued his cautious inspection, and then almost inaudibly whispered, "Shit," beneath his mask. As he lifted the sponge a fraction of an inch more, there was another torrent of blood. "We're into the sagittal sinus," he announced matter-of-factly. "How's the pressure, Ed?"

The brain's largest vein, the sagittal sinus, occupied the space between the two lobes of the brain. In Felix's case, a much smaller vein draining the skull communicated directly with the sinus, an aberration of normal anatomy that Lionel could not have predicted before the operation. When the plate of bone was removed, the traction on the vein had torn a hole in the larger vein.

"Not hearing it at all. The computer reads out at forty systolic. I've given the first unit and pumping in the second. He's a skinny kid, and we've lost more than a third of his blood volume." A graceful man even under pressure, Sweeny had used the collective "we" in referring to a problem he had done nothing to cause. "But we're still way behind him, Lion."

"Problem is I've got to fix the tear, and to do that he's going to bleed some more. Maybe a lot more. I can't clamp the sinus or I'll stroke him out," Stern said. He took several deep breaths.

"Then you better give me some time to get his pressure up," the anesthesiologist said. "That is, providing I can."

For the first time Lionel looked away from the operative field and saw Peter's face, completely bleached of the deep brown Southern California tan, his eyelids wide open in fear. "Peter?" he said firmly.

"I'm fine," Peter replied quickly, but less than convincingly.

There was little choice but to believe him. At that moment, Lionel could not afford to worry about his friend's reaction. "Flo, I'm going to need some vascular suture. Seven-O silk on an atraumatic needle." The Flash was already placing the delicate suture in the needle holder.

Several minutes passed, each second somehow extended lazily in time.

"The monitor says sixty systolic, but I don't hear it very strong." Some anesthesiologists would simply have relied on the computer. Sweeny was listening hard.

The room was silent again, except for the soft blowing of the respirator. Lionel stood quite still, gently placing pressure on the sponge on the top of Felix's head.

"Okay, Lion," Sweeny said after five minutes. "He's had a thousand cc's replacement and the pressure is one hundred and strong. I'm still behind, but not by much. He has a young heart and I'm pushing it in fast. Might as well let 'er rip."

Maltry put his hands over the sponge, and Lionel carefully pushed his fingers forward, maintaining the delicate pressure, until the tear became visible. Quickly, Lionel caught the two edges of the vein with the suture, and as soon as the knot was tied, the flow of blood slowed perceptibly. Without thinking, Lionel said, "Cut," a reflex that always followed tying a suture—the most basic surgical maneuver.

Peter Dalway reached over, suture scissors in his shaky hands. Suddenly, the flow of blood welled up in the wound. In his attempt to cut the suture just above the knot, the unsteadiness of his hands had stretched the thin silk thread, causing it to tear through the delicate vein. Lionel quickly reapplied the pressure, but by the time he lifted his head, he could only see Peter's back as he left OR 9, still fully gowned and gloved.

Lionel took a deep, audible breath trying to suppress his anger, which was not directed to Peter but to himself. He repeated the maneuver with Maltry, again gaining control of the blood loss. It required only eight sutures to completely repair the tear in the vein. To put them in took more than an hour. "How's everything, Ed?" he asked when finished, in the same calm voice he always used in the OR regardless of what was happening.

"Like a rock. Didn't turn a hair. If you're thinking of going ahead, which I know you are, I don't see any reason why not. We've come this far."

"Hate to pay for the same real estate twice," Stern said, taking the chisel from Flo.

"General George Smith Patton Jr. Seventh Army. Battle of the Bulge. Belgium. December 1943."

"Something like that," Lionel said as he continued. "But it was the Third Army and it was in Bastogne, France."

Just before he took the mallet to make the facial bone osteotomies, Lionel thought about Peter Dalway.

# 8

"Stephanie, I'm terribly sorry to keep you waiting, but the doctor has been called on an emergency." Mrs. Evans, Morrie's office manager, lowered her voice reverently. "NBC," she whispered.

Elise Evans, with her snow white hair, flawless complexion and pale blue Adolfo suit, greeted each patient with a serenity and warmth that reassured them Dr. Morrie Gold was no less than the right hand of God. And that she was no less than Saint Peter.

Stephanie's eyes lit up. "NBC?"

"The studio called to say that he would be leaving any moment now."

"Oh, that's all right." Stephanie laughed nervously. "I've waited this long . . ."

Mrs. Evans took Stephanie's hand and spoke to her as though double entendre were a recognized language. "You won't have to wait much longer."

What Stephanie Green had been waiting for was a rhinoplasty. She wanted a new nose. "Can I ask you something?"

"Of course."

Even though they were alone in the waiting room, Stephanie leaned close. She pointed to the picture of Liza Minnelli and whispered, "Did Dr. Gold really do Liza?"

Mrs. Evans smiled warmly. "We never discuss our patients." She raised an eyebrow. "Confidentiality."

Stephanie understood perfectly. She knew she had come

to the right place. Danny Arnold, her agent, was right. Dr. Gold was the right plastic surgeon, but if he didn't show up soon Stephanie thought she would die.

It was long ago that Stephanie had decided her nose must have been some kind of genetic mutation. When she was a young girl, her home was filled with photographs. They were on the walls, on the bookshelves, arranged on tables. The special ones of her mother and two older sisters sat proudly in the center of the mantel. They were symbols of Stephanie's expectation that she would follow the same beautiful genetic path. Stephanie waited patiently. As patiently as she was now waiting for Dr. Gold.

But when she was ten, around the time little girls assume the first suggestions of what they will look like as women, when round lines become gradually replaced by more angular forms, something happened to Stephanie's nose. Rather than forming a gentle concave line extending from her forehead, as had been tacitly promised by the black and white images on the mantel, the contour of her nose began to project outward. Looking back, she was certain that it didn't happen overnight. But it seemed as though it had. Suddenly, Stephanie recognized she was ugly and two entities emerged: Stephanie's nose and Stephanie's body. People no longer spoke about Stephanie without reference to one or the other. By twelve, she felt like a failure. In an effort to compensate, Stephanie fine-tuned her body as though preparing for world-class competition. She ate carefully, exercised, vaporized and moisturized. She became the most devoted daughter in the world, the best friend anyone could want, the funniest girl in her class. Everything about Stephanie was perfect until she turned around and looked at herself.

"Tell you what," Mrs. Evans said, handing her a leather-bound looseleaf notebook. "Why don't you look through this until Dr. Gold gets here?" Mrs. Evans quietly disappeared into the back office.

It was the nose book. More wondrous than all the Sears catalogs she had read from cover to cover as a child, Dr. Gold's book contained the one thing she most wanted in life: beauty. She turned each page slowly, time standing still, comparing herself to photographs of high fashion models and before and after shots of ordinary people like her, imagining and then sharing vicariously their happiness.

"I had my nose done when I graduated high school." The voice exploded in the silent room.

Stephanie gasped, startled, as though someone had been reading her mind. The attractive woman settling into the deeply cushioned, gray ultrasuede chair opposite her was a flight attendant. Her uniform was impeccable, her makeup flawless. Stephanie smiled nervously. She hadn't heard any footsteps. It must have been the thick carpeting. "I'm sorry. You scared me."

"Hell, I didn't think I looked that bad!" The woman rolled her eyes and picked up a copy of *Cosmopolitan*.

Stephanie closed the nose book, studying the young woman opposite her. "I've always wanted a nose like yours."

The woman shrugged. "It better look good. It cost a fortune."

"I'm not usually so talkative with strangers, but I guess it's nerves. I'm scared to death."

"Talkative? Honey, talkative is a salesman who's flying home after he just lost a deal. I ought to know," she said, pointing to her flight badge. "My name is Rochelle. So relax. I'm not a stranger anymore."

"Is this your first time? I mean, have you seen Dr. Gold before?"

"You bet I have."

"Did he do your nose?"

"Not exactly." Rochelle unbuttoned her jacket, took a deep breath, and pointed to her breasts. "Voilà!"

"Wow!" Stephanie sat back and instinctively folded her arms in front of her. Not that she had any cause to worry. Indeed Stephanie had earned a decent living for years as a "body parts" model. Her breasts had appeared in bra commercials, her derriere in swimsuit ads, her legs in lingerie catalogs. Anywhere her face was not required. She had also recently appeared in her new agent's bed. Danny

Arnold had put her on a budget and this was the week she'd finally had enough money. If she got her nose fixed, he'd promised to launch her acting career by getting her an audition for a part on "General Hospital." She had the right agent, a chance at a part and the money for surgery. It was now all within Stephanie's power to turn her life around and face the camera head-on. There was only one thing she was afraid of. "Did it hurt?"

Rochelle waved her hand. "Didn't feel a thing."

"I'm such a coward when it comes to pain. I have to take a Valium before I get my hair cut," Stephanie said, with a nervous giggle. "I can't believe I actually got up the courage to come here. But I can't live with this nose one more day. It's so ugly. I've seen Dr. Gold's ads on TV for months now. *Be good to yourself. Cosmetic surgery can change your life. Be happy.*"

Rochelle made an exaggerated frown. "That's my problem. I'm too happy." She moved next to Stephanie, checking to see that Mrs. Evans wasn't within earshot. "What do you think? They're not too big, are they?" she said, unbuttoning her jacket and thrusting her chest forward again.

"No. Not if you don't think so," Stephanie said, mildly shocked and amused.

"My point exactly! You do this kind of surgery for yourself, right? Not for somebody else." Rochelle paused. "And Dr. Gold's been terrific about everything. He's not like other plastic surgeons." Rochelle whispered, "He does important research." She cupped her breasts in her palms and smiled. "Would you believe, these are research?" Then Rochelle's expression became serious. "But they're still mine."

"I don't understand."

"Listen, you don't earn enough money as a flying waitress to pay for this kind of surgery. I could never afford breast implants if it weren't for Dr. Gold. He's developed a new technique. Some kind of special operation so the breasts won't get hard. I know two girls on the Paris–New

York run who have boobs as hard as rocks. They could run a marathon and they wouldn't bounce on inch."

"I thought they put in those soft bags of silicone."

"It's not the silicone that gets hard. That's what Dr. Gold's research is all about. The breast forms some kind of lining around the implant. Dr. G. calls it a capsule. So what he does is put in implants that are larger than you need. He waits a month for the breast to form the lining, and then he takes out the bigger implants and puts in smaller ones. That way they stay soft. Don't ask me why. All I know is I like 'em big."

"*Two* operations? That must really hurt."

"It's a breeze. You go back to work the next day. A little sore, but what the hell. The price is right. He's done four of my friends. We're all flight attendants on the Bogotá–Lima run."

"South America?"

"He has this clinic in Cartagena where he does surgery for free on the poor. And I have a hunch he does the first operations down there because it's still experimental. I guess you would say I'm one of Dr. Gold's guinea pigs. I'm supposed to have the second surgery here today."

"Today? And you're just sitting here so calmly?"

"I'm thinking the same sort of thing." Rochelle stood up. "I signed a contract with Morrie before the first implant that said I'd agree to have the second. Don't get me wrong. I think Dr. Gold is a great doctor. But I just met this guy, and you know how it is, he likes 'em big." She picked up her purse. "I'm not kidding myself, I doubt he'll ever marry me. But I didn't have enough money to go to college to find a husband." Rochelle's eyes grew slightly moist. "What the hell am I supposed to do?" She shrugged. "He likes them big! And now that's what I got. Why change?"

Before Stephanie could say anything, Rochelle came over to her, smiling, gave her a hug and in three strides was out the door. Mrs. Evans's voice was suddenly shrill as she called after her, "Wait, Miss Whitaker!"

# 9

THE ACCOMPANIST WAS playing the opening bars from Act Two of *Swan Lake* on the piano. Faster, Luisa thought. Da dum, da dum. One, two. One, two.

She heard the grind of tires against the gravel driveway and stepped out onto the balcony. Her driver parked the car at the front door and began to load her luggage. Luisa walked back into her bedroom, careful to lock the balcony door.

She appraised herself in the full-length mirror, smoothing the silk dress against her breasts, her small waist, her hips. The loose fit and bright multicolored pattern would hide the inevitable wrinkles resulting from a long flight. She paused to look around the room and then locked the door behind her.

As Luisa descended the marble staircase, the two young men in tights who were sitting at the bottom looked up. She shook her head impatiently at the rehearsal room as she slapped her palm loudly on the banister. *"Uno, dos, tres,"* she counted, correcting the piano player's tempo. *"Uno, dos, tres."*

The boys smiled at one another, flanking the stairs as they offered Luisa their hands. She kissed each one on the cheek and without turning back waved good-bye.

Luisa strode out of the house, a hand held upward to shield her eyes from the bright sun. Though she loved her spacious house, leaving it she couldn't escape the sensation of being liberated from prison. The driver helped her into the sedan and shut the door. No more *Swan Lake*.

The only sound was the gravel beneath the tires as the car turned slowly down the long tree-shaded driveway to the gates. Luisa waved at the two guards, small bearded men dressed in white T-shirts. Uzi submachine guns hung from their necks on leather straps stained black with sweat. One of them pulled the heavy wooden gate open.

As the car passed through, Luisa glanced down the street. A late sixties Buick, its chipped metallic blue paint almost completely obscured by a heavy coat of street dust, was parked one block away, as it had been for the past six weeks, to watch her every move. Bastards! she thought to herself. Within moments, the Buick started up and pulled out into the street following close behind. The police no longer made any effort to conceal their surveillance.

At the airport, the driver took her luggage and followed Luisa as she walked through the crowd. She presented her ticket and passport to the clerk behind the Pan Am counter. The man examined it for a moment, looked up, smiled and excused himself. Luisa had barely enough time to realize that something was wrong when three armed policemen surrounded her. Without a word, they took hold of her arms and gently ushered her back through the crowd, down a long corridor and into a small unmarked room where, just as suddenly, they left her alone, sitting on a straight wooden chair. The room was not air-conditioned. There were no windows. The air hung thick, pressing in around her, competing for breathing space with her own fears.

Determined not to give in, Luisa sat erect. Rivulets of perspiration traveled slowly down her back, gluing the thin silk dress to her skin. After twenty minutes of silence she heard whispers outside the door. A man wearing mirrored sunglasses entered. He was tall and thinly muscular, his sleek black hair combed straight back. He wore a neatly pressed uniform of an army colonel, his cap cradled in his arm. His cheeks shone from a recent shave, and in the small, unventilated room, there was no escaping the heavy fragrance of his cologne.

Despite the dim light, he did not remove his mirrored sunglasses. A single lightbulb overhead reflected from the center of each lens like small glistening beams. He nodded at Luisa. "What language do you prefer?"

She smiled. "The language of farewell."

*"Adiós. Adieu. Auf wiedersehen."* He turned the pages of her passport as though reading a novel. "Still saying good-bye."

Luisa tilted her head. A strange phrase for him to use. "Who are you?"

He glanced up. "The question is, who are you?"

"One of your people follows me wherever I go, searches my packages, questions clerks in shops, threatens my servants. Surely you know everything about me."

"I don't know why you go to Los Angeles."

"Business."

"May I ask what type of business?"

"You may not. I wish to leave."

He smiled. "More good-byes." Turning the pages of her passport, he said, "Three trips to Los Angeles within the past three months."

"You don't need my passport for that information. You know that from the men who search my luggage each time." Luisa stood up angrily. "They found nothing!"

"Perhaps they are looking in the wrong places, señora." He put down her passport.

"I can't imagine where else you could look."

"There are places," he said softly, lighting a cigarette, then offering her one. Luisa shook her head.

"Señora Obregon," the colonel said slowly, smiling, "you have a great deal of money that belongs to the Colombian government. I know that. You know that."

"I have no such money. By now you should have convinced yourself that I am telling the truth." Her voice grew tight. "Since my husband died, your people have followed me everywhere and they have found nothing and—"

"Your husband did not just die, señora. He was shot in the face twenty times. An extraordinary death, even in the violent area of the world where we live. He was murdered because he took a great deal of money from men who are not as reasonable as myself."

Luisa turned away. She spoke softly. "Why aren't you trying to find the men who killed him instead of some fictitious buried treasure?"

"I am trying to do both. You have no doubt heard about the unfortunate plane crash three days ago."

"No."

"No? We found one hundred thousand dollars in gold bullion."

"Planes do crash, don't they, Colonel?" Luisa said, looking at her watch.

"Yes, but few try to take off from the top of the Cordillera mountains, an altitude of twelve thousand feet, in the middle of the night, loaded with gold bullion. We identified the serial number of the engine. The plane belongs to your cousin."

"I have many cousins. I still don't see what all this has to do with me."

"Neither did I until I questioned some of your husband's former associates." He paused. "His associates in the export business."

"My husband exported coffee."

"He may have enjoyed coffee in a cup, señora, but that was likely his only dealing with coffee."

"I know only what he told me."

The man smiled. "Maybe I believe that. Maybe not. That is why I'm here. Some of the information I was given suggests another relationship."

"Relationship?"

"That you were not the innocent wife but rather a full partner in your husband's so-called export business."

"This, Colonel, is insanity."

"Furthermore, we believe you enjoyed a position of great

authority, not to mention the money, and finally, that you yourself arranged your husband's execution while you were in Florida setting up delivery points."

Luisa shifted her weight so that she faced the man squarely. She folded her arms and said nothing for several long moments. "Well then, Colonel, I do not wish to miss my plane."

"Unfortunately that is not all I was told. You see, the individuals we questioned said that your husband gave you the difficult responsibility of getting a very large sum of money out of Colombia. A very large sum that rightfully belongs to the Colombian government."

"It is quite simple. They were not telling the truth," Luisa said calmly.

"That is still to be seen. How much money are you taking with you?"

"A few thousand in traveler's checks. But you know that. One of your men was behind me at the bank yesterday. You probably know the serial numbers. Who are you?"

"Please come here. Closer."

"Do you want to look in my purse?"

"No. In your eyes."

"Who are you?"

"When does your flight leave?"

"Ten o'clock," Luisa said flatly.

"That allows only twenty-five minutes. I will be happy to wait for our physician, but you may well miss your plane."

Luisa's eyes narrowed, blazing at the man as he approached.

His hand darted out, curving around the narrowest part of her back, sweeping up and then down. Instinctively, he pulled her close, as if to kiss her. The man hesitated, staring from behind the mirrored lenses in which Luisa could see only a reflection of herself. Suddenly, he put a hand to her breast. Pressing hard, lingering too long. And then he swept her dress upward as his index and middle finger probed inside her.

Luisa gasped but did not struggle, watching the man coldly.

"You call that reasonable?" she hissed when he was done.

"You're still alive."

She spit in his face, splattering his mirrored lenses. "My plane," she said with the thinnest of smiles.

# 10

It HAD BEEN nearly half an hour since Mrs. Evans showed Stephanie into Dr. Gold's study, a wood-paneled room filled with books. They sat at a highly polished table while Mrs. Evans took Stephanie's history with the warmth of a long-separated mother and daughter out to lunch for the first time in months. Mrs. Evans took her on a brief tour of the institute, gave her a brochure on rhinoplasty and showed her a video about the surgery. Then, like two best friends picking out a party dress, they pored over the "nose" book together, trying to decide on what style would be most suitable for Stephanie's face. All the while, Stephanie studied the older woman, searching for a sign of cosmetic surgery but not at all certain what to look for.

Mrs. Evans got down to business. "Now, let me explain exactly what's going to happen. You arrive here on the morning of the surgery—"

"Here? I thought I'd be going to a hospital."

"Most people don't realize that you go home a few hours after a rhinoplasty."

"Every time you say that word, rhinoplasty," Stephanie laughed nervously, "it sounds like something you do to a rhinoceros." Her face grew dark as her voice wavered. "And that's exactly what I feel like with this ugly thing in the middle of my face."

"My dear. You're a lovely young woman who's going to

leave all those bad feelings behind you." Mrs. Evans leaned close. "Forever."

Stephanie wiped the corners of her eyes and shrugged. "Then why am I so afraid?"

"This means a new life for you, Stephanie. All the nos become yeses. All the what ifs become reality. You're nervous, my dear, because suddenly the whole world is opening up for you. I assure you, it's quite a normal reaction."

"Thank you." Stephanie took the Kleenex offered by Mrs. Evans and blew her nose. "I really appreciate your being so understanding."

"Now after the surgery, you're to remain in bed at home. Of course, someone must stay with you for that first twenty-four hours. There'll be a small amount of oozing."

"But I live alone. That's why a hospital would be so much better."

"Oh, I'm certain you can have a friend stay over with you. Besides, if you have any questions at all you may call us at any hour of the day or night."

"I still think I should be in a hospital."

"My dear, that's the last place you'd want to be. You're not sick. We have everything you need right here at the institute"—Mrs. Evans patted Stephanie's hand—"without all that overhead and the chance of infection."

"I just thought that—"

"Stephanie, none of Dr. Gold's patients go to the hospital. And for good reason. Who's going to get all the attention? The patient who's in for a pretty new nose or the one who's seriously ill?"

"But what if . . ."

Mrs. Evans sighed. "Dr. Gold does make arrangements for patients to stay at a small, discreet hotel. Of course, that's usually for patients from out of town or celebrities who don't wish to be seen coming or going."

"Is it very expensive?"

"Not for a night or two, if that would make you feel better."

Stephanie smiled. "I read about a place where celebrities go to recuperate."

"But your surgery is so simple. All you have to do, dear, is apply cold compresses for the first day and use two pillows to keep your head elevated."

"I think I'd feel better at—"

Mrs. Evans smiled. "—L'Etoile."

Stephanie sat back. She said the name over again to herself. "Yes. The Star."

"Do you have any questions before seeing Dr. Gold?" The tone of Mrs. Evans's voice presumed that Stephanie had none.

Hesitating, Stephanie asked. "That other woman? Rochelle?"

Mrs. Evans spoke in a soft, gentle voice unlike her shrill tone in calling after the flight attendant. "A little misunderstanding. Everything is all right now. And I thought only you actresses were high-strung."

Exactly, Stephanie thought to herself. She nodded, took a deep breath and smiled. Through the large picture window, despite the haze that covered the hills, she could make out the gigantic letters that spelled HOLLYWOOD. It was precisely what Stephanie wanted to see.

# 11

Luisa stepped on the Pan American flight to Los Angeles with a radiant smile and was warmly greeted by all the flight attendants. She took her seat in the first-class cabin. The one next to it was, as usual, empty. Whenever possible it was kept vacant so that the flight attendants could sit and talk to her as they so commonly did.

As soon as the 747 was airborne, one of the young women approached her, introduced herself and asked if she could sit down. "My name is Melissa. Melissa Eckhart." She leaned close. "I'm a good friend of Rochelle Whitaker."

Luisa nodded. "It's such a pleasure to meet you, Melissa. I thought I hadn't had the pleasure of meeting you on one of the other flights. I'm sure I would have remembered someone as lovely as you." Luisa sat gracefully in the well-padded seat, hands relaxed in her lap. "And I'll bet you want to know all about Dr. Gold's research. I can see it on your face."

"And on my chest." Melissa laughed. "After seeing Rochelle's new figure and hearing about how her whole life has changed. It's fantastic. It really is. All the girls on this run admire you so, señora Obregon. The work you do for Dr. Gold, flying back and forth to raise money for the clinic so that he can continue his research." Melissa rolled her eyes admiringly. "It's so . . . 'forties.' "

Luisa smiled modestly. "I don't pretend to understand all the applications of his new surgical techniques, but I know how important his work is, and I have learned to trust Dr. Gold."

"Do you think that Dr. Gold . . . you know, would he use me for one of the operations?"

"I will speak to him. When you get to Los Angeles call the institute and ask for Mrs. Evans. I'll do my best. He is a busy man, but I'm sure he will make the time."

Melissa reached over and embraced Luisa, squeezing her tightly. "Oh, señora, thank you. You do such wonderful things for so many people. It must bring you great pleasure."

Luisa reached out with the expressive hands of a prima ballerina and touched Melissa's cheek. "It is the most rewarding work I have ever done."

# 12

THE GOLD INSTITUTE of Surgical Rejuvenation/N.A. was located on a corner lot on the part of Sunset Strip just a few blocks east of where Beverly Hills ends. The eighteen-unit apartment building that formerly occupied the premises had been the first of Morrie's many real estate investments. Without question, it was his most successful.

The BE GOOD TO YOURSELF, BE HAPPY ads that ran in the L.A. *Times* and *Los Angeles Magazine* all featured the BE GOOD TO YOURSELF address and the BE HAPPY phone number. Morrie once joked to Mrs. Evans that if business ever got bad, they could convert into condos with one of the most recognizable addresses in town.

The institute, attractive by virtue of its simplicity, was a bold example of postmodern architecture: round corners and reflective glass and plaster that formed smooth, flush lines. It was not only Morrie's office, but a monument to his achievement. Aggressive advertising and favorable financing terms had made plastic surgery, once the fountain of youth only for the rich and famous, as accessible as a haircut.

It had taken him nearly twenty years. After graduating from medical school, Morrie began a residency in dermatology. But after one year it became clear that this training would only impede his progress. He knew much more than those who were supposed to be his teachers, and the salary was ridiculously low. "Why punish yourself?" he thought. During that year he dated a nurse who had received silicone injections to enlarge her breasts. It was that simple. The key that unlocked it all for Morrie was a clear, inert, oily liquid easily introduced to the body with a syringe. He immediately went out and opened an office. He began performing the procedure for friends to supplement his income while building his dermatology practice. Suddenly, his waiting room and office were filled. Not with rashes and allergic reactions, but with flat chests. A new and rewarding career had presented itself to Morrie. Silicone also confirmed what he had already known to be true about the repressive attitudes of organized medicine. It had failed miserably to recognize silicone's advantages. The medical hierarchy served only those within its structure and was consistently suspicious of any physician who stood up to it. The establishment had questioned him then as they did now. But the state of California had given him a license to practice medicine as a "physician and a *surgeon,*" and that was exactly what Morrie intended to do. Even though his license did not specify plastic surgery and even though he had no formal training as a plastic surgeon, it was primarily a question of legal right. In this case, *his* legal right.

Morrie Gold had, over the years, carefully constructed for himself a pyramid of surgical experiences. He was self-taught. The transitions and his own educational process were orderly and gradual. He had waited three years before he inserted the first pair of silicone breast implants. Morrie was patient in his personal commitment to self-improvement. It had taken fifteen years for the institute to become a reality. Fifteen years of premieres and benefits and endless smiles and putting himself on call twenty-four hours a day. Hollywood fantasies and surgical fantasies intertwined neatly. Morrie became a presence, someone on whom the studios could depend. He understood their problems and they helped him shape his TV persona. And over those fifteen long years, Morrie refused to be intimidated by the medical establishment. He had flourished in spite of them. He owed nothing to anyone.

He was innovative and, yes, unconventional, and because of that he was persecuted. For being different and being better, it was necessary to pay a price, Morrie Gold told himself. It was the same with his research. Through ground-breaking experiments he had discovered how to avoid the common problem of hard, uncomfortable breasts following augmentation mammoplasty. It was a simple matter—do the operation in two stages. During the first procedure a larger implant than was needed was placed behind the breast. Wait until the body became accustomed to the new shape and then, under local anesthesia, replace the larger implant with a smaller one. Voilà! Soft, natural-feeling breasts. He had done the operation for two years in Los Angeles with great results and had submitted his findings to a plastic surgery meeting. But because he wasn't a member of the fraternity, not "board certified," the paper was rejected. They had said that there were no proper "controls" and other academic double-talk, but Morrie knew the real reason for the rejection.

He vowed to get even. First, with the help of a clever lawyer, he established his own board: The American Board of Surgery for Rejuvenation. No longer could anyone say he wasn't board certified. And the second step had come as so many things come to great people—by accident. While on vacation in Florida six months earlier, Morrie had met a striking woman from Colombia. In fact the most beautiful woman he had ever seen. As often happens, the subject of plastic surgery arose and during that conversation he disclosed his theory about breast hardening. Luisa Obregon instantly saw him as the visionary he in fact was, and proposed a second institute in Colombia, where he could continue his research without the scrutiny of the Los Angeles medical community. With Luisa's help Morris Gold would show them, one way or another, that he was not to be taken lightly.

Morrie drove back from NBC, knowing he was already backed up with patients. Still, he made a U-turn on Sunset in order to pass the Gold Institute from the other direction.

His last name was printed in the triangular pediment and he wanted to appreciate it fully. Morrie smiled. Not bad for a kid from the Bronx.

He parked his white Mercedes in the space reserved with his name and went into the institute through a private entrance that bypassed patients in the waiting room and led directly to his office. He carefully hung up and smoothed the jacket to his Bijan suit and put on the lab coat made for him at Giorgio. He glanced at his Rolex watch and paused for a final check in the mirror.

Time had been kinder to Morrie than genetics. At forty-six, he had a full head of curly reddish brown hair, with distinguished graying sideburns. His skin was still as pink and soft as a baby's. But his watery, nearly colorless eyes were too small for his face. He had a very short neck, a square, stocky body that his tailors tried to reshape by nipping in the waist on all his clothes and advising him to wear elevator shoes. Morrie had successfully deducted his clothes as a business expense, along with his weekly hair rinses and dental work. The son of an accountant, he had adopted his father's philosophy: if it isn't deductible, it isn't worth doing. Morrie ran his tongue over his perfectly capped teeth and pronounced himself open for business.

As he entered the conference room, he noticed the look of relief on Mrs. Evans's face. Ignoring her he spoke directly to his patient. "Stephanie, how nice of you to visit me. I'm very flattered. I guess you know who I am. I'm surprised each and every day by how many people actually do. I've been blessed by so many grateful patients." As she turned to him, and Morrie saw her nose full front, he mentally upped the price. "You must forgive me for being late, but I ran into your agent, Danny Arnold, at NBC, and he wouldn't stop talking about you."

What Danny Arnold wouldn't stop talking about was how fast could he get his kickback from Morrie for recommending Stephanie to him. Morrie had an elaborate network of "thank-you's" worked out with numerous casting agents, talent coordinators and hairdressers that ranged from cases of champagne to free nips and tucks, and, as in the case of Danny Arnold, to a percentage of the fee.

Stephanie's nose was a horror. Fleshy. Misshapen. It was huge. Why the hell had she waited so long? Hadn't she seen his ads?

"Dr. Gold?" Stephanie asked nervously.

Morrie bowed slightly from the waist, feet together. He reached out to grasp her right hand and held it firmly as he looked into her eyes, smiling. "A young Natalie Wood. Dark, sultry, but with a very innocent sensuality. God, if they ever did a remake of *Splendor in the Grass,* I'd speak to someone about you."

Morrie let go of Stephanie's hand. She put it to her forehead as though she had an itch. It was clear she wanted to cover her nose. He reached for Stephanie's hand and took it away from her face. Her eyes were filled with tears. She couldn't look up at him. Mrs. Evans knew it was time to leave the room. She closed the door soundlessly behind her. This was the moment Morrie liked best. One on one with the patient. Whereas volume was emphasized to the staff, this was Morrie's quality time. Should a patient desire collagen injections, a chemical peel or a prescription, that service was performed by a nurse specialist. But there was no clock ticking when Morrie made his pitch—he enjoyed it too much.

"You're going to have to get used to that kind of talk, Stephanie. From what Danny tells me, you'll be hearing a lot of it."

"Did he say that?"

Morrie looked at her intently. "You wouldn't believe what he said." Danny Arnold had given Morrie a full accounting of Stephanie's finances, including the fact that she had a very generous father. His attention fully focused on Stephanie, Morrie stepped straight backward and sat down. His eyes narrowed into a studied squint. Then he got up and began to walk slowly around her, making throaty sounds as if he had identified something very important. "When I was young, I didn't like my nose, either. I can empathize with the way you feel." He reached over to touch her nose and she pulled back. "I'm not going to hurt you," he said, the tone reminiscent of a sexual advance. "Don't be embarrassed." He put his thumb and forefinger on the bridge of her nose, aware of her discomfort. Very slowly, and for no reason other than to impress the customer, he ran his thumb and forefinger down her nose. She was shaking.

"Can you do something?" she whispered.

Morrie nodded. At least thirty-two hundred dollars, maybe he could get away with thirty-five. If only he knew more about the father.

"Dr. Gold?"

"It will be difficult, but not impossible," he said, appraising the substantial dimensions of her nose. Difficult was a major understatement. The skin was thick, the profile a gigantic curve, massive alar cartilages that made the tip wide and hanging down. It would not be an easy procedure. "We usually operate through the nostril, avoiding visible scars." But as he spoke Morrie recalled a diagram of a similar rhinoplasty he had seen in one of the texts in his library. "In your case, Stephanie . . . there may be small scars on the outside of the nostrils. That will let me see exactly how much cartilage and bone I should remove."

Although he had no formal training in plastic surgery, Morrie had remained a faithful student of the field. He attended every plastic surgery meeting and symposium whose registration did not require completion of a residency. He was the first there in the morning, the last to leave in the late afternoon. When there was a break in the program, Morrie did not stand around drinking coffee. He went to the video displays and studied the various surgical procedures and took meticulous notes on his Gucci leather pad.

The very last block in the pyramid of his surgical education was rhinoplasty. The progression had been gradual and disciplined. He had ventured first into the simplest operative procedure: breast augmentation. It was more than seven years later that he took the next step into face-lifting. He proceeded gingerly, doing no more than removing an inch of skin in front of the ear to tighten the cheeks a bit. After a few more years, he removed a small ellipse of redundant upper eyelid skin: Morrie Gold had performed his first blepharoplasty. Each case had been a carefully selected learning experience. The blocks fit neatly in place. After nearly twenty years of practice, he was ready for his first rhinoplasty. More than ready.

It was generally agreed by anyone who did aesthetic surgery that rhinoplasty, the reshaping of a nose, was the most difficult of all operative procedures. Being an avid student of plastic surgery, Morrie was well aware of that reality. And he was also aware of the latest trends and developments that had recently swept this particular kind of surgery. Quite recently it had become increasingly popular to perform rhinoplasties by the "open" method. He had read about it. At medical meetings he had seen the videos. The concept made sense. The objective of rhinoplastic surgery was to reshape the cartilage and bone that defined the shape of each individual nose. Rather than the conventional approach first described in the early 1900s, where incisions were made inside each nostril to remove cartilage and bone, the open approach offered better visualization of what the surgeon was doing. It entailed an incision inside each curved nostril rim and then across the skin of the central columella, lifting the skin away from the tip of the nose to allow direct visualization and sculpting of the cartilages. It was the "hot" procedure performed by most plastic surgeons in Los Angeles. The results were more precise, primarily because it was easier.

He had thought about it for several months, just waiting for the right case. Now he had it. But Morrie Gold would go one step further. In the literature he had uncovered a description of a bold approach in which the distal end of the nose was divided by an incision that lifted not just the skin but all of the nostril and the columella away from the cheek and upper lip. Any irregularities could be worked on directly. Morrie was certain that the other plastic surgeons were not aware of the literature as thoroughly as he was. Once again, he was one step ahead of them. Innovative and agile.

Stephanie's nose would be a substantial challenge. Morrie knew from his reading that there were many variables in nasal surgery and they were often unpredictable. Morrie also knew that rhinoplasties paid well. But it was, in fact, the very complexity that made such a procedure attractive to him. Stephanie's nose was another, but much more difficult, opportunity to be a sculptor of living tissue. The ultimate confrontation. His first rhinoplasty would go down in the history books as a magnificent and unprecedented surgical feat.

"Will you have to break my nose? I'll just die if I hear the bones break," she said, bringing him out of his reverie.

A screamer, Morrie thought. "Why don't you leave the surgery to me?" he responded, holding his smile firm. Screamers were bad for business. Other patients hear them and when the surgery's over most of them go running around town saying, "It was the most horrible experience of my life. He hurt me." And God forbid, if they didn't like the result, they'd tell everyone they could find that you'd butchered them.

"I hate pain," Stephanie blurted out.

"Oh, my, is that all you're worried about?" Morrie could not have sounded more casual. "My sweet girl, I have all kinds of medication for just that very purpose. Stephanie, I already sensed that you were afraid. I sensed it as soon as I walked into the room. I have a special feeling for this kind of thing. Trust me, I understand. I'm a doctor. I have responsibilities to my patients, and there is no responsibility more basic in the practice of medicine than to soothe pain. Or better yet, avoid it altogether. That's my job. That's what I was trained to do." His soft blue eyes looked squarely into hers, not blushing, not looking away. "Medical science has developed all varieties of medications. If one doesn't work, another one surely will. There will be no pain, Stephanie, my dear." Morrie knew how to handle screamers—snow 'em. If they're out of it, they didn't scream, they didn't scare other patients, and they told everybody, "I didn't feel a thing, not one thing." Snowing was good for business.

"Someone as attractive as you shouldn't worry." Morrie reached out and again took her right hand between his palms. His hands were soft and warm. "We call this operation a rhinoplasty. My dear, it's been around since

1910. It's simply a matter of taking a little cartilage and bone away from here and there. A Chicago physician made this kind of surgery popular back then. Did it at night in a room over his pharmacy. People were quite secretive in those days. I daresay we've improved the technique since then," Morrie said confidently. "I promise you won't feel a thing. Please trust me. You are much better off not thinking about it."

For Stephanie it was magic. This middle-aged man had effortlessly dismissed her greatest fear, demonstrated his power as the ultimate masculine protector, her dragon slayer. Stephanie looked into Morrie Gold's soft blue eyes and saw happiness. Stephanie saw her doctor.

Barely missing a beat, Morrie asked, "Do you have any trouble breathing, my dear?"

"No."

"No trouble at all?" he asked with surprise.

"Not really."

"Sometimes at night perhaps?"

"No. Well, maybe a couple of times . . ."

"I can fix that."

"Fix what?"

"Stephanie, you must stop worrying." He would tell Mrs. Evans to get as much up front as possible and then bill the insurance company full tilt. With a nose like hers, she ought to have trouble breathing. He smiled at her. "Now we come to the fun part. Have you selected a nose?"

"Oh, yes!" she said excitedly.

"Good. Show me the nose you want."

Stephanie lunged at the nose book, almost tearing pages as she turned them. She stopped and pointed to an elegant, chiseled profile.

"Aha!" Morrie said. "Very sophisticated. Very Morgan Fairchild. I can see you're a young woman with champagne taste."

"You mean this one costs more?"

"No. I was admiring your choice. It may be a little more difficult, considering the existing configuration."

"But you can do it?"

"Stephanie, a great plastic surgeon is not unlike an artist. We interpret according to the medium. You have a very lovely face. Results are evaluated as part of the total landscape. Let me show you what I mean."

Morrie motioned Stephanie over to the computer. He had a videocam set up and two monitors. Before she knew what was happening, he turned on the lights and her image appeared on one of the screens. Stephanie gasped. "Turn sideways, sweetheart, I want your profile."

"No."

"Stephanie! Trust me. Do you want to be a star?" Morrie waited while she slowly turned her head to the side. "Just hold it for a minute." After recording the picture, Morrie sat down at the keyboard. "All right. Now watch this."

After investing a small fortune in state of the art equipment, he would now finally put it to practical use. Morrie copied the image of Stephanie from one screen to another. Then he picked up his light pen and began to redraw her nose on the second monitor. He heard her gasp as he contoured and shortened her nose.

"Oh, my God!"

"Now, do you want to see how the nose you picked out would look on you?"

Stephanie glanced back at the page in the book. "Yes," she said softly.

Morrie reached for the keyboard. "Number twelve it is!" The image on the second monitor was that of a beautiful young woman. Someone who resembled but clearly was not the Stephanie Green on the other monitor.

Suddenly Stephanie began to cry. Ignoring her, Morrie began typing on the keyboard with the dramatic intensity of an organist accompanying a silent movie. Above him, the two "before and after" on-screen faces began rotating slowly from left profile to full face to right profile. Stephanie sobbed uncontrollably. Morrie sat back and listened to her tears with great satisfaction.

# 13

THE SURGERY TO reshape Felix Enriquez's face required slightly more than ten hours. During all that time, Lionel had stood in one place with his shoulders bent over the young boy's head. Only his hands had moved. When it was over, Lionel wasn't sure which part of his body hurt worse. The small bones in his feet felt like they had been crushed. He shrugged his shoulders forward to break the ties of his paper gown, and the muscles between his shoulder blades ached as if they had solidified. But as Lionel stepped away from the operating table he was more than satisfied with what he saw. The bone grafts now defined new, pleasing prominences on the boy's cheeks and nose. Nobody would ever again say that Felix resembled a frog.

"This kid is steel," Ed Arnold said as he removed the plastic anesthesia tube from Felix's trachea. "He bounced right back like there was nothing to it. Must have lost half his blood volume, but you'd never know it now." Felix gave a reassuring cough and fluttered his eyelids against the lingering anesthetic.

Lionel glanced at Felix's electrocardiogram and the brilliant red numbers that flashed his heart rate and blood pressure, and nodded his head affirmatively.

"Was that a friend of yours who scrubbed in for a while?"

"A very good friend."

"Looked a little shaky."

"Did pretty well, actually."

"Could have fooled me. When he left, he was pale as a sheet."

"He's had a rough time. A year ago he made a big mistake. Came into the operating room one morning and took out the wrong kidney."

"Christ," Sweeny whispered.

"The kidney was shriveled up so bad it was causing hypertension, and the patient was plus-four sick. The blood pressure was moving around like a Ping-Pong ball. So the internists called Peter to take it out," Lionel said. "Nobody knows what really happened. I've talked to Peter about it, and I don't think he knows himself. The scrub nurse said she thought he just reversed the X ray and mistook the right for the left. Anyway, post-op the patient had a hypertensive crisis and the pressure went right through the ceiling. The patient had a stroke and became paralyzed on one side of his body. Two days later they did another Intravenous Pyelogram and realized what happened. Peter had to take the patient to the OR again and remove the remaining kidney to control the blood pressure. They planned a transplant, but by that time the patient was entirely too sick and they had to settle for chronic dialysis."

"Was he drinking?"

"Absolutely not," Lionel said firmly. "At least not then. Never drank much at all. He was an extremely conscientious surgeon. He just made one careless mistake." Lionel shook his head. "He started to visit the patient in the hospital. Peter went every day. And every day the patient slid downhill just a little bit further. That's when Peter started to hit the sauce pretty hard. I haven't seen much of him since. Don't think anyone has. He just started to get out and around a few weeks ago. Trying to get a practice together again. Today was the first time he's been in an operating room since the whole thing happened."

"No wonder he looked spooked," Sweeny said as he snapped closed the fishing tackle box containing his IV medications. "You never know, do you? But I'll tell you one thing, Lion. I didn't know it at the time, but I was real glad you were holding the knife this morning. That was some piece of work."

"I appreciate that, Ed. Thanks," Lionel said as Sweeny left with the orderlies who wheeled Felix to the recovery room.

Flo was in the corner of the OR, cleaning the surgical instruments with a brush and soapy water, getting them ready for the next sterilization.

"Flo, you were great," Lionel said under his mask. The Flash merely shrugged her shoulders, offering a token acknowledgment for what was obviously true.

Lionel was accustomed to tangible results achieved in the operating room. Some people were repulsed by the sick and deformed. Lionel Stern was attracted to them, driven by a compulsion to repair the damage, to restore the humanity. It wasn't altruism that made him love surgery, but rather a basic satisfaction that came from setting things right. By surgically intervening in a patient's life, his efforts resulted in a visible improvement that was gratifying.

But Lionel took equal pleasure from the technical challenge that his hands had been trained to meet. He knew very well that surgery was a performing art. Each time he stepped into an operating room, he savored the quality of that performance. He had substantially improved the quality of life for Felix. Mrs. McWaters was another matter entirely. At that moment in her life she didn't need surgery; she needed a husband. It was all too likely she'd find someone out there only too eager to bill her for what she wanted. That was the problem—he resented deeply having to share his profession with the Beverly Hills Nose Brigade, the Sunset Boulevard Liposuction Lotharios.

Lionel pushed his palms against the tiled wall and began to slowly stretch the muscles in his calves. OR 9 was empty again and, with the exception of the clock, looked exactly as it had early that morning. He stretched some more. Flo loaded the instruments into the steam autoclave, continuing to work as if he weren't there. He said good-bye, got another shrug from her and ran up the stairs, taking four at a stride.

In less than three minutes, he swallowed two cups of coffee cooled by tap water, changed into thin nylon running shorts, New Balance sneakers and a blue cotton T-shirt that was soft and faded from countless washings. He jogged out of the loading dock of the mail room located at the back of the hospital and headed across the sprawling university campus toward the stadium.

Lionel ran easily at first, allowing his muscles to warm and loosen, and by the time he reached the track, he was in full stride. Although the lanes were only partially illumi-nated by the lights of the adjacent dormitory, the artificial surface was smooth and predictable. His body began to surge, the effort of his legs pleasing, and soon all thoughts that tumbled noisily in his mind disappeared.

It was only after he completed his twelfth lap that he thought of anything at all. But after the final turn, it wasn't Felix's surgery that occupied his mind. It was the unsettling image of Peter Dalway, ashen white.

The two men had first met in the basement laundry room of Johns Hopkins Hospital as they picked up their allocation of white pants and coats. They put on the heavily starched, absolutely white cotton—the billboard that labeled them as new, untested interns. Over the next year, although sharing jokes about too little sleep, sex and sunlight, their perspec-tives were quite different.

Nothing came easily for Lionel. He was an adopted child, whereas Peter's father was the head of one of the largest film studios in Hollywood. Lionel had to work his way through college, barely able to keep up with his studies, while Peter sailed through and spent vacations in the exotic locales where E. R. Dalway's films were being shot. Lionel couldn't even get into a U.S. medical school. The most important part of Peter's application for admission was the understanding that his father would break ground for The Dalway Research Center upon Peter's acceptance. Lionel spent the first two years in Guadalajara, where the living was so cheap he could work less and study more to bring his grades up in order to transfer back home.

Johns Hopkins University Hospital was located in a bleak part of Baltimore. The buildings were old and the inside of the hospital was quite ordinary. But from the moment Lionel first walked through the front door, four days after graduation from medical school, he recognized the rich heritage of this very special place. The walls were covered with photographs of men who had conceived and developed the surgical operations that were still used long after they had died. There was an unmistakable pride within the old building and a sense of medical history that could be felt even in the depths of the laundry room where the ceiling pipes ran in all directions and were covered with layers of cracked paint.

Peter took it all for granted. His perspective came from special casual luxury unique to Southern California. His father had carved out his own definition of tradition at a time when Los Angeles was still a young city. Because the family tradition was so solid and formidable, Peter concluded at an early age that it was unlikely he could ever make an impression on it. So he simply chose to ignore it. As if out of reflex, when he walked through the monumental front door of the hospital, Peter looked at it very quickly and never gave it a second thought. Lionel breathed it in with a silent and modest reverence that he kept carefully hidden from view.

Within days after they put on those first starched whites, the cotton was stained by every fluid that flows through the bodies of sick people. But each day they put on the whites, they did so with very different feelings.

"What's your first rotation?" Peter asked as they left the laundry room.

"Emergency room."

"The Pit," Peter said, nodding solemnly. "Some interns never leave that place alive. The weak ones don't last more than a few days. From then on they just wheel you out with the rest of the stiffs that submarine in there. I heard that hospital administration doesn't even notify your family. They just assume that if you're dumb enough to apply for this internship you deserve anything you get. This place is crazy. As you may have noticed, we are not situated in one of the better neighborhoods of the fair city of Baltimore. Would you believe some social workers decided to give the neighborhood kids, each and every one of them, mind you, a pair of roller skates? Can you imagine? I guess this nice lady thought it would make their lives more meaningful. I don't know what the nice lady was thinking when she came up with the idea, but what I do know is they skate around here in groups of ten or twelve kids and you could write a book on the management of trauma on account of that do-gooder social worker." Peter used his chin to steady the stack of starched whites cradled in his arms. "Caused three auto accidents and more broken arms and sprained wrists than you can count. The worst thing happened yesterday. Two of 'em lost their balance during a race along the sidewalk and fell into a store window. They brought one in DOA, literally in two pieces. The other one they saved in The Pit and is up in the ICU after nine hours in the operating room."

"Sounds like a busy place." Lionel was suitably impressed.

"The Pit?" Peter's voice grew deep and solemn. "You'll love it." Peter stopped as they reached the tiny on-call room, which was almost completely filled by a set of double-decker metal bunks and a sink. "*We* will love it. Heads or tails?" Peter asked, flipping a coin he took from his pocket.

"Heads."

"You, Dr. Stern, win the prize. You are, as of now, the medical custodian of the East Baltimore Chapter of the Knife and Gun Club. And, friend, to make you feel welcome—it's Saturday night! Which is meeting night. From what I hear, you'll be busy. And, remember, we're not medical students anymore. Things change quickly after they give you that diploma. Now we are the guys we used to call for help just a couple of days ago. Think about it. Scary, huh?" Peter hesitated. "Actually, I hope things are slow because I'm your backup. If things get warm out there, call me. Don't hesitate. Believe me, when your twenty-four hours are over and you get a chance for some sleep, I'll call you if I have to put on two Band-Aids at the same time."

Lionel gave a nervous laugh and unfolded his whites and shoved his legs and arms between the thick starchy layers before walking into the emergency room.

It was a long rectangular room, lined on each side by ten narrow beds mounted on wheels, with thin mattresses covered by precisely folded sheets. It was noon and the room was quiet. Empty. Five hours later, true to Peter's prediction, all of the gurneys were occupied by either sick or injured people. Stern moved methodically from patient to patient, looking at X rays, molding wet plaster around broken legs and wrists, suturing cuts, and placing neatly taped bandages on wounds.

The hours had flown by when Lionel saw Peter walking toward him. "You should have called me three hours ago," Peter said, rubbing his puffy eyes as if they had just opened.

"Lost track of time," Lionel said as he carefully knotted the last in an orderly row of black silk sutures that perfectly approximated what had been a gaping forehead laceration.

"You know, Stern, you're very slow," Peter whispered over Lionel's shoulder, one of his boyish smiles covering his face. "But, on the other hand, you do very poor work."

And so it began, the friendly rivalry. Neither was simply a good surgical intern—each was extraordinary, in very different ways. Stern, methodical and steady. Dalway, quick and unconventional.

Within a few months, Peter had become a phenomenon. The mechanical aspects of the performance of a surgical procedure, the sequence of maneuvers and the command of anatomy, often difficult for young physicians in training, never posed the slightest obstacle for Peter. He absorbed what he saw in the operating room and read in surgical journals so quickly and easily that it appeared entirely effortless. It was not difficult to make the erroneous assumption that he didn't care as much as the other interns. In the early months of his internship, some of the senior residents, particularly those from eastern medical schools, referred to him as "California Casual." But in the operating room, Peter was a natural surgeon, blessed with an almost mystical sense of what to do with a scalpel.

Surgeons in training learned how to handle fine suture material by sewing up the abdominal wound after the completion of a surgical procedure. As time went on it was customary for a senior resident to reward an intern for his long hours of patient care by allowing him to perform part of a surgical procedure—the first steps in a graduated surgical education. In the fourth month of Peter's internship, a senior resident allowed him to stand on the right side of the operating table and make the abdominal incision that began a cholecystectomy. Thirty minutes later, Peter had neatly removed the patient's gall bladder and it was lying on the scrub nurse's table. The senior resident was in a mild state of shock.

Lionel and Peter became close friends during that first year. By midyear, they had also become rivals—not because of direct competition, but rather because they were so frequently compared to each other due to their outstanding talent and skill. Lionel was aware that in the cafeteria and the coffee room, the other residents and nurses spoke quite highly of his own technical abilities. He also knew that the same residents spoke of Peter in terms that bordered on pure awe.

At the end of each academic year, the department of surgery held a formal banquet where there were toasts and awards handed out. It was a black-tie celebration capping twelve months of very hard work. The highlight of the ceremony was a medal given to one of the sixteen interns for being the very best in his group. In Peter and Lionel's year, there was no question in anyone's mind that one of them would receive the coveted badge of courage and excellence for performance during a year when the demands were measured by superhuman standards: dedication, intelligence, judgment, maturity, technical ability. So as to be complete, "devotion to humanity" was also listed by the chairman when he rose to announce the winner.

It was a contrast in style. Who would win the Heisman Trophy? The flashy quarterback who could sidestep and scramble for nine yards when his receivers were covered just as easily as complete a touchdown pass, or the hard-running, straight-ahead fullback who averaged 3.1 yards a carry?

The award went to the quarterback.

"I'm disappointed they didn't give it to you," Peter said to Lionel after the festivities, his face quite solemn.

"It went to the best man," Lionel replied, a bit surprised that there wasn't any joy in his friend's face.

"No, it didn't."

After his run, Lionel showered and changed. It was nine o'clock at night and he was on the way back to his office. As the elevator doors opened, he found himself standing face to face with Ellsworth Crawford, "the old man" who was everyone's old man at University Hospital. It seemed to Lionel that Ellsworth must have always been an old man, even in kindergarten. He was head of surgery, but now all Lionel could think about was the fact that he was also Casey's father.

"It was a dumb thing to do," Ellsworth said.

"Peter couldn't help it. I owe him one and right now he's having a rough time."

Ellsworth stepped off the elevator and took Lionel's arm. "I don't expect anything from Peter. I'm talking about you." He spoke in a voice that was modulated but made no effort to cover his upset. "The OR is not to be used as a halfway house."

"How the hell did you find out so fast?"

"How? I keep my ear to the ground. That's how."

The two men stared angrily at one another. Finally, Ellsworth spoke. "You want to go to dinner?"

Lionel couldn't help smiling. "Casey would kill me."

Ellsworth rolled his eyes. "What the hell are we going to do about Casey? I figured a year ago back that she'd marry you and I'd be off the hook. God knows, Lion, you're worse than I ever was."

Lionel wanted to change the subject. "Who told you about Peter?"

"You know I can't reveal my sources." Then, as though remembering, Ellsworth said proudly, "I hear you did one hell of a job on Felix."

Suddenly, Lionel knew who had told Ellsworth about Peter. "Sweeny!"

Ellsworth shrugged. "You know what an old lady he is."

# 14

It HAD BEEN hours since Stephanie entered her apartment, closed the door gently and sat down on the sofa, tightly holding her purse as though she were on a park bench in a dangerous neighborhood. The sun had been bright, then faded and set. It was dark. Stephanie was still shaking.

What's wrong with me? The question repeated itself over and over again. Dr. Gold had promised there would be no pain. She trusted him more than she had any of the others. The other doctors with whom she had scheduled surgery and then canceled were so cold. So businesslike. But Dr. Gold really understood her. His soft blue eyes had seen beyond her face and into her dreams. She didn't understand why she should grieve. After all, it was finally going to happen. She was going to be beautiful. The dream was within reach. Right in her lap. Just like her purse. The thing she wanted most in the world was about to come true. But as much as she tried to rely on reason, Stephanie's emotions were on the downslope of a roller coaster. Her mind was filled with a single image, that of her face, her new face, on Dr. Gold's computer. And a single thought, *Splendor in the Grass*. What if she had the surgery but didn't become a star? Then who or what could she blame?

That had always been the problem. But Dr. Gold and surgery would eliminate the excuses. She would have to take full responsibility for her life and could no longer blame a genetic accident for her success or failure. Stephanie would have to redefine rejection as an enemy rather than a familiar friend. The explanation for living alone or not getting a part would no longer be as plain as the nose on her face.

The single element that made it different this time was her new agent, Danny Arnold. She was sure that Danny wouldn't have set up the appointment with Dr. Gold if he hadn't been serious about her testing for the part on "General Hospital." The reason she felt sure about Danny had nothing to do with sleeping with him. It had everything to do with Dr. Gold. There was no doubt in Stephanie's mind that Danny had been right about him.

Stephanie was outnumbered. Her fear of surgery, her parents' admonitions against being vain and frivolous, even her own fear of the future paled in comparison to the show-business biological clock against which she was racing. It was a business that bought and sold youth. Her youth was running out. If there was one thing she had learned as a body model it was to forget all that "inner beauty" crap. Cosmetics, hair dressing, clothes, perfume or even surgery—it didn't matter which—they differed only in degree. You had to have a beautiful face. Stephanie had always felt she deserved a beautiful face. Now she could afford to buy one.

Stephanie put down her purse, reached over and turned on the light. She went to the closet and took a box from the top shelf. It was dusty. She slowly opened the box and one by one took out photographs of her mother and her two sisters. The tears fell down her cheeks as she put the pictures on a shelf. It was the first time in years that she had been able to look at them.

# 15

Lᴉᴏɴᴇʟ ᴀɴᴅ Cᴀꜱᴇʏ never spoke while making love. Words, like medical explanations for the swirl of emotions they were feeling, had no place and were erased from memory. Only their senses were operative. What Lionel enjoyed most was that he and Casey made love like grown-ups. They trusted not only each other but themselves.

Casey had been the first and only woman with whom Lionel had slept since his divorce from Ginny. They could not have been more different. Not just in the obvious ways: Ginny was country-club pretty, a woman totally dependent upon appreciation and compliments. Casey was pure country, strong features, honey-blonde hair cut short, stylish but simple clothes, with a sense of power that surrounded her.

Ginny always talked during and after sex, constantly telling Lionel how wonderful he was. Casey never did. There was a tacit understanding that if he were not wonderful, she simply wouldn't be with him.

In many ways Lionel felt more confident with Casey. But also more challenged. Casey watched his every move while they made love, her blue eyes focused on him as he pushed deep inside her. Physically, the way they fit was a horizontal paradise. But he never felt as though he possessed her, even when she was wrapped within his arms. There were times that she seemed to consciously, by an act of will, maintain a distance. And when it occurred, he suddenly felt lonely. Casey had the power to move him around like an emotional yo-yo. It was at the same time both attractive and unsettling.

Lionel kissed her gently on the lips, then lowered his head to feel the warmth of her neck. Casey's hands moved slowly down his sides, turning her head to face him with an open mouth. As his lips touched hers, the phone rang.

Casey whispered, "I didn't hear a thing."

Lionel froze, his consciousness returning from deep within this magnificent woman, up from his belly and into his brain. "Shit." He sighed heavily.

She tightened her legs around him as the phone rang again. "Don't talk, Lion. To anyone."

Lionel pulled away slowly. "I have bad news. There is an outside world."

"What outside world?" Casey picked up the phone, hesitated and looked at Lionel. "Is this your house or mine?"

He lay back on the bed and covered himself. "Yours."

Casey shrugged and spoke into the receiver. "If you're selling magazine subscriptions . . ."

It was Ellsworth. "Get you at a bad time?"

"No," she said impatiently. "The trouble is you got me at a good time." Casey put her hand over the receiver and whispered to Lionel, "It's my father."

"Should have known better. I told him I was seeing you tonight."

"Then you should have known he'd call if you were here. He's playing matchmaker again." She took her hand away from the receiver. "Hi, daddy."

"Lionel there?"

"Yes, I'm fine, thank you," she said sarcastically. "How are you?"

"What's the matter?" Ellsworth asked. "You two have another fight?"

"No. But if you don't watch it, I think we're about to."

Lionel sighed deeply and took the phone from her. "Ellsworth."

"I wanted to talk to you about Felix."

Lionel sat up. "What's wrong?"

Casey groaned and put the sheet over her head. "Doctors!"

"I thought you might be stopping in to look at him on your way home. That is, if you're going home."

"Ellsworth, is there something wrong?"

"No. I just thought . . ."

"Listen, I left the hospital less than two hours ago. I've got Felix covered better than King Tut's mummy."

There was a pause, then Ellsworth said, "I was concerned about the amount of fluid he's received. It's not difficult to give too much, you know."

Lionel covered his mouthpiece and whispered to Casey, "Now he's giving a lecture on postoperative care." Lionel smiled and shook his head. "Is there a problem, Ellsworth? I mean with Felix?"

"Well . . . not really . . ."

"Listen, as long as there isn't an emergency, I mean, this isn't the best time for me to come down to the hospital."

Casey nodded her head affirmatively and kissed Lionel.

"No problem," Ellsworth said. "I'll come over."

Lionel's voice became tense. "Ellsworth, that is not a good idea."

"Why what's the matter? Didn't you kids eat yet?"

"No," Lionel said quickly, thinking he had found an out. "We didn't eat yet."

Casey opened her mouth wide and chomped on Lionel's shoulder.

"Great!" Ellsworth shouted. "I'll bring Chinese."

Lionel put his hand over the receiver and spoke to Casey. "He wants to come over."

"Not tonight, Josephine," she whispered.

"Casey, *you* tell him. He's your father."

She reached for the phone. "He's your mentor!" she whispered. Changing her tone, she spoke into the receiver. "I'd love to have dinner with you, daddy. How about tomorrow? Seven o'clock? I know this great place on Melrose. We can catch up what I've been doing since I was twelve."

Lionel flopped back on the bed and groaned. "Oh, Christ!"

There was a pause on the other end of the receiver. "You know I can't make it at seven o'clock."

"Seven-fifteen?"

"Your mother really did a job on you," Ellsworth said.

"Wasn't anybody else around, as I recall." Another pause. "So, Pops? Can I buy you a bottle and a bird?"

"I don't think so, Casey. Not as long as you're offering cyanide and crow. Sounds to me that's all you've got an appetite for." Another pause. "You okay, kiddo?"

Casey spoke softly. "Yes. I'm fine. We'll talk tomorrow." She hung up the phone and whispered, "Couldn't be better."

Lionel sat up. He put his arms around her. "Why do you keep doing that to him? Listen I know how you feel, but he needs some support right now. He'd kill me if he knew I told you, but there's been some talk at the hospital that he should retire. Couple of different staff members have gently suggested it to him. So, to change their minds, he puts in eighteen hours a day, which only convinces everyone they're right."

"Damn them. Don't they know he's got no life outside the hospital? He sure as hell never did and never will."

"Except for you. That's why . . ."

"That's why nothing. I gave up a good part of my childhood because my father was a surgeon. I'm not going to give up the rest of my life because he isn't." Casey emerged from the sheets and quickly put a pillow over her face. "Oh, I can't believe this. I'm complaining about Icarus to Daedalus. What the hell kind of sympathy am I going to get from you?"

"You're not the one who needs sympathy!"

"You're right. What I need is my head examined for ever getting involved with another doctor! And it has to be of all things a fucking surgeon!"

"Casey, are you going to be mad at him for the rest of your life?"

"Dear God, I hope so."

"Why?"

Casey held tight to Lionel. "It's the only protection I have."

"Against what?"

"Against you."

Lionel forced a laugh. There was something suggesting a finality in what she said, but more in the way she said it. He coaxed her to lie down with him. "Come here."

She pulled back from him. "No. Lion, no. You lie down with doctors, you wake up with patients. I saw what kind of life my mother had. I don't want to marry a surgeon whose responsibilities make him a husband by proxy. I'm the real thing, Lion. I want the same back."

"Casey, I'm not Ellsworth."

"No, you're not. You got here an hour before he would have. But it was still late at night. Need I remind you I still had to go to the party by myself. Solo. Alone. A cappella." Casey sat upright in bed. Her eyes focused on Lionel. "And, I have a confession to make. I met a man tonight at the reception. Businessman, stocks, that sort of thing. Very nice. Sort of average looking, maybe average all the way around. But nice."

"So what do you see in him?" Lionel said, perplexed, a sinking feeling pulling at his stomach.

"I see a man who doesn't have patients or, in his case, clients calling him in the middle of the night with a financial crisis. He doesn't have to rush down to the bank to count mutual funds at two in the morning. He could probably make love without his beeper going off! Oh, Lion, it's not what I see in some stranger. It's what he saw in me! When I talked to him I felt important, as a woman. He wants to see me. This weekend. *Anytime* this weekend, not just in the middle of the night. I got the feeling I would be very important to him. I'm afraid, Lion, afraid of not being very important to you."

Lionel sat on the edge of the bed, facing away from Casey. "I didn't know things had gone this far."

"Nothing happened."

Lionel didn't say anything, content to tuck the pillow

beneath his chest. "Yes. Yes it did," he said with a sigh. "Six months ago, when we started seeing each other, you would never allow someone to get that close. Whatever it was he had to say, you listened."

"I had to."

"Why did you have to?"

Without missing a beat, she said very simply, "Because . . . I . . . am so in love with you."

"Then for God's sake, let's get married!" He turned to Casey and smiled. "Make an honest man out of me."

She put a hand to his cheek. "Oh, Lion, you don't need me for that. You're the most honest man I've ever met."

At that moment Lionel realized that while he wanted a lover, he needed Casey as a wife even more. She was bright and smart, ambitious and loving. A whole person, a woman who defined herself. She didn't have to fit into Lionel's life, she had her own. She was the perfect wife for someone who couldn't be around—except, she wouldn't live that way. And it was now quite clear that a line had been drawn. He had tried in the months before to understand Casey's not wanting to marry him, but it had been difficult—probably because he had always clung to the belief that she would eventually change her mind. But what it amounted to was that he was unwilling to believe what she kept saying. Casey had suffered as a child because of medicine and had never forgotten it. She had no intention of becoming a surgery widow. She had said it over and over. This time she had sounded different, harder, just a little bit farther away. What sent panic deep within him now was the thought that time just may have run out. "So tell me. How do I stack up against Mr. Businessman?"

Casey kissed him gently. "Dummy. It's no contest. It's more a question of availability. You're by far the better man."

"But not necessarily the winner." Lionel got up to dress, wondering whether he had made an accurate diagnosis of what had, before this evening, been going on between them. Now there was some nondescript gray-suiter to complicate the picture. He understood why Casey had said she loved him. She had risked nothing by admitting it. She was safe in the Kingdom of Unless. But he wasn't.

"Why are you going?" she asked.

He hesitated. "I have to stop in and see Felix," he said absently, suddenly realizing that this might be his last time in Casey's bed. It also occurred to him that he was very dumb.

# 16

PETER DALWAY WAS at home. More accurately, at his condominium overlooking rows of sailboats in the marina. It was the place where he slept most often, had a closet filled with expensive clothes, and stacks of paperback novels lining the walls. A decorator had brought in the kind of tasteful but mindless furniture one finds in a motel suite. It had never occurred to Peter that he might rearrange anything because he never felt in possession of the premises. He often wondered why he bothered to lock the door when he left. Inside that place there was nothing of value to him.

The sun had long since set, fading out the armada of sailboats in the marina, their masts swaying in the calm water. The end of the nightmare that had been his day. He felt the fade-in of a very elite film noir at the same time he realized he was out of cognac. He would have to buy some. But he hated buying liquor, the same way he hated buying condoms. It was an invasion of privacy. A public declaration that he was about to be fucked, one way or the other.

But there was a solution. A bar. And Peter knew the very best bar in Los Angeles. He called for a taxi, grabbed his jacket and walked out of the condo, smiling to himself. He left the door unlocked. Wide open.

Slouched in the back seat of the taxi, Peter directed the driver north on the San Diego freeway, across Sunset Boulevard and into Benedict Canyon. He rolled down the window to inhale the scent of pine trees. "Stop here, please."

The driver looked at Peter and shrugged. No one stopped in the middle of a deserted street in Benedict Canyon. Peter gave him a twenty and walked along the tree-lined driveway. As he approached the heavy wrought-iron gate, he stopped and put his hands on the bars. Like a prisoner in a cell, he looked through at the house. This was a real home. Home was a place you kept locked.

Peter took out his key, turned it in the small box at knee level, and the gate swung open slowly. He closed it behind him and continued up the incline of asphalt, gray and cracked with age. The house, partially hidden by trees, sprawled in several directions. San Diego red bougainvilleas climbed up the heavily textured white plaster walls and crept over the adobe-tiled roof. He stood in front of the house, staring at the doorway as if trying to remember something. Then he heard the sound of screeching brakes behind him.

"Hey! What the hell do you . . . Peter? My God!" the man yelled as he jumped out of the shiny black Mercedes sedan and embraced him. Homer was the last of Edgar Dalway's previously enormous staff. A portly black man, he started to laugh. "I was just going out when I see this man on the TV monitor. Thought you were a prowler. They come around every now and then. Why didn't you let me know you were coming?"

Peter put a hand on Homer's shoulder. "Keep you on your toes."

"Toes?" Homer began to laugh again and patted his belly. "I haven't seen my toes in years." He became serious. "Why don't you come back home, Petie?"

"Too big, Homer. I'd get lost. Anyway, it's not my house."

"It is, if you let it be. Mr. Dalway wanted you to have it. This used to be a happy house, Petie. Needs to have parties, people, a few stiff belts."

Peter considered for a moment. "Now that's one hell of an idea."

"A party?" There was glee in the man's voice.

"Yeah, that too."

Homer took the car back to the garage after Peter promised to call him soon and talk about a party. It was the same promise he had made to Homer at least half a dozen times. Once alone, Peter punched in the combination on the digital alarm code, opened the thick wooden door and went into the house. He took one step onto the white marble floor and stopped. An intruder, Peter Dalway was trespassing on what used to be, loitering on what might have been.

Peter once described the decor of the house as a cross between Versailles and Hitler's bunker—"Early Mogul" he would often tease his father. It was lavish, dangerous, vulgar and breathtaking. A copy of Tara's staircase in the foyer. Mirrors from *The Great Ziegfeld* and urns from *The Good Earth*. A tastefully gaudy backdrop for all the movie stars and politicians who wouldn't dare miss one of E.R.'s parties. Without turning on a light, Peter walked in shadows toward his father's study.

The walls were filled with photographs of E.R.'s friends and with books E.R. had never read but which were selected for their covers. The floor had carpet upon carpet— Tabriz, Kashans, tribal Caucasians—covering the walnut inlay and part of each other like a deck of playing cards someone had dropped casually.

Peter walked to the bookshelf that extended from floor to frescoed ceiling and pressed against the large red leather dictionary. A segment of five shelves slid up to reveal a mirrored panel lined with cut crystal decanters and sparkling goblets. As Peter reached for the cognac, he caught a glimpse of himself. His eyes were red. Pouchy. Moist. Like some old rummy. He poured a drink quickly and downed it in a single gulp. Goddamn. It *was* the best bar in town.

Holding the decanter in one hand and a glass in the other, Peter sat down at the imposing mahogany desk in front of a wall of photographs. The size of the desk was compelling. It was a desk at which one did important things. Like pouring another drink. With a deep sigh of resignation, Peter took out a pad of yellow legal size paper and his father's gold pen. He hesitated and exchanged the pen for a plain wooden pencil. He began a list.

For one thing, he was not going to see Irene anymore. And that included her kinky roommate. And, he vowed, pushing the decanter away, he would stop drinking.

Peter took the telephone book from the top drawer and wrote down the names of all the hospitals in West Los Angeles in a disorderly column. Under each entry, he made space for the time of the urology conferences and a schedule of visits to each of the doctors' dining rooms. Peter swallowed hard against his dry throat. He had tried the lunch routine before, good God he had tried, and how he hated the feigned comradery with other doctors whose dull personalities only made his depression worse.

He uttered a brief curse and reached for the cognac. He filled the glass half full. What the hell. One out of two wasn't bad. He definitely would not call Irene and he would have lunch in every doctors' dining room in Southern California if he had to. Peter swiveled the leather desk chair and faced the wall of photographs.

There were his mother and father at the beach in Santa Monica, at the Oscars, on location. There was his father with Errol Flynn. Shit, anyone who knew Errol Flynn ought to be able to get his son a job. Dead or not. Being dead was nothing new for E.R. It had happened to everyone in the picture business. Often for years at a time. His father with John F. Kennedy. All varieties of banquet tables, black bow ties, puffy-shouldered evening dresses, smiles, cocktail glasses. His father with Streisand. With Speilberg. Where the hell was Einstein? Salk? There was a banquet photo with his father sitting next to Morrie Gold.

Peter's eyes moved over the orderly arrangement of familiar faces. There was Peter Dalway, young surgical resident, one year out of medical school, in starched whites. A man who still had a future. The picture had been taken the day Peter learned he would enter the United States Army. The news had not made him unhappy. Within the next frame, Peter with his dog tags glistening as he leaned against his tent in Vietnam, sweat making a dark circle in the center of his olive drab T-shirt.

Time had passed so quickly. He sighed, making a futile wish that somehow, by the silent utterance of his wish, he could retrieve the past. Peter felt the onset of the comforting oblivion of the cognac. It offered hope that he was not permanently connected to things, places, people.

Leaving the C-131 after it landed in Qui Non was like stepping into a steam bath. Captain Peter Dalway held five copies of his orders, combinations of unintelligible numbers and letters separated by diagonal lines. They rustled in the gusts of wind like a refugee tag. Within minutes, the noise stopped, the sheets of paper joined together by the heavy moisture in the air.

It had been seven months since the U.S. destroyer *C. Turner Joy* had been torpedoed in the Gulf of Tonkin. The episode had started a military draft of doctors and a small panic among Peter's fellow residents at Johns Hopkins. Several friends were there one day, gone the next. Lionel had been drafted. One medical resident moved to Canada. Others searched for ways to be classified 4F. For anyone other than a doctor, the task of draft avoidance was difficult but not impossible. If you had a heart murmur, you were 4F. If you had diabetes, you were 4F. Indeed, if you were taller than six feet six, you were 4F. But if you were a physician, none of the medical loopholes applied. You were considered suitable for military service even if you required a portable oxygen tank to breathe.

Avoiding service to his country was not an issue for Peter. He knew a great deal about surgery after that first year, and the prospect of doing something dangerous was attractive. Randolph Scott and John Wayne had been ready to go to war. So was Peter Dalway. Ann-Margret had promised to write, and Debbie Reynolds was going to send cookies.

"Captain Dalway?" The voice could barely be heard as it was blown away by the thick wind. "I'm Sergeant Hill. Step in and we'll get your gear." Hill led Peter around to the passenger side of the jeep as if there were a door to open. The jeep was short and square, no doors, no top, no windshield. Hill smiled. "You can write home and say you were picked up in a convertible."

Peter laughed more than the joke was worth. He felt giddy. For the first time in his life he was alone, separated from his family and his name. And until Debbie Reynolds's cookies arrived, he was anxious to be accepted on his own.

Months passed. But instead of surgical breakthroughs, Peter became adept at treating venereal diseases. He spent his off time alone, reading. He devoured war novels, seeking the excitement of battle vicariously. It was during this time that Peter concluded that war was not, as it was in the movies, a rewarding drama of men in constant combat. Rather, it was for the most part a dull experience punctuated with occasional episodes of terror.

One windless night, Peter snapped awake as a medic burst into his tent shouting, "Captain, we just brought in some casualties. Special Forces. On some kind of secret operation. They got hit in the jungle. Hill is with 'em now." He rushed out. The chopper's flashing lights were barely visible through the dust that swirled around the landing pad. Hill was in the cabin on his knees. Peter pushed by him. Three men lay inside, each almost completely covered with layers of mud. A pool of blood spread over the floor, deep enough to cover the corrugations in the metal. The soldier lying behind the pilot's seat was very still, his eyes open and staring at Peter.

"I wonder how old he was," Peter said absently, feeling a wave of nausea.

"He's dead, Captain," Hill replied. "That's as old as you get around here." Hill was working on another man, cutting away his grimy fatigue jacket. "Son of a bitch!" Hill muttered, exposing the man's chest. "Captain?"

Peter felt the blood soak through his trousers as he knelt next to the soldier. Just below the right clavicle was a purple-red wound about the size of a nickel that slowly oozed small pools of nearly black blood mixed with bubbles of air. Peter reached for the man's wrist and felt its cool temperature and barely perceptible pulse. "It's not going to stop by itself. You have instruments for me to open his chest?"

"Five minutes, Captain," Hill said, jumping onto the ground. "That's all I need."

Caught up in the blur of motion he had set in progress, Peter shouted, "That's all he's got!"

Peter had assisted on several thoracotomies, but he had never performed the procedure by himself. Now, in the dust of Delta Med, in the middle of the night, Peter was the best chance for survival the man had. For the first time in his life, Peter had an opportunity to accomplish something in a place where no one recognized or cared about the Dalway name.

The sandbagged tin operating room was small, completely filled with sweaty bodies and the drone of a marginally-effective air conditioner. The soldier was lying naked on the operating table, still covered by splotches of drying mud, a black rubber anesthetic mask over his mouth and nose. Peter, eager to be tested, quickly scrubbed his hands while the corpsman began to wash away the sticky dirt from the dying man's chest. He nodded to the anesthesiologist, who lifted the rubber mask and inserted the endotracheal tube. It was only a matter of seconds that the mask was raised, but Peter's heart began to race as he looked down at his patient. It was Lionel Stern.

Hours later, when Lionel's eyes opened, Peter was sitting on his bed. Lionel's eyes wandered, then fixed on Peter. His mouth moved, but no sounds came out.

"I know you missed me," Peter said, "but a phone call would have done."

Lionel looked down at the tape that covered his chest. "You did this?"

"Neat little bit of needle and thread work, if I do say so myself. I may go into dressmaking."

"It's a miracle."

Peter nodded. "You were lucky all right. One helluva mortar wound."

Lionel shook his head. "No. It's a miracle I survived your

surgery." He grinned weakly as the corpsman brought in a stretcher to move Lionel back to his MASH unit. As Peter followed alongside and helped put him on the waiting helicopter, Lionel said, "I owe you one."

Peter laughed. "Don't worry. I'll send you a bill."

# 17

$L$IONEL STERN AND John Maltry led a loose procession of white coats walking along the polished linoleum corridors of University Hospital. They were followed by two third-year students making early morning rounds. The patient they had just seen was watching television.

Brian Abraham whispered to his classmate, "How's this for a little nostalgia? I can remember watching 'The Today Show' when I got up in the morning. Not before I went to sleep in the morning."

Lionel was accustomed to hearing the residents bitch. It reminded him of that first year at Hopkins with Peter, and it gave him great satisfaction to be on the other end. He knew it would probably be time to give up teaching when the residents stopped complaining.

"Look to your right," Abraham continued, "and you may notice that there is sunshine outside this institution. And I use that word intentionally. Are you aware that a statistically significant segment of greater Los Angeles is getting up, fully rested, after a good night's sleep?"

"Keep it down," the other whispered back. "My feet are killing me. If we were on the medicine floor, we would be home like normal people," Abraham said, his shoulders slumped forward as he walked.

"That's one of the reasons internists think surgeons are very dumb," his classmate replied from the corner of his mouth. "You know how to tell the difference between an internist and a surgeon trying to catch an elevator when the doors are closing?" he asked. "An internist stops it with his hand. A surgeon uses his head."

The procession went down two stairwells and onto the pediatric floor. As the group entered Felix's room, he raised his fist above his head into what had become his familiar greeting. But he raised his arm very slowly. Felix's usually bright eyes were barely visible and what little could be seen of them was quite dull. It had been three days since the surgery and the edema fluid still lingered, distorting all of his facial features. The young boy resembled a caricature from a science fiction movie.

"Give the nurses a hard time today?" Lionel asked as he gently patted the boy's swollen cheek. Felix shook his head slowly and made a feeble and ineffective effort to smile.

The cluster of white lab coats formed a semicircle around Felix's bed, and the first-year general surgery resident began his presentation. "This nine-year-old boy has had extensive facial reconstruction with iliac bone grafts for the congenital deformities of Apert's syndrome," the young resident said in a confident, smooth delivery with a deep resonant voice that had more than a hint of affectation. "With the exception of a brief temperature spike to 102 degrees last night, he's doing extremely well—the usual smooth course for one of Dr. Stern's patients."

The obsequious compliment irritated Lionel. In fact, Franklin Upton, with his eternally smiling, fresh face, irritated Lionel. The young physician was always eager and immaculate, and he used just the right amount of oil to keep his blond hair in place. When he spoke he sounded like a self-satisfied preacher. It was not the resident's prissy appearance that irritated Lionel, but rather the overly confident and mechanical way he approached patients. To Franklin, patients were problems to be solved rather than people. He was ambitious and always wanted to appear to be in complete control of any medical situation. Lionel had never heard him say "I'm not sure" or "I don't know." Upton always had an answer, and right or wrong he was absolutely certain that he knew what he was doing. For a first-year surgical resident, it was a dangerous attitude.

As far as Franklin Upton was concerned, patients were merely a means to an end. If they got better because of his efforts, Franklin felt the pride of achievement, but he never shared any of their joy. Lionel doubted he even noticed it.

"What do you think about the fever spike, Dr. Upton?" Lionel asked carefully.

"Not much, sir. It's like pulmonary due to the general anesthetic and of no consequence." Franklin was a machine.

"I see. So you believe it's all smooth sailing for Felix?"

"Absolutely. Yes, sir," Franklin said enthusiastically.

As he listened, Lionel looked over the group of white coats and noticed that one of the medical students had carefully maneuvered himself directly behind the chief resident to hide that he had fallen asleep standing up. "What do *you* think about it?" Lionel directed his voice at the sleeping medical student. The student's body reeled, his eyes exploded open, terror on his face, pupils narrow.

"I'm not sure I understand the question, Dr. Stern," he replied plaintively, scrambling for time.

"The question is, Doctor . . . ah . . . "

"Abraham, sir. Brian Abraham."

"The question is, Doctor Abraham"—Lionel always addressed his medical students as Doctor, a title that was always gratefully received—"the significance of a fever on the second postoperative day. Doctor Upton here seems to believe it is of very little significance. Do you agree?"

"Could I ask if the patient is on antibiotics?"

"Yes, starting the night before surgery. Any other piece of information you might want to know?"

"Well . . . was a chest X ray taken?"

Worried about Felix, Lionel knew the answer, but folded his arms and turned back in the direction of Upton.

"Yes, it was taken. Clear as a bell. I undertook a complete fever workup, urinalysis, white count, complete physical exam. Nothing. *No* positive findings," Upton recited confidently.

"Well, Dr. Abraham, anything else?"

"As I recall this patient also has a cleft palate. Are his ears clear?" Abraham asked cautiously.

"Why do you ask?"

"It is unusual to have a cleft palate with Apert's syndrome but even if it is repaired, these patients have difficulty with chronic middle-ear infection."

"Why?" Lionel asked.

"Because the muscles within the soft palate don't form the usual sling and can't function properly to open the eustachian tube and equalize the pressure between the throat and middle ear."

"What are the ears like, Dr. Upton?"

"I . . . didn't look, sir. Cleft palates are—" ·

"Isn't an ear examination in your fever workup?"

"Of course, sir . . . but . . ." Upton realized he had erred and hastily examined Felix's ears with the otoscope. Lionel and the group waited. "They *are* clear, sir."

"So it looks like everything is okay, nothing on physical exam, nothing on fever workup. What do you think? Would you be worried?" Lionel asked the question directly to Abraham.

"I'm afraid I would be concerned, Dr. Stern. Mostly because I can't explain it. I'd feel better if one of the tests showed something."

"The surgical incision seems to be healing nicely," Upton interrupted nervously, anxious not to leave anything else out.

"I'm interested in knowing what Dr. Abraham thinks," Lionel asked, purposely ignoring Franklin Upton.

"Well, I don't know, sir, and that's what bothers me. And because I don't know, I'd watch the patient very carefully."

"I like the way you think, Dr. Abraham. Perhaps you can help Dr. Upton out with the patient." The sarcasm hung in the air as Lionel realized he'd have to keep a close watch on Felix. He looked at his watch. He was late for a consultation. Lionel took hold of Felix's hand and squeezed it good-bye. As he stepped away from the group, Lionel motioned to Maltry. "I don't like the way Felix looks," he whispered. "I know you've come up with nothing, but I'm worried that something is wrong. Watch him, John, will you?" Maltry nodded soberly.

Lionel headed down the corridor feeling less self-satisfied than before; not only was he worried about Felix, but the one thing he couldn't teach the residents was a sixth sense that despite all medical evidence to the contrary, something was wrong.

As he passed the nurses' station, the head floor nurse looked up at him. "I know. Keep an eye on Felix."

Lionel raced for the elevator, catching the doors with his hands. He smiled. He should have used his head.

The consult for which Lionel was late was with Melissa Eckhart. A second opinion. That was all he knew until he buzzed his secretary and a pretty blonde flight attendant walked into his office. Lionel stood up and extended one hand as he took the file from Gloria with his other.

"Ms. Eckhart, I'm sorry I was late."

She smiled. "Oh, I understand."

Lionel motioned to her to be seated. "Well, the least a doctor can do is show up on time. I do apologize."

"Apology accepted, Doctor." Before he could close the file, she was chattering nervously. "Perhaps because I'm a flight attendant, I'm always early. It's as much a curse as being late, which, by the way, I am as of right now. Not that I'm blaming you, Doctor, but I have to get to the airport . . ."

"How can I help you?"

Taking a deep breath, she unbuttoned her hospital gown. "I'd like to be a little bigger up here."

"We can do that kind of surgery . . ."

"Well, that's not exactly what I'm asking your opinion about. God knows I've got a lifetime of opinions about that. What I want to know," she said, slowing down as she consulted a 3 by 5 card, "is whether you think the incision should be under the arm or under the breast?"

"I can see you've come well prepared." He smiled, motioning to the thick folder of newspaper and magazine articles. "I use both incisions. In thin women like you, I prefer the incision under the arm."

Melissa nodded. "That is exactly what I've read." She rolled her eyes. "I've been cutting out articles for years."

Lionel pointed to her copy of *Cosmopolitan* and smiled. "The working girl's *New England Journal of Medicine*."

She leaned forward as though asking a very personal question. "Do you put the implant under the muscle?"

"There seems to be less hardening under the muscle than if the implant is placed in front of the chest muscle, behind the breasts." Melissa began to take notes. Lionel, usually careful to tell a patient as much as they wanted to know, realized this was about to be a long consultation. "Any time you put something foreign in the body, it responds by forming scar tissue, what we call a capsule, around it. It's one of the body's defense mechanisms." She wanted more. "The silicone implant stays soft, it's the body tissue that gets hard. The implants are shaped like a hemisphere, round on one side, flat on the other. And they are very soft. But if a capsule forms, the scar tissue shrinks around the implant and squeezes it into a sphere. When that happens, the breasts become hard."

"I certainly don't want that!"

"I don't either. But it's out of my, or any other plastic surgeon's, control."

"Doctor, what I really wanted to ask was, what would you think"—she spoke cautiously—"of the idea of doing the operation in two stages?" She consulted her card again. "Let's say you put in large implants, much bigger than anyone, me included, would need. And you let the capsule form around them. And then you replace them with smaller ones several weeks later?"

Lionel thought for a moment. Who the hell had she been talking to? "An interesting theory, but I'm afraid that's exactly what it is. A theory."

Melissa sat back thoughtfully. "Maybe. Maybe not." She looked directly into Lionel's eyes. "But you're not saying it couldn't work."

"No, I'm not saying that. Melissa, I assume this has been proposed to you by another plastic surgeon?"

"By someone who's doing breakthrough research on this very problem."

"Well, perhaps if I could speak to him—"

A sharp intake of breath. "Oh, no! If he thought for one minute that I was here." Quickly, she put her card back into her purse. "The thing is, Dr. Stern, that this doctor is so famous I just know you know him and I would die of embarrassment." She stood up. "I can't thank you enough. I know just what I'm going to do." She smiled. "Actually, what I'm going to do now is work a flight to Dallas. And back. You want to know work, you ought to be on a plane with all those cowboys."

Lionel shook hands with Melissa. He held the door open and said, "I hope I've been some help."

"I need all I can get," she said cheerfully as she left.

# 18

STEPHANIE HAD HER suitcase carefully packed. She had been up nearly all night, cleaning out the refrigerator, dusting the shelves, washing the woodwork. She repotted two plants and pruned the others. She had arranged for her neighbor to come in to water the plants. Stephanie worried that the neighbor would look in her closets or drawers. They were practically empty.

As she checked again that there was no garbage, the bell rang. It was her agent. A short, rumpled man in his late forties, Danny Arnold stood impatiently in the hallway, widening his eyes as he said, "So, come on!"

Stephanie shook her head. "You have to come in for a moment."

"Kiddo, this is not a social visit. I've got to get to Century City after I drop you off. So, come on!"

"Danny, I want to show you something. Please. It means a great deal to me." She coaxed him into the apartment and quickly ran to the closet. She opened the door. "Danny, look!"

"Look at what? An empty closet? What happened to all your dresses?"

"Danny, come here. Wait till you see this!" She opened two dresser drawers. They were almost empty.

"You get robbed?"

"I threw them out. I threw out everything I didn't like."

Danny shook his head. He narrowed his eyes. "It's a

good thing I didn't come over last night." He took a deep breath. "You threw them out?"

"I went through the fridge, the cupboard, the closets and the drawers. I threw out everything I didn't want."

"Did they pick up your garbage yet? Maybe you can still get it all back."

"Danny, don't you see? Out with the old, in with the new. It's New Year's Eve for me!"

He waved a finger in her face. "It's the booby hatch for you, if you're not careful." Danny opened the refrigerator and stared at the empty shelves. Then he turned quickly to her. "What happened to your food? Is this some kind of crazy new diet? Stephanie, what is going on?"

Stephanie smiled. She spoke softly. "It's my nose."

"It's your nose," he repeated.

She nodded. "Yes."

He nodded. "Oh."

"Danny, don't you see? I'm finally wiping the slate clean. A new nose. A new face. A new life."

There was a long silence. "Happy New Year, Stephanie. Let's get in the car before I get a ticket."

"Well, aren't you the early bird?" Mrs. Evans sang as she walked into the waiting room. "Good morning, Stephanie. Everything is ready. Let's get started. Follow me, and I'll give you some medication that will take the edge off."

Only the day before, sitting on the same sofa, Stephanie's feelings had been an equal mixture of raw nerves and hope. Now, as she walked down the narrow hallway toward the operating room, the anticipation she had savored all the way over with Danny was completely displaced by panic.

Mrs. Evans showed her into a small room. "Please take everything off, dear, and put on the surgical gown." Reluctantly, Stephanie removed her clothes. The thin paper gown tied in the back, offering little protection from the cold of the examining table. "Now lift it up a bit in the back," Mrs. Evans chirped.

Stephanie gasped, not expecting an injection in her hip.

Then, two blue capsules and a sip of water from a paper cup.

"Don't go away."

Stephanie hunched her shoulders. The chill penetrated deeply and brought with it a very lonely feeling that was much worse than the injection. She waited in the cold, staring at the acoustical tiles on the ceiling until their borders blurred.

She did not recall ever being moved, but suddenly she was in another room. It was very bright. Dr. Gold was standing over her. Through the fog that floated in front of her face, Stephanie thought she detected something about his smile that had changed. During their first meeting, she had memorized his face. So understanding and warm. But now everything was suddenly cold. As though she were covered over by a layer of ice. Did he know who she was? Why didn't he speak to her?

"Evans, get me an IV. I don't want this one moving around."

The sound of his voice made her feel colder. She was sure he didn't know it was her. Stephanie struggled against the smothering medication. She did her best to fight it. Just as she thought she couldn't bear the cold for another minute, there was a sharp pain in her left forearm. She opened her mouth. She thought she opened her mouth. She screamed. She thought she screamed.

"Evans, give her more Valium."

Pharmacology won the battle.

# 19

Peter Dalway had spent two days pondering his future as he weaved in and out of a drunken stupor. He was continually surprised to awaken in a strange bedroom. His own. The one in which he had grown up. Growing up was a time that Peter's father had likened to the comradery of the preproduction period on a movie before the principal filming began. The actors still loved the director, and the producer still loved the writer. It was a time when the bloom was on the rose. Hung over, his mouth feeling like a wad of cotton and his head pounding, Peter knew he was well into production.

Although he couldn't recall everything that happened the past couple days or even putting himself to bed last night, the moment he saw the glass of tomato juice on the night table it became apparent who had. Reaching for the glass, Peter wished Homer could be there for every facet of his life, for all the different hangovers.

One thing Peter did remember, for Chrissake, was tearing up his list of hospitals. Hoping that the pieces might still be in the basket, he flung aside the covers. Holding both sides of his head, he walked slowly downstairs. Midway on the staircase, he realized, with some amusement, that he was naked. Of all the things Peter had been in that house: young, idealistic, rebellious, he had never been naked outside of his room. At least not physically naked.

As he walked down the corridor toward his father's study, Peter was overwhelmed by a sense of déjà vu. His nakedness had recreated a knot in the pit of his belly that he got whenever he walked into his father's study. One way or another, it was a room he had yet to enter feeling fully clothed.

The room was empty. So was the basket. Homer was still as efficient as ever. Peter slid down into the desk chair, still holding onto his head. Through the fog in his eyes, he caught a glimpse of a photo of his father and Morrie Gold. Morrie had always been around the house when Peter was growing up. And now Peter would definitely put Morrie's name on his list of doctors he was going to arrange to "bump into." Peter shook his head. Morrie Gold! A very, very high-priced hairdresser. But very successful in what he did. He had made his way from dermatology to cosmetic surgery. He must know something about building a practice—and that's precisely what Peter needed.

Peter thought bitterly of all the times he had walked quickly past the study just to avoid having to say hello to Morrie. Now he was going to chase around town after that son of a bitch? The hell he would. Morrie owed him. His father was the one who had put Morrie on the map. Peter reached for the phone. He was going to call Morrie and tell him to get his ass over there.

Peter hung up the receiver. He would call Morrie, but first he'd have to put on some clothes.

# 20

LUISA OBREGON LOCKED the door to Bungalow 5 at the Beverly Hills Hotel and walked through the garden with a graceful stride. Her silk dress clung to her, accenting firm, feminine lines as she opened the lobby door, took a few steps and stood at the entrance to the Polo Lounge. In a town where much of everything of importance is skin deep, and in a room accustomed to the finest skins, Luisa made heads turn.

And that was precisely what Morrie liked to see. He watched Nico, the maître d', greet her. Luisa was entirely too elegant to look around the room for him. Morrie smiled. Many beautiful women do not risk eye contact with strangers. They do not check to see if anyone was looking at them. The assumption is, and quite correctly in Luisa's case, everyone is looking.

Her head tilted slightly to the side, a Giselle lost in thought, Luisa glided down the aisle behind Nico, past the cracked crab and the banana daiquiris, ignoring the agents who stared at her talking on telephones in their booths. Morrie greeted her by kissing the air in front of each cheek. She took a deep breath, slid gracefully onto the seat next to him and, without missing a beat, took a large swallow from the waiting glass of champagne.

Morrie whispered, "Now kiss me."

She turned to face him. "What?"

"Just so that I can taste the champagne," he said, pretending innocence. "I might have to send it back."

Luisa smiled. "And what happens if you don't like the kiss?"

"Impossible."

She slid his own glass closer to him. "You didn't pay for the kiss. Only for the champagne."

He clinked glasses with her. "But that doesn't preclude—"

"Nor does it guarantee," Luisa said sharply. "What happened to Rochelle Whitaker?"

Morrie didn't want to be sidetracked. "You know, we are the perfect couple."

"The implants must be removed."

He ignored her. "You're the merry widow and I'm the king of big tits. The *Los Angeles Magazine* couple of the year."

"Morrie . . ."

"Need I remind you that I've taken very good care of my three ex-wives? I fixed their eyes and chins and gave them all the chassis work they wanted. And then I married them off very well. I come to you unencumbered. A financial virgin. No community property. No settlements. No alimony. Not even any hard feelings. I've handled it all extremely well. Not one of those bitches ever got a penny out of me."

"That's precisely what worries me, darling." Luisa smiled. "What would I get when I leave you?"

He laughed. "You're too smart to leave me."

"No, you've got it wrong, Morrie." She sipped the champagne. "I'm much too smart to marry you."

"But you will go to a party with me?"

"*Con mucho gusto.*"

That was all Morrie really cared about. He wanted Luisa on his arm even more than he wanted her in his bed. Sexual conquest, like money, was a very public thing for Morrie. He was not one to savor inner satisfaction. Except, surprisingly, for Stephanie. The surgery on her nose had taken all morning and required more skill than he had anticipated. Although it was a procedure he had not done before, he had sailed through brilliantly.

"The party is at the Dalway house," Morrie explained. "I was very close to E.R. while he was running Fox. He, with his casting couch, and I, with my scalpel, went into the starlet business," Morrie announced with considerable pride.

Luisa interrupted him. "Rochelle is not returning my calls. She has canceled twice."

Morrie shrugged. "Stop worrying. You'll change her mind on the flight back to Bogotá."

"I am not going back there."

Morrie paused. "That's impossible."

"I am not going back," she repeated. "You will go by yourself, do two more implants, and that will be the end of it."

"Don't be ridiculous. What about the rest of the money?"

Luisa looked up at him. "It is too dangerous for me there."

"It's always been dangerous for you."

She became upset. "You have enough money, Morrie."

He began to laugh. "Enough money?" Morrie took her hand. "'Enough' is a word used with food, not money."

"I will deal with Rochelle. The next two, the last two, are Melissa Eckhart and Sharon White."

Morrie sat back. "Are you sure you know what you're doing? Things were not going well before we met."

"I am sure."

"I worry about you, Luisa."

"Please, Morrie. Save it for the patients."

"You want to stop? Fine. There's always something else to do. We live in a world of opportunities limited only by one's imagination. Come to think of it, this may even work to my advantage." He smiled. "Our advantage?"

"I'm listening."

"I've thought for some time now about putting together a line of cosmetics. Skin products. Collagen. Call it 'Something' Gold."

Luisa patted his cheek. "My little Rumpelstiltskin."

Morrie laughed. His mind was racing ahead. Always ahead. Images of Luisa on television, advertising his creams and lotions. She would be ideal, if he could get her cheaply enough. Luisa made heads turn. People always stared at her, and that was one of the many reasons he enjoyed her company.

# 21

CASEY WAS BUSY at her desk at the Board of Medical Quality Assurance, amid uneven stacks of letters and scattered legal briefs. As chief investigator for the BMQA, she had a staff of seven to handle over two hundred complaints a month from dissatisfied patients. Only the more urgent cases wound up on Casey's desk. There were tall piles of medical records on the floor. Three walls were bare, her diplomas and certificates from medical school and residency training stacked neatly in the corner. The window looked out over Sepulveda Boulevard, close enough to Los Angeles International Airport for the high-pitched whine of jet engines to fill the room. Lionel stood in the doorway, waiting for her to look up. "Knock knock," he said.

Casey was surprised to see him. "Who's there?"

"I came to apologize."

"I came to apologize who?"

Lionel closed the door behind him. He walked to her desk and leaned over to kiss her, half-expecting Casey to pull back or make an excuse. She didn't. Lionel winced at the sound of another plane coming in for a landing. "How can you work in here with all that noise?"

"What noise?" Casey replied, almost yelling.

He smiled. "Let me take you away from all this."

"I knew there was a catch." Jokingly, she threw down her pencil and sat back. "I leave my door open, hoping that someone will come in and kiss me, and the first person who does . . ."

"Are you kidding? It's practically lunchtime. You mean, no one else has been in here to kiss you?"

"It seems I tend to put men off."

"Only the dumb ones."

She squeezed his hand. "Thank you, Lion."

"Hey, I hear the sand dabs are running at Chez Jay."

"I can't."

Lionel slumped down in a chair and picked up a handful of files from her desk. "Why can't you?"

Casey got up and took the folders from him. "You're not supposed to look at these," she said, putting the files back on her desk. "They're not open for public inspection."

"Oh, come on, Casey. Stop being such a bureaucrat." He smiled. "I just wanted to see if you had any complaints about me."

"Personally? Or on file?" She held up a folder. "If I were writing to the BMQA to complain about Dr. Lionel Stern, I would say that I was afraid of seeing much more of him. He was everything I ever wanted and everything I promised myself to stay away from. I would say that I didn't know what the hell to do anymore."

"Why not just follow doctor's orders and have lunch with me?"

Casey looked at him lovingly. "Because I have a very low pleasure threshold."

Lionel stood up. "Obviously not low enough." He turned away and found himself facing a blank wall. Literally. "Why don't you hang up all these diplomas?" he said, annoyed.

"I already know who I am. I don't need any reminders."

He swung around quickly. "Well, then, maybe you can let me in on the secret. Who are you, Casey? And how do I fit into your life?" He picked up a handful of files from her desk. "How come you've got room for all these people's problems but not mine? You're in the complaint business? How about this? Dear BMQA," he shouted, "I'm hungry and I'm in love. Is anybody listening?" He tapped his finger on the files and looked at the names. "Or do you only care what happens to Dr. Harry Kincaid, Dr. Arnold Barstow,

Dr. . . . Morrie Gold?" Lionel stopped for a minute and looked again at the last name. "Morrie Gold?"

Casey reached for the files, but he held them back. "Lionel, please!"

"God, I'd love to see what you've got on that son of a bitch."

She walked quickly around the desk. "That's none of your business."

"Are you kidding? Just about everyone in Southern California thinks he's a real live plastic surgeon. That makes it my business. Morrie Gold scares the hell out of me. Have you seen this month's issue of *Los Angeles Magazine*? Twenty-two ads for cosmetic surgery and only two or three of the guys advertising had any training. See Dr. Gold's ads for cosmetic surgery: *It will change your life?* Never saw so much bullshit. You watch television? You see Morrie Gold's commercials for his 'Rejuvenation Institute'? One of these days, somebody's going to get hurt real bad."

She took the files back from him and sat down.

Lionel was angry—not entirely about Morrie Gold. It occurred to him that much of the explosion was because of what was happening between himself and Casey. Or more accurately, what was not happening. "I thought your office was under the State Department of Consumer Affairs? Isn't it your job to protect people?"

"That's precisely what it is. *My* job. Not yours. You waltz in here, you're in my office for five minutes, and you're telling me what my job is. Just the way you tell me what my life should be."

"I tell you because I love you."

"Then love me enough to *ask* me."

Lionel sighed. "Christ, next thing you're going to want me to do is burn my bra. Okay. I'm asking you to go to lunch with me."

"I told you why I can't."

He nodded slowly. "Because you love me."

"Yes."

"I've got an idea. Suppose we go and I do something like

eat real sloppy or yell at the waiter and you'd begin to love me a little less. Who knows, you might even begin to dislike me and then before we knew it, we'd be having breakfast together."

She smiled. "I could never dislike you that much."

Lionel walked to the door. "It doesn't sound fair to me."

"Fair has nothing to do with anything."

He thought for a moment. "Oh."

# 22

LIONEL MADE HIS way through the thick traffic to return to University Hospital, to the environment that he understood and in which he felt secure. Completely lost in thought about reconciliation and perhaps accommodation of his career to the woman he loved, he barely noticed as someone entered the passenger side of his car as he was waiting for a stop light in front of the doctors' parking lot. It was Peter Dalway.

Lionel looked over at him without any visible surprise. He hadn't spoken to Peter since the near disaster with Felix. After repeatedly getting no answer at the condo, Lionel had played a hunch and called Homer, who told him about Peter's brief vacation from reality. He had been tempted to go over there and force Peter to snap out of it, but he knew that Homer had a special place in the Dalway family and that Peter was in the safest of hands. Lionel now felt reassured about his decision as he looked at Peter, who was clearly sober. He decided to let the matter drop. For the moment. Besides, his mind kept racing back to Casey. "Want some lunch?" he asked flatly.

"Just had some. But when you make an invitation like that, with all that enthusiasm, it's hard to say no."

"Come to think of it, I'm not hungry either." Stern growled.

"Bad day, eh? Put someone's nose back in the wrong place?"

"No, I could handle that kind of problem," Lionel replied.

As Lionel stopped the car at the gate, Peter ran his hand across the dashboard. "When are you going to get a real car, Lion?"

"Fuck you. This is a collector's item. One of Dr. Porsche's best years. 1964. C model Cabriolet. Original enamel, original leather seats." The bright blue car was indeed one of Lionel Stern's prize possessions.

Peter nodded. "Should be in a museum."

"They don't make them like this anymore."

"There's a reason."

Lionel pushed down on the accelerator, the vibration transforming into a smooth throaty hum. "Listen to that engine."

"I don't have to. I can feel it."

Lionel shook his head, then parked the car and shut off the ignition.

"Now I know why you drive this thing," Peter said, stretching his neck. "It feels so good when you stop."

Stern glanced over at Peter, noticing for the first time how nattily he was dressed: chocolate raw-silk sports coat, tan gabardine slacks, gold paisley tie. "You look like you're applying for a job at GQ magazine."

Peter brushed the sleeve of his jacket. "Just the good life showing through. You know, Lion, a big-time plastic surgeon like you ought to dress better. That, whatever it is that you have on, looks like one of Dr. Porsche's original 1964-model suits."

"Great. After we have some lunch, let's go shopping," Lionel snapped. "We'll make a goddamn day of it."

"Oh, oh. Somebody piss on your toothbrush this morning? What's up, Lion?"

"I don't know what it is she wants." Lionel's head dropped.

"She?" He had never seen Lionel in such a mood. "Short for Casey?"

"I've spent a long time getting to be the best surgeon I can be. Casey doesn't seem to understand that's what I do.

I'm a surgeon. Somehow I remind her of her father, and she thinks I spend too much time at the hospital. Now, every time I'm with her I'm on the defensive. For the first time I'm beginning to think maybe, just maybe, she's got a point. So I'm taking a hard look at surgery and what I'm doing—"

"Oh, my God," Peter interrupted. "You into one of those male menopausal things about reevaluation and not being able to handle success?"

"Hell, I don't know. I don't think so. I'm just not so sure how to handle Casey. She's not someone I can walk away from."

"I thought things were good with you two."

"They *were*. Past tense. I think, as far as she is concerned, it's beginning to look like things would be much better if I quit operating and started doing insurance physicals for a living." Lionel sat back and took a deep breath. "I offered to take her to lunch today. You know how many times I go out to lunch?" he said sheepishly. "Turned me down flatter than a pancake."

Peter laughed lightly. "Well, you can give it another try and make it up to her on Saturday night. I'm having a party at the family manse. A blowout Hollywood party."

"Oh, Peter, I don't know about that. Haven't you done enough partying lately?" Lionel said slowly.

Peter winced and quickly changed the subject. "Lion, trust me. You and Casey will have made up by then."

"That's not what I'm talking about."

"I'm having the cocktail party to help drum up some business, get the practice rolling. Create a little positive PR for myself. Let people know I'm still alive. Maybe some of the Bev Hills docs will throw some business my way."

"For Chrissake, Peter, let *me* help you."

"For Chrissake, Lion, you tried! And I fucked it up. God, how I fucked up. All I've been doing lately is fucking things up."

"Is the cocktail circuit the way you want to get started? You had an accident, a bad one, but that is behind you now.

Goddamn it, Peter, you don't know shit about how to help yourself."

"And you don't know shit about the world outside your nice little operating room. Just more of that nose-to-the-grindstone. For you, Lion, things are just too simple, too black and white." He sighed in resignation. There was silence for a long while.

"Sounds like you been talking to Casey."

"Look, I'm sorry, I don't know what got into me," Peter said, clearly backing away from Lionel's intensity. "Lion, you're my best friend. The only person I can trust. Goddamn it, you know what an asshole I feel like because of what happened in the OR. I wasn't sure what I was going to say to you, how I was going to apologize. And here you are still trying to help."

Lionel slammed his fist on the steering wheel. "You know what gets me mad?" he shouted. "You're so goddamn wound up in yourself that you can't see anything else. Right now at this very minute I am not here to make *you* feel good. I am talking to you to make *me* feel good. I need a friend, Friend."

Peter turned to Lionel. He was dumbfounded. "I thought you were doing . . . all this . . . for me!"

"Fuck you!" Lionel said. "I was doing it for me. I see, and I wanted, no, I *needed* to talk to you, you self-centered son of a bitch. In fact, before you got in this car I was planning on calling you because I realized how much *I* really needed you. Period."

They stared at one another, looked away, then stared again. Peter's eyes were red and now teary. He held out his left hand. Lionel hesitated and then grabbed it with his right, the two men held tight to one another's wrists. Peter sniffed, cleared his throat and whispered, "Faggot." There was silence for a few minutes then both men began to laugh uncontrollably. As they got out of the car, Peter hesitated before he closed the door. He leaned over to Lionel. "I know you hate cocktail parties, but I'd really appreciate—"

"What time?" Lionel said.

# 23

I<small>T HAD BEEN</small> nearly two hours since Lionel completed evening rounds and nearly a lifetime since he first caught himself hoping Casey might call. Trying to put off facing another evening by himself, another night alone in bed, Lionel stayed at the hospital long enough to clear off his desk before making his last stop of the day at L'Etoile, the small hotel that had become a way station for those who preferred to recover from plastic surgery away from the prying eye of the press, friends or servants.

Security at L'Etoile was as impeccable as the Porthault linens on the beds. Lionel parked his car in one of the many empty spaces: guests at L'Etoile usually arrived and departed in limousines with darkly tinted glass. He nodded to the man at the front desk in the expensively understated lobby and turned the corner to the elevator.

Andy had been standing guard in the lobby for years. "Evening, Doc." Then a whispered "How's she doin'?"

Lionel smiled. "She's doing fine, Andy."

"She gonna look like she used to?"

"Andy, nobody looks like they used to."

"Gloria Swanson did. When she died, she died with the same face she had for fifty years. And that's the way it should be with those people."

Lionel stepped into the elevator and pressed 4. When it came to a stop, he got off and nodded hello to Mrs. Riaz, a day nurse at University Hospital who worked nights on the

113

floor at L'Etoile. Like a Russian hotel, there was a woman at a desk on every floor.

"Evening, doctor."

"Good evening. Any complaints?"

Mrs. Riaz smiled. "Nothing but."

Lionel nodded. "Sounds normal." He walked down the hallway and knocked on the door to Room 410. His hand reached automatically for the knob, but he waited until he heard that unmistakably brassy voice.

"It's about time!"

Helene Hudson was every inch a movie star. The problem was that Helene had too many inches. A fifties glamour girl, she was now on her sixth husband, third comeback, fourth facelift—and, most important at the moment, second box of chocolates in as many days.

"Helene!" Lionel walked over to the recliner and took the TV remote control from her. He turned off the set, adjusted the chair and put the lid on the box of chocolates. The bandages around Helene's mouth were stained dark brown. Her bright blue eyes and fluorescent orange hair were all the billing Helene needed.

"Don't 'Helene' me, you quack. My face feels as though you stuck it in a blender."

"Your face feels fine. If you'd stop eating chocolates you wouldn't have to go through this all the time."

"Everybody wants to be Selznick!"

Lionel pulled up a chair. "How do you feel?"

"Like Mae West cruising Sunset Boulevard."

"Helene."

"How the hell should I feel? I have my manager checking out my agent, and a private detective checking out my husband." Her voice broke as she nervously began to smooth her hair. "You're the only one I can trust, and I don't even trust you."

Lionel smiled. "So, you're all right."

"The hell I am. I'm as horny as Kansas in August. I want to take my new face and get out of here. I've got a gorgeous twenty-three-year-old pool man waiting for me at home."

As he unwrapped the bandages to check the incisions, he cautioned her, "No rough stuff for a while, Helene."

"Yes, mother."

"You want to look?"

She took the mirror from him and stared into it. "The bride of Frankenstein."

"You see how the liposuction got rid of those jowls? The eyes are healing nicely. You can see the definition of the chin line."

Helene shook her head. "I feel like I'm being judged at a dog show."

He smiled. "And the forehead is smooth. The cheeks are nice and tight."

Instinctively, she put a hand to her thigh. "How soon can you do my ass?"

"Helene, if you'd only give up the chocolates—"

"I didn't hire a dietician. How soon?"

"Give yourself a few weeks. A month."

"Christ! A month? He'll be twenty-four by then!"

Lionel finished putting on a new dressing, all the time thinking how different Helene was from so many other patients. A woman without illusions. She realized that her pattern of self-abuse and her constant search for youth were losing battles. But she was determined to go down fighting.

After a few words with Mrs. Riaz, Lionel pressed the elevator button. He noticed a young woman sitting near the elevator. Over her nose was the pattern of white tape used for rhinoplasties. But something caught his eye. The tip of her nose, normally exposed after such surgery, was discolored. Careful not to be caught staring, he looked again. It was black.

Just then the elevator door opened and Lionel found himself face to face with someone who looked very familiar. His first thought was that the square, chubby man was a doctor he knew. Then, as he heard the young woman's voice, he realized it was a doctor he didn't know.

"Dr. Gold," she called out.

Morrie Gold greeted Lionel with the professional-courtesy

nod that one general makes on passing another. Then he turned to his patient. "Stephanie, my dear."

Lionel stared straight ahead, disquieted that there had been no opportunity for a formal introduction, no chance to say something to the man he had already said so much about.

# 24

"Dr. Gold," Stephanie said, once they were back in her room, "I can't stand that funny smell."

Morrie smiled as he unwrapped the bandages. "You actresses! You're all the same. So dramatic. So sensitive."

"But it's making me sick."

"I can see you've got quite a future ahead of you." Morrie kept the smile fixed on his face as he stared at Stephanie's nose. He was careful to breathe through his mouth, not wanting to inhale the strong odor that came from beneath the tape. Something had gone very wrong. The tip of her nose had already discolored. Pus was coming out of the sutures. It looked to Morrie as though, for some reason, the blood supply was insufficient to keep the flesh of the tip alive.

"Dr. Gold?"

"Yes, my dear?"

"I know you said I'm not supposed to see my nose for a few days, but—"

Morrie began to laugh. "You can't be serious! Miss Sarah Bernhardt wishes to see her nose a few hours after surgery when it's never looked worse? Stephanie, if you have ever trusted anyone in your life, trust me now. It would simply be too unnerving for someone with your esthetic sensibilities. I speak from experience."

Morrie had never before seen anything so horrifying as Stephanie's nose. Must be some aberrant anatomical variation. Perhaps what was going on was some unusual virulent infection. There was no doubt that most of the skin of her nose was dying. There was also no doubt that she would become quickly hysterical. One good look would be enough. The best thing to do, Morrie reasoned, was keep her from looking for as long as possible. And begin preparing for a lawsuit. He had certainly done all he could. Morric Gold could not be held responsible for some extraordinary act of God.

"Do you know who's here?" Stephanie whispered excitedly. "Helene Hudson. She's right next door."

"Yes, I know," Morrie said absently.

"Is she your patient, too?"

He smiled. "Now, you know my policy about patient confidentiality."

"I've seen every one of her pictures at least three times. Oh, God, Dr. Gold, I'm just going to die if you don't let me see my nose!"

The thought occurred to Morrie that perhaps he should let her see it and explain away the discoloration as bruising, giving her at least a moment to appreciate the wonderful sculpting he had accomplished with such agility and finesse. Perhaps then she wouldn't think it had all been a failure. And then slowly introduce the possibility of infection. It might prove less of a shock.

No. There was no telling with someone like Stephanie. He'd have to get her sedated first. Certainly he should make certain the check had cleared before doing anything. "Absolutely not," he said, preparing to rebandage her face. "But I will do this. Give me some perfume."

"Perfume?" She reached over to the night table and handed him a small bottle of Elizabeth Taylor's Passion.

"Ah," he said approvingly. "I knew you had good taste. And besides, Elizabeth would be so pleased to know you like this."

"Oh, no! You're Elizabeth Taylor's doctor, too?"

"Stephanie, Stephanie. Please. Confidentiality." He poured a few drops of perfume onto the tape that covered the bridge of the nose. "There. Now everything will be fine. That is, if I have your word not to peek."

She smiled. "I was always the kid who looked in the closets before Christmas." Then her face grew dark. "What you've done for me is the Christmas present I've been waiting for forever."

Morrie left an order for Valium with Mrs. Riaz, advising her that Stephanie was in a highly excited state and was to be kept under sedation. Mrs. Riaz said she would begin administering the pills immediately.

No sooner had Morrie stepped into the elevator than he heard a long piercing scream. Mrs. Riaz rushed out of her chair and down the hall. Another scream. And another. And then Stephanie cried out, "Dr. Gold! Dr. Gold!"

Morrie stepped back into the corner of the elevator. He shook his head. Why didn't they ever listen? He pressed the down button.

# 25

LIONEL SAT IN the corner of the hospital cafeteria, staring into his coffee cup as if a message would come from the depths of the dark brown. It was his tenth of the day, and it wasn't quite ten o'clock in the morning. From out of his peripheral vision, he saw someone standing opposite him. He looked up. It was Casey.

Four miserable days had passed without a phone call. And now she stood before him, on his turf, smiling. In her hands was a large wicker basket that she put down on the table. Without a word, she took Lionel's paper coffee cup and threw it into a waste bin. She opened the basket and took out a red-and-white checked tablecloth. Two red mugs. A thermos of coffee. A plate with croissants. A jar of jelly. Silver knives and spoons. Linen napkins. She closed the basket, put it on the floor, sat down, opened the thermos and poured them each a cup of steaming coffee.

"Croissant?" she asked, holding up the plate.

Expressionless, he nodded yes. She put one on a plate and looked directly at him for the first time.

"Jelly?"

He nodded again.

Casey opened the jar, scooped out a dollop of strawberry preserves, put a knife on the plate and handed it to him. "I don't know what I've missed more, the breakfasts or the sex."

He smiled. "The sex."

"I'd have cut your heart out with this butter knife if you hadn't said that."

He reached for her hand. "Speaking of my heart . . ."

Casey held tight to him. "We weren't speaking about your heart. We were speaking about sex." She let go of his hand. "If you don't mind, I'd rather not talk about your heart while I eat."

Lionel shook his head. He had truly never met a more infuriating woman. "Since you brought the breakfast, you pick the subject."

Casey smiled. She reached down, took a thick file from the basket and slammed it victoriously onto the table. "The subject is Morrie Gold. I think I can finally nail the bastard."

Lionel stared at her for a long bewildered moment. "That's why you came here?" He pushed his plate aside. "That's what all this is about?" motioning at the table setting.

"Lion, I need your help," she said simply.

"Why me? You could go to dozens of other plastic surgeons."

Casey narrowed her eyes. "You're really going to make me sweat this out, aren't you? All right, since you won't be satisfied until you hear me say it, I came to you because you're the best. Your reputation is impeccable. You're honest. I trust you—in professional matters, that is. And you do the best nasal reconstructive work in town." She sat back angrily. "There, does that do it for your insatiable male ego?"

"No." He leaned across the table and whispered, "My insatiable male ego was dumb enough to think you came here to apologize for your irrational female psyche. Damn it, Casey. I thought you missed me." Lionel had given her the opening. All Casey had to say was yes. Yes, Lion, I missed you so much I had to drum up an excuse to see you. That was what he wanted to hear. No, that was what he *needed* to hear.

"Oh, please, Lionel! This is important." She pointed to the file. "There's a young woman, practically catatonic, in the psychiatric ward at L.A. General because she's about to lose her entire nose. All of the soft tissue and the skin are completely black and necrotic—the result of a rhinoplasty, are you ready for this, performed by the eminent Morris Gold."

Lionel studied Casey, wondering whether she had any idea how much that remark had hurt him. He hoped not. "Her name is Stephanie."

"How did you know?"

"I saw her at L'Etoile. I knew something was wrong."

"How?"

"The tip of her nose was black."

"What did you do?"

"What do you mean, what did I do? Did I go up to her and say, 'Excuse me, miss, but your nose is dying'?"

"When did you see her?"

"Two days ago."

"And you did nothing?"

"What the hell was I supposed to do? She's not my patient."

Casey picked up the file and dropped it with a thud in front of Lionel. "She is now."

"She asked for me?"

"I'm asking for you."

Lionel smiled. "Yeah, but will you respect me in the morning?"

"Ask me in the morning."

Lionel picked up the file and balanced it from one hand to another. "I'll stop by tonight when I'm through with rounds. Since you brought the breakfast, I'll bring the sex."

Casey leaned close to him. "What happens to Stephanie Green if I have other plans tonight?"

He shook his head and whispered. "You are the goddamnedest woman I've ever met. You're narrow and rigid and suspicious and totally victimized by your so-called independence." What was happening swirled past him like the thoughts of a drowning man. As much as he loved her, he seriously wondered how much longer he could stand in the crossfire of the ghosts Casey was battling. It hurt too much.

Casey kissed him lightly on the cheek, a pacifying gesture. His heart sank a bit more. It was back to business, a transition she made so easily. "Lion, I've gone out on a limb on this one. I pulled a few strings and got the attorney general's office to issue a temporary restraining order on Morrie Gold. Pending a hearing, he can't operate."

Lionel whistled softly. "That's a very big string to pull."

"You going to help me reel him in?"

"Why me?"

"I asked Dr. Daddy for a referral. He thought I was crazy. He said I should call you." She put her hand on his knee. "Why didn't you call me?"

"I figured we were all washed up. I didn't think I'd ever see you again. I was thinking about building a new life without you."

"Me too."

"Did you?" he asked.

"No. Did you?"

"Yes. I'm already going to a big Hollywood party on Saturday night."

"But you hate big parties, particularly that kind."

"What did I tell you?"

Casey turned away. "Lion, sometimes I think . . . I . . . need you."

"For Stephanie or for you?"

"For both?" she asked.

He nodded. "You going to go to the party with me?"

"Is this blackmail?"

He nodded.

Casey smiled. "Okay, but one thing at a time. Business first. We're friends. Nothing more, for now at least. Deal?"

Lionel felt a flush of anger, but managed to control it, muttering "Deal."

# 26

LIONEL CAUGHT UP with Ellsworth in the doctors' gym. Ellsworth was riding an exercycle, reading an article on desserts in a women's magazine. Having changed into his sweats, Lionel took the bike next to Ellsworth.

"Pure porn," Ellsworth said, seeing Lionel sit down. "They ought to sell these magazines in video stores next to the dirty movies. For old men like me. Can't even eat anymore. You have lunch yet?"

"No."

"Good. A few more minutes here and we can go downstairs. They have butter pecan today."

"Ellsworth—"

"What the hell's going on with you and Casey?"

"Nothing."

"That's what I mean. I've had dinner with her two nights in a row and she's been so attentive it's driving me nuts. I know my daughter. Something must be bothering her."

"Ellsworth, I didn't come here to talk about Casey."

"I don't want you to talk about Casey, I want you to do something about her. Before it's too late. Listen, do you know when I developed my love for ice cream? It was after my little cardiac episode. Before then, I wouldn't go near ice cream for fear of plugging up my precious arteries. Well, you know what I learned while I was gasping for breath as I lay on the tennis court? There are some things worth dying for. I wish to hell I had realized it a lot sooner."

"Casey spoke to you about Stephanie Green?" Lionel asked.

"She spoke to me about Morrie Gold. *I* spoke to her about Stephanie Green. My daughter has lost all sense of priorities since becoming a doc cop. You're the best plastic surgeon around this town. I told her you were the only one in L.A. who could help the girl."

"That's a lie."

"I know. But she sure as hell wanted to believe me."

Lionel tried to change the subject. "You ever meet him?"

"Gold? Yeah. Greedy bastard. I tell you, I've been bitten by lots of mosquitoes, but that son of a bitch really makes me itch."

"What I don't understand is his doing this kind of procedure. He doesn't strike me as being dumb. Nasal surgery? Seems like this is just begging for trouble."

Ellsworth stopped pedaling long enough to decrease the pressure on the wheels. "Ego. Pure and simple. He's smart. Shrewd. With an ego as big as the Grand Canyon and twice as deep. He's the kind who convinces himself he can do anything. Talked himself into it without help from anyone. The worst kind. Back in the mid-sixties, none of us in plastic surgery would even consider injecting silicone into women's breasts. Gold pumped more silicone than an Oklahoma gusher pumps oil. Bought it from some Japanese warehouse in San Pedro. The same stuff airplane mechanics use to lubricate jet engines, if you can believe that. They looked good for a few years. Then the inflammation started. The redness, hardness. Can't get that stuff out once it's injected. A lot of those breasts have ended up in pathology lab buckets by now."

"I've seen breasts like that," Lionel said with disdain. "Started turning hard in about five years and in another five the skin began to break down. Ulcers formed and most of those women had to have some kind of mastectomy. I still get one every once in a while."

"I'd pay to see them boil Morrie's balls in oil. He's rich as Croesus and all he wants is more. Kid goes in to have a bump taken off her nose and comes out ruined for life. I tell you, Lion, this'll be the first time I'll be glad to see one of those scumbag malpractice lawyers go to the bank." Ellsworth stopped pedaling. He took his pulse and stepped on the bike, motioning toward the locker room. "Come on. I want to get down there before they run out of butter pecan."

# 27

MORRIE HAD JUST seen his last patient, an outrageously fat woman who worried that her ears had been pulled too far forward after a face-lift. He had listened patiently while she went on. He nodded knowingly. Then a suggestion, a compliment, another suggestion. Within thirty minutes the woman was ecstatic about the prospect of having essentially total body liposuction. How stupid they all were, Morrie thought as he scanned the computer screen to check the week's installment payments received. By offering lower interest rates than the bank, and despite occasional collection problems, he was able to net significantly more per procedure. And besides, checking the computer daily kept him in closer contact with his patients than most doctors. It was Morrie's way of making rounds.

Not that he wanted to be in contact with them. As the names scrolled down the screen with the procedure, price and payment received, his head moved imperceptibly as though reviewing a checklist of vanities. All they needed to make them happy was money. Not even his plush surroundings convinced Morrie of the power of money more than the roster of imperfect people cured by having available cash. Some were happy after their surgery, many were not. Morrie Gold was always happy.

He looked at his watch. It was time to pack. Reluctantly, he turned off the computer and went upstairs to his penthouse. The apartment was everything he had dreamed of as a kid. It was huge, it was dramatic, it was elegant, and most of all, it not only looked, but was indeed rich. Ultrasuede walls, leather sofas and chairs, antique Chinese rugs and a dazzling collection of rare African masks. A little macho, yes, but good-taste macho. There were solid brass pots filled with flowering plants and a wet bar with crystal decanters in a neat line in every room. He walked quickly up a winding brass staircase to his loft bedroom. The Hollywood hills sprawled out on one side of a glass wall that led onto the terrace, and the city lights dazzled beneath him on the other side.

His dressing room was paneled in mahogany, orderly shelves filled with underwear, socks and sweaters. Suits and shirts hung on brass hangers. Freshly shined shoes were on cantilevered wall shelving. Morrie surveyed the landscape within the ample room. It was time to pack.

Morrie had a duplicate wardrobe in Bogotá. There was no need to take any of his clothes. He opened one of the drawers. It was filled with soft finery. Pink lace teddies. Black silk panties. A bra to match. A red lace garter belt. The very best from Juel Park on Robertson Boulevard. His hand crushed the black panties. He brought them to his face, inhaling their fresh scent, rubbing the silk across his lips. He smiled at the thought of one of his mestizas wearing the $150 panties. Those young women took such delight when they put them on.

He tossed the lingerie into his ostrich attaché case, glanced at himself in the mirror and then splashed some cologne on his face. Morrie was pronouncing himself ready to go when he heard the unmistakable sound of Luisa's feather-light footsteps on the staircase.

"My darling," he said, not needing to turn around, "I wish you would change your mind and come with me."

Luisa's eyes were ablaze with anger. "I just spoke to Mrs. Evans. Is it true?"

"Is what true?"

"Morrie! The court order. Is it true you cannot practice medicine? You cannot operate?"

"Yes. It is also true that many people are killed when

crossing the street. True, but meaningless. Just another day in the war. Just another skirmish."

"Not in my war it isn't," she said. "I don't lose, Morris." A concrete mask seemed to cover her face for a moment. Then she softened, but only slightly. "I cannot afford to lose. Particularly now."

Morrie put his hands on her shoulders. "Nothing is at stake. Nothing will be lost. The restraining order limits me only until there is a hearing. Remember, I am not without friends in this town. Jason Berwick has done some networking. The hearing is scheduled for Monday afternoon."

"But Morris, I don't have to remind you there are two replacements scheduled for Monday morning. And, believe me, there is absolutely no way I can change my appointment with Lu."

Morrie put his index finger under her chin and spoke as one would to a child. "The ballet is so tragic, my darling. But so unreal."

Luisa pulled back in a rage. "You want to talk about *real?* Real are the guards in the mines at Muzo. Real is smuggling out the very best quality merchandise from that godforsaken jungle. Real is the pilot being shot down. Real is the police in Bogotá watching my every move. Real is Mr. Lu waiting. And you don't make a man like that wait."

Morrie smiled. "My plans are unchanged. I'll go to Bogotá for the scheduled cases and be back in time for the party on Saturday night. I already have someone in mind to do the replacements Monday morning. After the hearing on Monday afternoon, everything will be back to normal." He bowed slightly. "Choreography by Morrie Gold."

Luisa stared at him. "And who will do the replacements on Monday?"

"Our host on Saturday night. Which is why you must be especially nice to him. It won't be difficult. He's an attractive man. More importantly, he's a physician with a most exploitable problem. But nothing that will prevent him from handling the procedures. Voilà!"

She began pacing. "How serious is the business about your license?"

"My darling, how many times have I told you that medicine is not a perfect science. If you do enough surgery, there will be occasional problems. This is an occasional problem. No more."

Luisa stared into his attaché case. "You could not have picked a worse time."

"I didn't select the time."

"Morris, I have a great deal . . . everything in the world at stake."

"We all do." He walked toward Luisa. "But I assure you, my darling, there is nothing more important to me than helping you. I gave you my word. How many times have I said you could depend upon me? How many times have I said you are the only woman I think about?"

Luisa's eyes had caught his luggage. "I hear what you say, Morris. Believing is another matter." She reached into the attaché case and delicately picked up a pair of lace panties. "What was it you were saying about you and I being perfect for each other?" Expressionless, her eyes fixed on Morrie, she stretched the panties slowly, then tore them up.

# 28

By the time the limousine pulled away from The Gold Institute of Surgical Rejuvenation, Morrie was in the back seat, talking on the phone to his lawyer, Jason Berwick.

"Morrie, what in hell do you think you're doing?" The voice exploded from the receiver. "No wonder you've gone through six lawyers in the past three years! It's going to be seven if you continue with this bullshit!"

"Jason, what in the world are you talking about?" Morrie asked with believable innocence.

"I'm talking about turning up at a hearing on Monday without representation, that's what the hell I'm talking about!" The voice grew louder.

"I have nothing to hide."

"You had nothing to hide eight months ago when I settled that case for one hundred and fifty thousand. And let me remind you you're not carrying any malpractice insurance. We were lucky as hell to get out for that figure. I thought you had learned something about the value of legal representation."

"It was my money, not yours, Jason. You got paid, didn't you?"

"From what I understand, you could lose a lot more in the situation you're in now."

"I can handle it, I'm sure."

"Look, Morrie, you may fancy yourself as Beverly Hills' answer to Albert Schweitzer, but Perry Mason you're not.

And let me remind you, you're not in the jungle, either. This is a sophisticated medical community, and from where I sit it looks like you don't seem to understand when you're in way over your head," Berwick barked. "I'm not going to give you any advice about how you conduct your medical practice—which seems to be doing very well, financially anyway. All I can do is try to protect your ass when you stick it out for people to take shots at. And my best advice is that you quit sticking it out there in the first place. This guy Soltano is no amateur."

"Soltano?"

"The lawyer for the BMQA. He called me yesterday afternoon to ask if I was going to show up for the hearing. He doesn't want this to be thrown out of court because you're not properly represented."

"There's an angle right there. If you find something you don't like when you read the transcript—"

"Angle, schmangle!" Berwick erupted. "Soltano is a barracuda and you're breakfast. I know this man, he's as good as they get. You can't give him *anything*, not one inch. I'm telling you that it would be in your best interest to postpone this as long as you can. We need more time to work up a defense. Soltano's moving very fast. He wants to catch you off balance, and you're letting him do just that. He sees this case as a very big number, and he's not afraid of publicity," Berwick's booming continued. "Is it true this patient of yours will lose her nose?"

"There  .  .  .  may be some loss of tissue."

"How the hell did that happen? Is that sort of thing very common?"

"Not usually, but this was not a usual case. Biggest nose I've ever seen. It was necessary to improvise—"

"Improvise! What the fuck does that mean?"

"You're not a physician, Jason. I am. Your help in establishing the American Board of Surgery for Rejuvenation has been invaluable, but in this matter it would take a great deal to explain the complexities—"

"*You* may not be a physician much longer, Morrie, if you run around inventing any more operations."

"What I did is described in the literature. I can document that. And the patient signed the usual surgical consent. If you perform surgery there will be occasional problems," Morrie replied, not the least bit flustered.

"How many nose operations do you do every week?" Berwick asked, slightly more calm.

There was silence on the other end.

"Okay, in a month?"

Silence, and then, "This was my first."

"First. What do you mean 'first'?"

"The first rhinoplasty I have ever done." There was a hint of pride in the statement.

"Oh—oh, my God! Are you crazy? Postpone the deposition!"

"I can handle it. I assure you."

"Soltano will tear you apart," Berwick said with a sigh as he hung up.

Morrie tapped the receiver to clear the line. He dialed quickly, waiting for the Pan Am customer-service rep to answer. "Good evening, Mr. Trent. This is Dr. Gold. I'm afraid my last procedure has delayed me slightly. I can't miss Flight 208. Can you hold it five or ten minutes for me? I have an important operation scheduled for this evening." Morrie needed the extra time to stop at the duty-free counter to buy a bottle of perfume to replace the black silk panties. The mestiza would kill him if he didn't bring her a present. "Wonderful. The little girl will be so grateful."

As Morrie put down the phone, the limo stopped in front of the Dalway mansion. Peter was leaning against the gate. Morrie waved him into the car, noticing that Peter was slightly unsteady on his feet. All the better.

"Sorry to be late," Morrie said, pressing the button to close the driver's window. "No need to rush, Dennis. They're holding the plane."

"Holding the plane," Peter repeated, letting Morrie know he was duly impressed.

Without asking, Morrie opened the bar and took out two glasses. "Bourbon?"

"Lucky guess."

"Guess, my ass," Morrie said, pouring two drinks. "E.R. and I drank enough bourbon together for me to remember." He raised his glass. "Like father, like son."

Peter hesitated. "Sure."

"I can't tell you how much I appreciate your making time to see me," Morrie said. "I'm sure your practice keeps you quite busy."

"I could be busier," Peter said into his glass. He looked up quickly and smiled. "Hey, no prob. I still like riding in limos."

"Well, as I said, it's yours for the night. I assure you, Dennis is always discreet."

"Morrie, I gave up secrets years ago."

"Well, I haven't. And I'm calling upon my close friendship with your father to share one with you."

"My lips are sealed." Peter smiled. "Except for an occasional sip."

"I've known you for a long time, Peter. You're almost family to me. I feel I can trust you."

Peter crossed his heart. "Trust away."

"The Gold Institute of Surgical Rejuvenation has been very successful."

"No secret there."

"I am on my way to my clinic in Bogotá, where I have developed a number of breakthrough techniques. You would think that I am a happy man."

Peter stared at Morrie. "I would think."

"I'm not. I am a driven man. Unable to rest. Some say driven solely by ambition. But I know better. When helping people brings rewards in our society, motives are always held suspect. But I know, Peter, just what I am."

Peter nodded. "I do, too."

"Regardless of what I'm about to say, I don't want you to interpret this as taking advantage of our friendship."

"Morrie, cut to the chase. You can count on me."

He turned to face Peter. "What's the most common urological problem in men over fifty?"

Peter sat back warily. "Enlargement of the prostate."

"Precisely! And how many men who have to get up two

or three times a night know that this is a condition that can be remedied?"

"I don't know. Probably not too many."

"My point exactly! Do they know the surgery can be done without an incision? No! Peter, do they know that The Dalway Urological Clinic can help them?" Morrie made a graceful arc with both hands outlining an imaginary marquee.

"The what?" Peter said as he suddenly sat forward.

Morrie paused dramatically as he refilled both glasses. He spoke softly. "But that's just the beginning. Prostate surgery merely pays the rent. There's something much better."

Peter took the glass and a large swallow, never breaking eye contact with him. "What's that?"

Morrie took a sip, fully aware that Peter's eyes were on his every move. He swallowed again, licked his lips and cleared his throat. "Impotence."

"Im-po-tence?" Peter said, eyes now wide.

Morrie shrugged. "Think of the numbers."

"The numbers?"

"The numbers are staggering. And that includes only those willing to talk about it. I've had men come to me, thinking they needed a plastic surgeon for such an operation. Naturally, I helped them. How could I turn them away when I knew that, with a single surgical procedure, the insertion of a penile silicone prosthesis, I could step into their troubled lives and instead of hopelessness offer them happiness. How better to define the practice of medicine?" Morrie sat back, confident in what was happening.

"The Dalway Urological Clinic?"

Morrie smiled. Bingo. "The *E.R*. Dalway Clinic," he clarified. "I'd like to create something that would honor your father. And have you in charge of it. That would have been your father's dream. I am simply trying to make his dream come true."

"Let me just get this straight," Peter said as he sucked at the bourbon. "Who bankrolls this?"

"I do. Naturally, if you, and only you, wish to become a partner, nothing would please me more."

"And you want me to head the clinic?"

"I don't mean to pressure you, Peter."

Peter put down his glass. "Do you know what's been going on with me?"

"We're all human, Peter. Today, with all the stress in the world, I'm surprised we survive at all." Morrie filled Peter's glass. "I'm sure that little problem is behind you." He handed Peter the glass. "The only answer is to move forward. That's all we can do, the only direction we can go. A young man with your looks and background. You could do anything you wanted."

"I wish other physicians felt as you do. I'm not exactly being trampled by all the referrals."

"What do you need referrals for?" Morrie snapped arrogantly. "Get your own patients. Don't think for a moment that everyone who plays golf on Wednesday is a colleague. They're all jealous little schoolgirls. Forget them. Strike out on your own. Don't sit there waiting for the phone to ring. Do as I did." He touched Peter's arm as he smiled and said, "Advertise!"

Peter drew back. "That would be quite a step," he said hesitantly. "It's one thing when you're dealing with cosmetic surgery. We're talking something else here. Urology is not—"

"You're a physician, Peter. You want to help people and there are thousands of them out there in need of the assistance you can so expertly provide. But how are they going to find you in a crowded city like Los Angeles?"

"I don't know. I haven't had much luck."

"Stop thinking of it as advertising. It's educating the public. Think of how many patients you see a day and how many you could be seeing." Morrie knew he had him. "Think about it," he said reassuringly. Morrie studied Peter's boyishly handsome face, the smooth skin of his cheeks flushed from the alcohol, the upper eyelid movements sluggish. Yes, Morrie thought, this young man has real promise. There was an appealing dichotomy about

Peter, so sophisticated outwardly and such a vulnerable innocence within. A potentially useful dichotomy.

"I'd want to put up some money," Peter said.

"Of course."

Peter's voice grew tight. Anxious. "So that I'd have control over things."

"Naturally."

Peter put a hand to his face, swallowing hard to hold back his emotions. "Christ. Do you know what I've been going through? Ass-kissing all those sons of bitches. Do you know how long it's been since I had control over anything?" His voice cracked. "Myself included."

Morrie picked up the phone. "Excuse me, Peter. I've just remembered something." Morrie dialed the weather. "Hello, Mrs. Evans. Did you get that business settled for Monday morning? What? Then find someone else immediately. Check my book, I'll hold." Morrie turned to Peter. "I'm trying to find someone to do a simple procedure for me on Monday. I have to be out of town again and  .  .  .  yes, I'm here. No. He's at a conference. I tell you what, I'll call you from Bogotá. But in the meantime, call the other number. I know it's short notice, but it's such a simple procedure. Just a replacement. Very good. Thank you."

Peter finished blowing his nose. "Problem?"

"It shouldn't be. Any second-year medical student could handle it. My nurse could handle it. But try to find a doctor who's willing to do a favor." Morrie sat back. Counting the seconds.

"What kind of procedure?"

Done. Morrie had landed his catch. "Peter, I'm embarrassed. It's like asking Jonas Salk to take out a splinter."

Peter leaned close. "Morrie, I want to do this for you."

"I don't know what to say. I'm very moved." He refilled Peter's glass and watched him empty it in a single gulp.

"No. That's a lie. I want to do it for me. Morrie, let me do it."

A deep sigh. Morrie shook his head. "On one condition. I'll let you do it if you promise to talk seriously when I get back about the E.R. Dalway Clinic."

Peter smiled and nodded. "You sure drive a hard bargain."

Morrie began to laugh. "What are friends for?"

The limo made the turn into the airport. *That* was choreography. To hell with the BMQA and their "temporary restraining order." No one was going to restrain Morrie Gold. All he had done was try an innovative procedure. It wasn't his fault that Stephanie didn't heal properly. Suddenly, like vultures, there were lawyers and threats, the government—little people for whom he was a most attractive target. But survive he would.

The driver stopped the car at the entrance to the terminal and rushed out to open the door. Morrie shook Peter's hand. "We'll talk more at your party."

"Don't worry about it. You can count on me."

Morrie nodded. He got out of the car and then stopped, turning back to Peter. "You know who invented plastic surgery?"

"Who?"

"The Jews."

Peter laughed. "Before or after they invented pastrami and MGM?"

Morrie shook Peter's hand. "Circumcision, my boy. Think about it. The first nip and tuck."

Waving good-bye to Peter without looking back, Morrie walked briskly into the terminal. He hadn't a thing in the world to worry about.

# 29

STEPHANIE GREEN, WEARING a ski mask and a restraining jacket, sat in a chair at the Glenview Convalescent Home. A male nurse on one side, her father on the other. Mr. Green extended his hand to Lionel. "Thank you for coming, Doctor. We couldn't move her."

A pungent odor of dead flesh filled the room. Stephanie's wrists were restrained by heavy cloth cuffs. The young woman's body was nearly limp, held upright because the restraining jacket was attached to the chair. Her head slumped to one side. There was an almost imperceptible sound of wailing, like a wounded animal that had given up any chance of being heard.

"She won't allow us to remove the mask," Green said. "When they called me from L'Etoile, I took her to the emergency room. An intern took the tape off her nose, the smell was so bad. Most of her nose came off with it. Then she took a mirror out of her purse," he said slowly. "She's been in this catatonic state ever since. Except when she comes out of it and starts to scream. Two doctors walked away from the case, said there was nothing to be done except skin grafts. That she would be deformed forever. They said it to her. I didn't know what to do."

Lionel nodded. "I'd like you to wait outside."

"I think I should be here. No offense, but after all she's been through—"

"I want you to wait outside." Lionel nodded at the burly male nurse. "Take him with you."

"But she may get violent. I'm afraid of what she might do to herself."

"Mr. Green," Lionel said softly, pointing to the door. Her father hesitated but then, as though swept by a wave of grief and despair, accepted that he had no choice and left.

Lionel pulled up a chair in front of Stephanie. He began to untie the jacket. "I am a doctor. My name is Lionel Stern. I am a plastic surgeon at the University Hospital. I have a great deal of experience in fixing the problem you have and I'm here because I can help you." The whimpering stopped. Lionel began to open the hooks, talking slowly, calmly. "I can rebuild your nose. There will be some scars, but makeup will cover them. We can make it okay. You will be able to go out into the world and look normal." As he undid the last of the ties on her jacket, she collapsed in his arms. He held her for several minutes.

"Stephanie, I want to take off the mask."

She shuddered, shoulders quickly bending over flexed knees so that her body formed the smallest possible physical size. She began to whimper again.

"Take off the mask."

Stephanie began kicking her feet. Softly, as though she had no strength left, she sobbed, "No. No. No. No. No. No."

Lionel took hold of her shoulders. "If you want me to help you, you have to trust me."

"I trusted the others. I let them see me. They didn't come back."

"I'm not going away."

"Who are you? A lawyer? A doctor? One of the zookeepers at this place? Aren't you afraid to look at me?"

Lionel repeated what he had said before. All the while, he kept his eyes on hers, those red unseeing eyes behind the knit mask. He knew that she would believe his eyes if she could focus on them long enough. "I have seen the pictures of your face. I'm not afraid. This kind of problem, your problem, doesn't upset me. This kind of work, this kind of reconstructive surgery is what I do. My job is helping people like you." Lionel felt her mind was wandering. "Stephanie, do you have any questions for me?"

"Yes."

"Ask me your questions and I will tell you the truth." Lionel's policy had always been to answer a patient's question. Not that he hadn't taken refuge at times in the definition of "medical truth." He wondered how much this fragile patient really wanted to know. Honesty, like molasses, was to be doled out a spoonful at a time and only in response to a request for more.

She raised a hand toward Lionel. "The truth?"

"Yes."

Stephanie paused to take a breath. But her emotions were still racing ahead. Her body convulsed. She began to sob uncontrollably. As Lionel reached toward her, she pushed him away. Above her own hysteria and the demons that had been unleashed inside, Stephanie cried out, "Why didn't Dr. Gold come back?"

Fifteen minutes later, Lionel opened the door and motioned for the nurse. Stephanie's father glanced in the room and saw his daughter sitting in the chair without her ski mask. Lionel walked down the hallway, followed closely by Mr. Green.

"Doctor?" he said soberly.

"She'll be all right," Lionel said, straining to hide his rage at Morrie Gold. "She'll have scars, and she won't be able to go out without makeup, but I can fix it."

"You can make her a new nose?" Green asked.

Stern nodded.

"The miracles of modern medicine. Thank God." Tears came to Arthur Green's eyes.

"Not . . . really, Mr. Green. In fact it's the oldest surgical procedure ever recorded," Lionel said. "The same operation was done in India two thousand years before Christ."

"But isn't there something more . . . up to date?"

"Mr. Green, sit down." Lionel massaged his hands together, an alternative since he didn't have Morrie Gold's neck to strangle. He spoke with his usual candor. This was not a time for anything but the truth. "Her entire nose is gone. Stephanie needs so much tissue in order to reconstruct it that it must be brought in from somewhere else. I can cut a flap of skin from her forehead and fold it down to reform the nose. But it must remain attached so we can maintain the blood supply. It will take at least two weeks for that forehead skin to develop its own circulation around the nose. At that time the attachment of the new nose can be divided from the forehead. After a few months I can use cartilage grafts from her ears to reform the curve of the nostrils. The scars on her forehead are precisely in the middle and usually heal extremely well and can be covered with bangs."

Mr. Green listened in astonishment. "That means she'll be all right!"

"On the outside, certainly. In time."

The two men talked about the surgery, about what it would look like, about Stephanie and what would happen on the inside during it all. Then Green shook his head. "If only there were some way I could get that bastard for what he did."

Lionel put his hand on the man's shoulder. "Mr. Green, you've been reading my mind."

Green smiled for the first time in many days.

# 30

THE AREA AROUND the pool was lit with large red Japanese lanterns. A band, dressed in white karate outfits, played "Poor Butterfly" on the violin, harp, trombone and drums. Waiters in black Armani suits with black mandarin collars carried trays filled with glasses of Dom Perignon while samurai-outfitted chefs noisily performed at a sushi bar in front of the cabanas. A young woman in a pink bikini swam in the pool, almost totally ignored by nearly two hundred very well-dressed people.

Casey, wearing a pale gray satin pantsuit that made her hair look almost platinum, held her hand on Lionel's arm as they walked onto the patio. "Expensive and unburdened by good taste. The perfect Westside Los Angeles party," she whispered. Even with the whisper she managed to keep some distance. "It is such a relief to get out of that Cuisinart you call a car," she said, stretching her neck.

Lionel watched the young woman jump off the diving board. "Look at that!"

"You mean, look at *those?*" Casey tugged at his arm. "Okay. We put in an appearance. Let's go."

"Are you crazy? And miss all this?"

"All what? These people are from Central Casting."

"Not *that* people." Lionel nodded toward Linda Evans.

"Oh, Lion. Has . . . she had plastic surgery?"

He laughed and then mimicked, "Oh, Casey. Does it make any difference?"

"Put me near a pool and I lose all my character."

Lionel grabbed two glasses from a waiter and handed one to Casey. "What do you lose when I put you near champagne?"

"My patience." She emptied the glass in a single gulp. "You sure you want to stay here?"

"We haven't even seen Peter yet." He leaned close and kissed her forehead quite lightly. She pulled away.

"Let's not get into that. We have a deal," Casey said.

"Okay, Dr. Crawford, we'll keep it professional. I know just how to handle it. All we have to do is talk to one another about incidental things that make no difference. Like during intermission at the opera."

"I hate the opera, and you know that. And you hate the opera. And this is going to be a long evening."

"That's the idea. You're doing very well." Lionel casually scanned the crowd, looking for Peter.

"You son of a bitch!" she whispered under her breath as she plucked another champagne from a passing tray.

"Excellent, Dr. Crawford! You're really getting the hang of it."

"What do I have to do to make you believe I'm serious about keeping some distance between us?" she asked.

"You have to marry me," Lionel said, turning to face her. "A lot of married people avoid each other."

"I see. You've decided to take no prisoners."

He smiled. "We'll announce it to the party. The band will play something stupid and we'll wish we had kept our mouths shut."

"I wish you would. We've been through all this. Why are we talking about this here? With all these people around?" Casey said, clearly annoyed.

"What people? I thought we were all alone." Lionel shifted his weight uncomfortably. Cocktail parties were a problem for Lionel. For one thing, he didn't drink. Alcohol slowed him uncomfortably, muddling otherwise clear waters. But drunk or sober, light cocktail conversation was a foreign language he was unable to sustain. That cornerstone of social interaction was a complete mystery to him, and he found such situations vaguely threatening.

He turned from Casey to watch with amazement as the girl in the pink bikini climbed out of the pool and stood, dripping wet, talking to a bald man in a tuxedo. She stood perfectly relaxed, a pool of water enlarging around her.

"My God, do you have to make it so obvious?" Casey said.

Lionel looked quickly away, unaware that he had stared so conspicuously. "I don't seem to be doing very well here tonight," he said, now clearly annoyed. He was out of his element. He much preferred the structured environment of the hospital, where people wore prescribed clothing and behaved according to established procedures. White coats. Operating rooms. Problems to be solved. He was infinitely more comfortable with patients in the hospital, people who needed a skill he could provide, rather than with strangers at a party who needed each other for only an hour or two. Lionel had been trained to deliver excellence. Easy smiles and surface glitter were unsettling. The delicate tinkling of glasses around the Dalway pool was an alien atmosphere where purpose was evasive and charm was the ultimate goal. It was an atmosphere he did not understand.

And Casey was also something he did not understand. "You know, I've never met anyone who ran as hot and cold as you do. Now we're friends. You seem to handle it without batting an eye. Just step back two paces and all of a sudden, presto! we're professional colleagues. I can't do things that way. I want more."

"What about what I want? What—"

"I'm a surgeon, damn it! That's what I am. That's what I do. I can't step from that." The boiling point was approaching.

"Neither can I," she said.

Peter interrupted, clutching Lionel's arms. "Glad you guys could make it." In his double-breasted white cotton suit and white silk shirt, Peter was a study in casual California elegance. But there was nothing casual about his grip on Lionel's arm. Peter held on like a man on a climbing expedition. A sudden flash of smile. "You ever seen so many people?"

Lionel put an arm on Peter's shoulder. "A few hundred of your closest friends?"

"Shh," Peter whispered jokingly. "I'm counting bladders."

"So that's what urologists count when they can't sleep." Lionel shook his head.

"Wrong, chum. That's what they count when they need work." Peter took a deep breath and turned to Casey. "You look sensational. How about us going upstairs for an hour or two?"

"I'm flattered, Peter, but I doubt either of us could last that long."

"Anyone here I know?" Lionel asked.

"Are you kidding?" Peter replied. "If a bomb went off now, University Hospital would lose half its staff."

Casey sighed with exaggerated disappointment. Looking directly at Lionel, she said, "Unfortunately, the chances of that happening are practically nil." Lionel Stern stiffened visibly. Casey's voice changed. "An impressive group, Peter. How did you get them all here?" She made an obvious effort to ignore Lionel.

Peter took them both by the arms and leaned forward. "I let it slip that there would be a few celebs. That's about all it takes." He looked around proudly. "But the ironic thing is, as it turns out, I didn't have to give this party at all. I've come up with the reddest lollipop in the candy store. How does this sound," Peter cleared his throat dramatically. "The E.R. Dalway Urological Clinic."

Lionel was astonished, remembering their conversation only a few days earlier. He looked at Peter. "Nothing halfway about you, is there?"

"I'm impressed," Casey said politely.

Peter was exuberant. "Well, I got some good advice the other day. 'If you can't join 'em, beat 'em.' "

"And who was giving the sage advice?" Lionel asked.

"Morrie Gold."

Lionel glanced at Casey. "Uh oh."

"How do you know Morrie Gold?" Casey asked quickly, her eyes narrowing.

Peter was surprised by the question, but more by the look on Casey's face. "He was an old friend of my father. They . . . did business together, you might say. I guess my dad got Morrie started with all this cosmetic surgery. From the start he was involved in the film business—" Peter caught himself and quickly slowed down. He turned defensively to Lionel. "Listen, Lion . . . I know how you feel. I know you don't like Morrie . . ."

"These days, Peter, it may be a little more than that."

Peter turned to Casey, his face a plea for support. "He's got this thing about Morrie. Always has."

Casey looked at both men, then at the party that surrounded them, and took a very deep breath. "Something tells me this is the prefect time for me to find the powder room."

They waited for her to leave. "I'd be careful, Peter. Even the best of us don't know when we're being used," Lionel said.

"Morrie Gold using me? Morrie Gold is not using me," Peter said with indignation. "I think you have it wrong, Lion. Not to mention a short memory. If anything, I'm using him. For Chrissake, the guy's known me since I was a kid."

"Then go out to dinner with him and talk about old times."

A look came into Peter's eyes that Lionel had never seen. "I—don't—need—to—go—out—to—dinner," he said with exaggerated emphasis. "I need to practice medicine. And *that* is what he is offering me."

Lionel stood there, unwilling to say anything. Peter was drawing a line. The question was, should he risk crossing it?

"Morrie's going to be out of town on Monday, and I'm going to sub on a few simple procedures for him." Peter Dalway said it—off the cuff, no big deal, but clearly happy.

Lionel looked at Peter, up to the brim in enthusiasm, and considered his response. "Peter, I'm going to give it to you straight. Morrie's not going to be out of town on Monday." Lionel felt his anger toward Morrie rise. "His license has been temporarily suspended. The court slapped a temporary restraining order on him. He's going to be at a hearing on Monday."

Peter took a deep breath. "How . . . do you know?"

"I know. That's all."

"What did he do?"

"Even to you, I can't talk about that before the hearing," Lionel said apologetically.

Peter lit a cigarette. "Aw, for Chrissake, there's nothing wrong with Morrie except he makes an ass of himself sometimes. Makes a big deal about who somebody is, big names, that sort of thing, particularly if they're Hollywood. It's important for him to hang around those kind of people. It's sort of his statement."

"Sounds like he should start a restaurant," Lionel replied.

"Well, yeah, there's no lack of self-confidence when it comes to Morrie."

"Or arrogance."

"Lion, you don't understand, surgery isn't the same for him as it is to you. To Morrie it's a means to an end. More than anything he wants what surrounds it. All the nice stuff. He likes the image. Limousines, good-looking women. Can't say he's wrong about that, now, can we?" Peter laughed. Lionel didn't. "Morrie's like a car salesman. Volume is what counts. For him everything is like a big-screen production. Money, flash, publicity. Morrie's ads? He really believes them. He thinks he's the best cosmetic surgeon in the world. He isn't, but he's talked himself into it. He believes what his PR people write," Peter said. "He goes for the publicity. If you read the L.A. *Times* you know who Morrie Gold is. To him, that's the most important thing. Don't think for one minute he'd be commuting to South America if it didn't get his picture in the newspaper. He needs to keep his name up there in lights. *Bigger* than life! That's Morrie." Peter motioned with his hands. "Believe it or not, Morrie's harmless."

Stern looked down at his glass and seriously considered drinking it. "There are a couple of patients around this town that would argue that one. Why do you think he's got the BMQA all over him like a tent? The guy is dangerous. I read one of his operative reports a few days ago. It made the hair on the back of my neck stand straight up."

"Well, I'm certainly not one to talk about making mistakes in the operating room," Peter said very quietly.

"You made a careless error. It was an honest mistake. What we're talking about here is very different."

"Say what you want, but Morrie is out there operating up a storm," Peter said. "He sure has more patients than I do."

"Not when I get through with him. The time has come to pull the plug," Lionel said firmly.

"You know that would include the Dalway Clinic?" Peter asked bitterly. "Why don't you get off your high horse for a few minutes? I finally had some good news and then my friend steps in."

"It's not good news, Peter." Lionel grabbed Peter's shoulder. "Trust me. You're better off not having anything to do with Morrie Gold."

"Why? Something to do with your lofty standards?"

Lionel let go of him with a slight push. "Yeah. Yeah, standards have something to do with it! They're worth something."

Casey returned. Peter put a finger to his lips and whispered, "Shhhhh." He leaned toward her and said, "You'd better tell your loudmouth friend to zip it about Morrie. I don't want any fistfights at my party."

She was horrified. "Morrie Gold is here?"

Peter smiled. "All my friends are here. And some who aren't." Then he turned toward Lionel. "Be sure to have some of the tuna. The sushi master says it's the best he's cut in years."

Lionel watched Peter walk back into the crowd, trying to negotiate his feelings about him. No matter how hard Lionel tried, they always seemed to be on different wavelengths. He owed his life to Peter, but still had been unable to make so much as a down payment.

Casey put her arm in his and leaned close. "Well, that just about does it for me," she said. "My job description does not include making small talk with the defendants. And as far as you and I are concerned, you're right. This isn't working." She spoke with a distinct finality.

"No, it isn't."

"But you did as much as you could for Peter. He obviously won't listen," Casey said, obviously wanting to change the subject.

"You should have heard him. He talked about Morrie as if he were some kind of god. Morrie's women. Morrie's money. Morrie's life-style. I just about threw up."

She put a hand on his arm. "You hated it. Or perhaps you feel a little . . . jealous maybe?"

Lionel stood in silence, stunned, both at the outrageousness of her statement and at the sudden realization that it was true. "I'm out of here," Casey said, looking inside her purse. "I'm not playing femme fatale with you. This whole thing is getting just a little too complicated. I'm the chief investigator for the BMQA. To be seen with Morrie Gold just before the hearing? Dating my expert witness, yet. This is jeopardizing my career."

"I understand," Lionel said, exhausted.

"But you don't care."

"Of course I care. You're beginning to sound like Peter."

"I'm beginning to understand Peter. Maybe someday you will." Casey reached out and touched his jacket with her fingertips. "You and I, Doctor . . . should be more than we are." She looked at him hard. "That's probably the worst thing I could say. But it says it all, doesn't it?"

"Casey . . ."

"What?"

"You never gave me an answer about marrying me."

Lionel noticed that when Casey cried, she did so quietly, without big sobs or any attempt to conceal it. "Sure I did. You just didn't hear me, Doctor."

Lionel watched her leave, painfully aware that he hadn't tried to stop her. Or Peter. They were the two people he loved most, and both felt he had betrayed them. It struck him quite hard that it was unlikely both of them were wrong. Lionel felt as alone as he had ever felt in his life. As he watched her walk away without looking back he realized that his future was rapidly becoming his past. He picked up Casey's glass and slowly poured the champagne onto the lawn.

"A rather expensive way to water the grass," said a sultry voice behind him.

Lionel turned quickly. The first thing he noticed about the woman was her skin, absolutely smooth and ageless. Tall and elegant, her jet black hair was combed straight back, each strand parallel to the next, drawn back in a bun by a black satin bow. Around her neck, a single large glittering emerald.

Lionel shrugged. "It's expensive grass."

She smiled and extended her hand in one of the most graceful movements he had ever seen. Minimal body movements. But the gesture had an unmistakable grace. Her torso was a textbook of feminine curves whose proportions made the shimmer of her floor-length evening dress explode with a primitive, animal energy. "Luisa Obregon," she said.

There was the slightest hint of an accent that complemented her dark eyes. Lionel took her hand as one reaches out to touch a marble statue. "Lionel Stern." He was surprised by the strength with which she gripped his hand.

"I know."

"You do?" he replied awkwardly, still trying to gather his senses as well as his wits.

"I asked Dr. Dalway to point you out."

"Oh," Lionel said puzzled. Clearly, she was not one of those women who corner doctors at parties in order to discuss plastic surgery. From what Lionel could see, Luisa Obregon needed absolutely nothing he could provide professionally. "I'm pleased to meet you."

She looked up at him. "You may not be when you find out who I am."

Lionel could not imagine, although there was something oddly familiar about her. In any case, it was shaping up to be an interesting game and a welcome breather after fifteen rounds with Casey and Peter.

Stern took a deep breath. "Then don't tell me."

She slipped her arm in his and oh-so-gently but persuasively led him back toward the house. "But that would be deceitful."

"Mmmm," he replied, unable to break eye contact with this beautiful creature.

"What shall we do?" she asked as if any answer would have been delightfully accepted.

Lionel, completely off balance, looked in the direction Casey had gone, then down at his shoes as if some answer would appear from them.

"I hope I didn't take you away from anything," she asked with genuine concern.

"Fine. I'm fine." It was over, Casey was over, he thought to himself. Might as well recognize it when the safe falls on your head.

Luisa stopped walking and let go of Lionel's arm. "I'm sorry. I'm not very good at this." After a moment's hesitation, she said, "I had a speech prepared." She looked up at him. Those eyes again. "But then I didn't know what you would be like."

"Disappointed?" He watched as she maintained eye contact with him. Not a flinch. But he thought he perceived a need. "Are you in some kind of trouble?"

She nodded slowly. "Perhaps," she said quite slowly. "I'm not sure yet." She let the words linger. "But I wasn't supposed to get into trouble. I was sent over to avoid a potentially awkward social situation, and now I'm afraid I've created one. I had no idea you were such an attractive man."

As a waiter approached, Lionel asked, "Would you like some champagne?"

"Later," she said quite firmly.

Later, he repeated to himself. The game was on. He hoped that he still remembered how to play.

"Dr. Stern," she began.

"Lionel." He very much wanted it to be a personal matter.

"Lionel." Luisa spoke softly. "A professional colleague

of yours, another plastic surgeon, Dr. Morris Gold, would like the opportunity to meet you."

The invitation caught him completely off guard. Then he realized he had seen her before, in society columns, on the arm of Morrie Gold. What was this woman, this exquisitely designed creature doing with that monster? Lionel smiled nervously, disliking the implied association of her calling Morrie a "professional colleague." Lionel almost never identified himself as a plastic surgeon. He had never forgotten that scene in *The Graduate* in which Dustin Hoffman was advised to pursue a career in "plastics." Ever since, he had disliked the very sound of the word, aware that most people thought of plastic as something toys were made of.

Suddenly, to his surprise, he did not want to meet Morrie. Because the invitation had come from Luisa? And what the hell *was* a woman like that doing with Morrie? Lionel looked at Luisa, searching for a clue. Instead, he felt a hand grab hold of his arm. It was Morrie Gold. Smiling.

"Dr. Stern," he began, his voice filled with urgency. "I can't tell you how I've been looking forward to meeting you. Please tell me, how is poor, dear Stephanie?"

Lionel couldn't believe his ears. It took him a moment to realize who had taken his hand and was shaking it. Lionel tried gently to get loose. But Morrie wouldn't let go. Polished and confident in mannerisms and carriage, the man spoke with a disarming and believable sincerity. There was a certain intensity about him that suggested credibility. Had he not known otherwise, Lionel might have guessed he was an evangelical preacher.

"I don't know how many times I've called," Morrie said. "But I can't get through. It's that father of hers. Of course, I was relieved to hear that you'd taken the case, but you know how it is. No matter how many times you tell yourself it wasn't your fault and that nothing could have been done, you just can't let go."

Lionel pulled his hand back. "You can let go now."

"Oh, please, don't misunderstand me. No slight intended, Doctor. I've followed your career for years. Brilliant! Sheer brilliance! I told Luisa, Señora Obregon," he corrected, reaching out and pulling her close to him, "that you were the only doctor I would recommend in such a delicate situation." Morrie leaned toward Lionel and lowered his voice dramatically. "Is there anything at all I can do?"

A stunning performance, Lionel thought. The son of a bitch may have his license revoked and there he was, in a dark blue silk suit with gold bracelets on both his wrists, convincingly displaying concern for his patient. It was art. Fine verbal sculpture.

"No," Lionel said, not even sure what the question had been. All he knew was that "No" was a reflex response. Lionel turned to Luisa, wondering what his response should be to her.

"At last!" Morrie said to the waiter as he took two glasses of champagne and handed one to Luisa.

She shook her head, never taking her eyes from Lionel as she once again said, "Later." The game was definitely on.

"Dr. Stern?" Morrie asked, offering Lionel a glass.

"Maybe later," Lionel said, looking directly at Luisa.

Morrie hesitated and then quickly put both glasses back on the tray. "Of course not. On call, that sort of thing. I understand completely." He held tight to Luisa as though she were a trophy.

"I think that's why doctors like to travel. It's the only time we don't have to worry about having a drink. Except, of course, when traveling to my clinic in Bogotá."

Lionel wasn't sure why he was still standing there listening to Morrie. Except his eyes kept moving toward Luisa. A fact which Morrie had taken note.

"No doubt Señora Obregon has been her usual modest self," Morrie began, "and has neglected to explain how instrumental she has been in helping me establish my clinic in Bogotá."

"I would be very interested in hearing about it," Lionel responded directly to Luisa.

Morrie continued. "As you may know, I fly down there as often as I possibly can. It breaks my heart to see those

poor children with cleft lips and scar deformities from
burns. I have my little clinic there, certainly nothing on the
scale to which you are accustomed at University Hospital,
Dr. Stern, but it is every bit as important to me. Luisa and
I are great friends and, aside from being the most beautiful
woman in South America, she is also one of the most
influential. Without her, my efforts in so poor an area would
not be possible."

Lionel had read newspaper articles featuring those trips to
Bogotá. Morrie often packed up his entire office to perform
reconstructive surgery on people who could barely afford
enough to eat. Certainly not by chance, a photographer had
carefully documented each excursion.

Was that it? Luisa Obregon, a member of the Bogotá
elite, soothed her conscience by supporting Morrie's medical philanthropy? It made sense that Luisa might do such a
thing, but the question still haunted Lionel. Why Morrie
Gold?

"Have you been to Los Angeles before?" Lionel asked
her self-consciously, feeling a need to say something.

"Oh yes, Dr. Stern. Many times. I'm here on a short
holiday. Morris was kind enough to ask me along this
evening." She had a soft throaty voice that made the base of
his spine vibrate.

No matter how Morrie held onto her, Lionel doubted any
romantic alliance between Dr. Gold and his patroness. But
somehow, Morrie must have tapped the right keys with his
polished, confident mannerisms. He spoke with an intensity
that suggested credibility. It wasn't difficult for Lionel to
understand how Luisa or anyone else for that matter was
taken in. He felt sorry for her.

"I hope you enjoy your stay here," Lionel offered, the
echo of his clumsy words a reminder of why he hated
cocktail parties where people rarely said what they were
thinking. She seemed to sense his discomfort, particularly
as people began to gather around Morrie.

"I find it interesting that although you and Morris are in
the same profession, you have just met for the first time
tonight."

Lionel wondered whether the observation was as perceptive as it seemed.

"Dr. Stern has a much different type of practice than I do," Morrie interjected casually. "Until a few years ago, plastic surgeons performed quite diversified surgery—burns, hand injuries, facial trauma, skin cancer, all kinds of reconstruction. The specialty began by taking what the general surgeons didn't want or didn't have time for. And plastic surgeons made a specialty of these leftovers." Morrie smiled broadly while he talked, a mannerism Lionel quickly found quite annoying. "But, about fifteen years ago, the consumer got into the picture. They began to ask for something different and special from medicine. Before that time the consumer—".

"Consumers? I always thought they were patients," Lionel snapped.

"I'm not sure the distinction is so clear these days. Times have changed. We live in an age of consumerism. We've been brainwashed by the concept that the customer is always right."

Lionel had quickly become angry. "Patients are different from customers!"

Morrie smiled. "Only to those of us naive enough to believe we're not retailers. I sell and you sell. Let's face it, Lionel. If the moneychangers outside the temple had belonged to the AMA, Jesus wouldn't have stood a chance. Perhaps I'm a bit more of a realist than you. I define a patient as someone stricken with a problem that requires the assistance of a physician. He has cancer, an ulcer, pneumonia—something he surely didn't ask for. But in the late sixties, people began to seek out the doctor for other kinds of problems. Call them problems of appearance. Psychological problems they believe could be medically treated. A woman with droopy eyelids wanted her husband to pay more attention. The plastic surgeon became the only physician with a product to sell. And when that happened, patients became customers."

"Surgery is not like buying a Buick," Lionel growled. "Whatever operation you're talking about, it still requires a scalpel, although you wouldn't get that idea from your ads. The moment you make an incision, you take a risk that something could go wrong."

"Surely you've had things go wrong during surgery," Morrie said with a smile, completely in control.

The playing field was not even, an imbalance that Lionel had, to a large extent, created himself. The realization only enhanced his frustration. "And when it happens I take care of the problem." Stern let the words hang in the air. He was certain that Gold got the message, but his face didn't show it.

"I suppose, Dr. Stern, that you and I have different perspectives. You are doing highly complicated reconstructive procedures every day. But in the real world, outside the University, we specialize. In my own practice, almost exclusively in cosmetic surgery. That's what I do *every* day. To you, after rebuilding one of those deformed children's faces, what is a face-lift?"

Morrie spoke to the guests around him, and Lionel's frustration began to grow into anger. Restrained by the social circumstance, he was unable to say what he really wanted to, what he knew to be the truth. He couldn't say Morrie had no training in plastic surgery. The now jolly, congenial man had just days before maimed a woman, ruining her life, because he incorrectly believed he had abilities he didn't possess. And there he stood confidently displaying an ego that would not allow him to recognize it.

"Dr. Stern, with the challenging work you do, I'm sure you don't have time for the indulgences of cosmetic operations. You don't know how lucky you are! I have patients who come back to the institute who find wrinkles after surgery with a *magnifying glass*." Laughter again, this time from people Lionel was certain had a magnifying glass in their pockets or purses.

"I do cosmetic surgery," Lionel said soberly.

"Be thankful you don't have to do it *all* the time like I do. It's rewarding, but"—Morrie sighed—"very demanding to contend with such detail constantly." Again he was playing to the crowd.

Lionel's anger had reached a point of no return. Attention to detail? He wondered what Morrie Gold would say if Stephanie Green in her ski mask were introduced to this gathering.

Morrie Gold stood squarely opposite him, calm, the ever-present smile larger. It was clear to Lionel that this angelic-looking, slightly obese salesman of plastic surgery was dangerous in a dimension that extended well beyond his initial assessment.

"Well, you guys look like you're having a good time." It was Peter, holding a glass of champagne in each hand. "Though how you could have a good time without some bubbly is beyond me." He offered a glass to Luisa and then, while staring at Lionel, offered the other glass to Morrie.

Lionel thought the message was clear. Peter was letting him know he was angry.

"I'm afraid Dr. Stern won't have the pleasure of another round with us," Peter said. He turned to Lionel. "The hospital just called."

He had picked up the wrong message from Peter. That realization was disconcerting to Lionel, and he began to wonder what other messages he had misinterpreted. Suddenly he was not sure if things, people, relationships were as he saw them. It was an extraordinarily rare circumstance for Lionel: uncertainty had reared its head. Had he misread Luisa? Grateful for the excuse to escape, Lionel looked at Peter and said, "I'm sorry."

"You never had your champagne, Doctor," Luisa said.

Lionel smiled. At least her signal was one he'd read loud and clear. "Later."

As he walked away, he heard Morrie say, "Such a dedicated man. I admire him tremendously."

His face tight and unsmiling, Lionel made his way with some difficulty through the noisy throng of people who jammed the Dalway foyer. It was the deception, Morrie's air of confidence, the facade of "the accomplished surgeon" that enraged him. But there could be no question, the performance he had witnessed was flawless. It was unsettling to Lionel that he was the only one who understood that everyone there was a potential victim. Including, he assumed, the enchanting Luisa Obregon.

Where the hell was the phone? As Lionel edged his way around the room, he was certain the voice on the other end would be John Maltry. University Hospital had its own well-defined chain of command not unlike the military. When an emergency arose, the hospital page operator would call the first-year general surgery resident. Franklin Upton would then call Maltry if he wasn't comfortable handling the problem and Maltry would call Lionel if he needed advice or if the problem required taking a patient to OR. But on a Saturday night, it could easily be an auto accident, a fractured jaw, nose or lacerated face. Lionel mentally reviewed a checklist of patients in the hospital. Not likely Stephanie Green. As he dialed, Lionel hoped to hell it wasn't Felix.

"The kid looks bad," Maltry said. "He threw up his dinner and he's getting sleepy. I checked him over and couldn't find any localizing signs. Reflexes were okay, pupils and extraocular movements were fine. Then about an hour ago, he spiked a temperature to one hundred four."

"What's he look like now?"

"Other than the fever, he looks the same. I contacted the radiologist on call, who was not overjoyed at the prospect of a Saturday night CT scan. They're setting it up right now. But regardless of what it shows, something tells me Felix has something bad wrong with him. We'll find it, but I hope it's not too late when we do. He doesn't look good to me. That much I'm sure of."

It was enough for Stern. "I'll be there in ten minutes."

Sitting deep within the soft, finely cracked leather of the bucket seat, the half oval car completely surrounded Lionel as he sped along Sunset Boulevard. He communicated with the expertly crafted machine through the clutch, the accelerator and the steering wheel he had carefully lacquered two months before. The car was alive, answering his commands with deep throaty resonant sounds and precise movements that allowed him to feel changes in the texture of the asphalt beneath him. It was a small miracle that there were no police along the seven miles and six minutes it took to get to University Hospital.

Lionel entered the hospital from the parking lot. The outer courtyard smelled of jet fuel: the Med-Evac helicopter had just landed on top of the South wing and looked like a giant dragonfly perched on the roof. Although he had seen it there dozens of times, it suddenly looked inexplicably ominous.

As inexplicable as Felix's temperature shooting up. The two elevations since his surgery had been the only measurable signs that something was wrong. Except for the way Felix looked. The swelling in the young boy's face had still not completely dissipated, and he remained uncharacteristically listless. Felix wasn't Felix.

Lionel had ordered the neurosurgeons and neurologists to go over him several times with their small rubber hammers to check reflexes, and with hat pins and wisps of cotton to check sensation. They had found nothing. The infectious disease specialists had taken blood cultures so many times it was difficult to find an open vein. No bacteria or fungi grew. They wrote two pages of notes in Felix's chart that said, in flawless ballpoint penmanship, they had absolutely no idea what was wrong.

Until recently, the hospital staff had become quite comfortable about calling Felix "the frog." Particularly after the surgery, when it was obvious to anyone that he would no longer look like one. The plastic surgery residents used the name most frequently. It was a compliment in reverse, defiant hospital humor that proclaimed, "We can fix frogs. Nothing to it. Bring on the next one."

But even the plastic surgery residents had become worried when the fevers began. Before that time they had thought, but never articulated—out of respect not to mention a small amount of fear—that perhaps Doctor Stern was overly concerned and too compulsive about this particular patient. Lionel personally examined the boy twice each day, and as the time of Felix's recovery dragged on, there was an edge about him that made the residents want to keep their distance. But it was now becoming apparent that although no one could find anything specific, *something* was wrong. Anyone who listened to the residents might have made that guess because they began to call him "Felix" again; no one referred to him as "the frog."

As Lionel walked down the corridor of the pediatric ward, he greeted John Maltry and entered Felix's room. It was a bad sign that the television wasn't on, but even more telling, it was the first time Lionel had not been greeted by the familiar outstretched arm and clenched fist.

"How's it going, slugger?" Felix didn't respond. His eyes were glassy. Lionel's pulse began to race. "Sit up for me, Felix."

"I don't want to," came the slurred reply.

"Watch my finger," Lionel instructed. Felix's eyes could not follow from side to side. Lionel took a penlight from his pocket and checked the pupil contraction of each eye. Both narrowed quickly as the light was focused on them, but the left pupil was slightly larger than the right. Using the ophthalmoscope he had taken from the nurses' station, Lionel flashed a narrow beam of light to look into Felix's eyes, focusing the series of small rotating magnifying lenses to the back surface of the interior of the eye, trying to see the retina and optic nerve. Holding his breath to keep the instrument still, he caught a glimpse of it. A pulsating orange ball instead of the small white round disc that should have been the optic nerve. It was a certain sign that pressure was building up within the skull, dangerously compressing the brain.

At that moment, Felix's body began to go rigid. His back arched. Legs straight. The boy's teeth suddenly clenched so violently they made a grinding sound, small pieces of rock being crushed.

"Get some help, John!" Lionel shouted out the door. "Call a Code Blue and get anesthesia up here fast."

Two nurses ran into Felix's room, and one handed Lionel wooden tongue blades wrapped several times with adhesive tape. Felix's lips had turned a deep blue color. Lionel thrust his index finger into Felix's mouth, and after several seconds of violent pulling, managed to wedge the spacer between the grinding teeth. Felix breathed noisily as gusts of air passed back and forth through the newly created space. After three breaths, the pink color returned to his lips. Maltry burst into the room, pushing the crash cart.

"He's building up pressure inside," Lionel said as he reached for a set of plastic IV tubing.

Maltry inserted a sharp metal needle into Felix's arm and then slid a narrow tube of silicone into a vein in front of his elbow.

"Got to be a slow epidural hematoma," Lionel said. "Must have been a blood clot from the surgery. It's starting to break down and draw fluid inside the skull." Lionel injected steroids into the IV. "If we move fast, he's got a chance. This will decrease the pressure for an hour."

Lionel picked up the phone, starting to speak before the person on the other end could say anything. "I need an OR and fast!"

"So what else is new?" the familiar voice asked.

"Norma? That you?" Lionel said, surprised.

"Who else is dumb enough to be here in the wee hours of Saturday night? Or is it Sunday morning? Two of the other nurses are out sick. I'm trying to keep this place going until the next shift. So what the hell do *you* want?" Norma barked gruffly.

"An OR, and fast."

"This better be good, Doctor Stern. I've got three surgeons that overbooked their cases and don't have the foggiest idea how long it takes the big hand to go around the clock. And I'm still working on two red-lines left over from the emergency room from this afternoon. I got more people coming and going down here than the airport."

"It's Felix. He must have a slow intracranial bleed. We need to open up his craniotomy. He just convulsed a minute ago. We've got to move."

"Bring him down. I'll bump the case in room four," Norma said. "This is not going to be my usual fun-filled Saturday night," she muttered as they both hung up.

While in the elevator going down to the operating room,

Maltry took Felix's pulse. It was thirty-five beats per minute, an urgent signal that the pressure had built up so that the brain was giving off reflex signals to slow down his body's metabolic rate. The pressure was now dangerously high and permanent brain damage was a real possibility. He began an infusion of mannitol into the IV, an inert sugar that, because of its large molecular size, draws water away from the blood clot, thus temporarily alleviating pressure on the brain.

Lionel was accustomed to surgical procedures that began in an orderly fashion. Nurses gathered tools and set up their tables, while an anesthesiologist arranged his drugs and double checked the monitors. But Felix's procedure began like an explosion. Things happened so quickly that it was impossible to identify any orderly sequence. He was placed on the operating table, anesthesia was begun, and his head was shaved and washed with antiseptic iodine solution, all simultaneously. Lionel began the operative procedure five minutes after Felix arrived in the operating room.

The usually tedious and lengthy process of entering the skull was accomplished quickly. Still in the early stages of healing, the old incision in the scalp was separated easily, Lionel using the handle of the scalpel rather than the blade. He quickly cut the stainless steel wires that had secured the rectangular piece of skull back into place, gaining access to the dura, the dense fibrous covering of the brain. As soon as the bone was loosened, the reason for the problem was obvious. In precisely the same area that Lionel had encountered bleeding during the first surgery was a large flat blood clot the size of the palm of an adult's hand. This had accumulated over the top of Felix's brain, but had spontaneously stopped sometime within the first week after surgery. However, over the period that followed, the body had begun to dissolve the clot and as it did, the hemoglobin molecule had divided into smaller particles, each having a natural attraction for the body's water. As the breakdown process continued, the clot behaved as a small sponge, slowly absorbing water and increasing the pressure within Felix's skull until he lost consciousness and convulsed. The hematoma was not large. In any other place in the body it would have been trivial. But within the unyielding encasement of the skull, the extra space it occupied was at the expense of the brain.

"How are the vital signs?" Lionel asked as he delicately suctioned away the clot.

"His blood pressure got up to two-forty over one-ten, but it's coming down nicely. The pulse is up to seventy-four now and seems to be stabilizing," the anesthesiologist replied.

Lionel examined the wound again to make certain there was no other bleeding. "Okay, let's close him up," Lionel said, his voice calm, disguising his satisfaction. He had snatched this one—at the very last moment. But there was more to it than a dramatic surgical extrication. He had been certain that something, although he could not be sure what, was wrong with Felix. He had always trusted that intuitive sense about people and, in particular, patients. But his uncertainty about the exact nature of Felix's condition had grown over the past few days and, along with Casey and everything else, it began to make him question whether that intuitive voice was thoroughly reliable. He feared that misperceptions might be spilling over into just about every aspect of his life. Morrie Gold had stood next to him, toe to toe, and he had more than held his own. Lionel was not sure what he had expected Gold to be like. But whatever it was, it was not as formidable as the reality he had experienced just over an hour earlier.

Lionel secured the piece of skull with stainless steel wire and closed Felix's scalp with metal staples. The entire procedure had taken twenty-six minutes. He looked up at the clock. Just about the time a woman like Luisa Obregon would require to finish a glass of champagne.

# 31

LUISA SLAMMED DOWN the phone and stared blankly at the bookcase in the Dalway library. Oblivious to the party going on outside, she massaged her forehead, wondering what to do next. Rochelle Whitaker had just refused to come to the institute for the second procedure. Not Monday, not ever, she had said. Those were the words Luisa most feared. In the pit of her stomach, Luisa had the feeling of being trapped. As though she were back in Colombia. As though she were in the customs office again. Morrie and the institute that had promised some security now became a potential noose. How she hated Morrie for not being smart enough to keep out of trouble. No, she corrected herself, it was not a question of intelligence, it was one of ego. That much was becoming very clear. Regardless of her predicament, Luisa never allowed such distortions of perception to get in her way. She always saw everything quite clearly. It was a question of survival. It had always been so. Kill or be killed.

"Morrie says I should get to know you." It was Peter, a champagne glass in each hand.

Luisa smiled at her host, wondering what it was that other women found attractive about boyish men. But then again, all men had a great deal of "boy" in them. It was a fascinating and reassuring characteristic. It was something to exploit.

"I'll be filling in for Morrie on Monday," Peter explained.

"I know. We've very fortunate to have a friend like you."
She took the glass he offered. "There is nothing I wouldn't
do for Morrie in order to ensure the continuance of such
important work."

Peter smiled. "Sounds as though you're really sold on
him." He moved closer.

"He is a genius. If only you could see the smiling faces
on the children."

"They couldn't be more wonderful than your face."

Luisa's smile hardened. "My work with Morrie is the
most important thing in my life."

"What about your play with Morrie?"

The game was on. "I am a free woman, and as a
gentleman you would not really want me to answer that,
would you? Divulge personal information so quickly? You
would get bored with me."

"I doubt that very much. But I would like an opportunity
to find out—"

"Life is filled with nothing *but* opportunities. But discre-
tion, my handsome young man. . . ." Luisa waved her
index finger lightly in the air. "You are entirely too
attractive. You must have a line of women just waiting for
your call. And I really must go back outside."

"Why don't you and I leave here and have a nice quiet
dinner?"

She sipped her champagne, running the tip of her tongue
along the rim. "There will be time. I look forward to seeing
you on Monday, Doctor," she said, offering a bright smile
that held some promise.

"But Morrie said we should get to know one another,"
Peter persisted, lunging at the prospect.

"Oh, we will, my charming doctor. On Monday." Luisa
smiled and left, making certain to close the door behind her.

Morrie was holding court near the pool. Four women stood
in rapt attention as he discussed using collagen to plump up
lips and wrinkles. As Luisa had seen him do many times
before, he picked the least attractive woman and framed her
face with his hands. "It's such a pleasure to see that sex is

back. Let's hope we're through with androgyny forever. Women who look like women, that's what it is all about." Then, quickly, he pretended to notice something. "Mmm. That line. It reminds me of Audrey Hepburn."

The women looked at one another. "Did you do . . . ?"

Morrie held up his hands and smiled. "Confidentiality," he sang.

Luisa took Morrie's sleeve as she approached. "You must forgive me, ladies. I'm afraid something has come up."

"A doctor's life," he said, bowing slightly to the women.

Once they were alone, Morrie said, "You could have waited. I was about to pick up all four of them. At the very least, my dear, you were looking at thirty, maybe forty thousand dollars' worth of surgery right there."

"What I have to talk about makes that look like small change. I spoke to Rochelle." There was no longer the slightest hint of the female enticement Peter Dalway had heard.

"Tonight?"

"I checked which flight she was on. She got home a few minutes ago. She refuses to come in on Monday." Luisa's voice was cold and firm.

"I'll call her," Gold offered casually.

"You should never have let this happen. You should have spoken to her before." Nothing was casual.

"I said I would call her."

"You'll have to do more than that. She's adamant."

"Have it your way. I'll frighten her. I'll remind her of the contract she signed."

"She's already figured out that we won't sue. She knows that legally your hands are tied."

"Luisa, I promise you that Rochelle will be in."

"When?"

"By the end of the week."

"That's too late. I need her there Monday morning as we had planned. I have an appointment with Lu and his people in the afternoon. They have already waited longer than I had asked, and they are not patient people."

Morrie narrowed his eyes. "My dear Luisa, isn't this a case of the tail wagging the dog?"

"In this particular case, Morris, I can assure you that the tail is stronger than the dog."

After a moment, Morrie smiled. "Or, at least, prettier."

"Damn you, Morris. You know what I have at stake. I do not intend to lose. I can't afford to."

"You also can't afford to frown. Does terrible things to the skin."

A waiter came over to Luisa. "Mrs. Obregon?"

"Señora Obregon," Morrie corrected.

"There's a telephone call for you."

"Who is it?" she asked.

The waiter shrugged. "The gentleman wouldn't say."

Luisa glanced nervously at Morrie and stepped away. "Hello."

"You ready to leave yet?"

Luisa's face relaxed into a smile as she recognized Lionel's voice. "And if I were?"

"Then I'd meet you in five minutes at the bottom of Peter's driveway."

Luisa said, "Four minutes," and hung up.

It wasn't until Lionel saw Luisa walk down the driveway that he realized just how tightly he was holding onto the steering wheel. Although his first impulse was to race up to her, he was frozen. He had never seen a woman move the way Luisa did. She came toward him, weightless, creating her own definition of motion and time. He looked down at her feet to be certain they touched the asphalt. It was a moment, a loop of film, that Lionel wished he could replay endlessly.

As Luisa neared the car, Lionel reached over and opened the door. In a single, unbroken, fluid movement she folded herself into the car and sat down. She looked at Lionel. They said nothing. She reached behind and slammed the door shut. Still not a word. Lionel leaned over and kissed her very hard. Luisa, as though choreographed, sat up on her knees, draped herself into Lionel's lap and put her arms around him. They kissed again. Harder. And again. Each gasping for air.

Luisa reached for his hand and pressed something into it. A key. As he kissed Luisa, Lionel raised his hand behind Luisa's back to see what the key was for. The key was for Bungalow 5 at the Beverly Hills Hotel.

After leaving his car with the valet, Lionel and Luisa walked into the lobby of the Beverly Hills Hotel. They had not spoken, touched or even looked at one another since he shifted into reverse and drove away from Peter's house. The desk clerk nodded at Luisa. Lionel's fingers were wrapped around the key clenched in his fist. Still without a word, they turned left and went out the entrance leading to the bungalows.

Luisa looked up at him for the first time as they stood in front of the door. Lionel opened his palm, showing her the key, as though giving her time to change her mind. Instead, she put her arms around him. No woman had ever held Lionel as tightly. He wondered for a moment whether it was passion or desperation. But it was also a fact that it didn't matter which. He leaned back against the door, almost embarrassed about the intensity with which he reacted.

Lionel was not a man who surrendered easily even to his own emotions, much less to someone else's. Yet something anonymous and quite compelling was playing havoc with all his familiar and customary responses. It was perhaps due to this confusion that all his normal defenses had abandoned him. The apprehension that came hand in hand with having to confront a whole set of new feelings made Luisa all the more fascinating. In the half-light outside her bungalow, her perfectly sculpted face shone like a figure in an unfinished painting: the artist had not yet shaded his central figure.

Luisa slid her hands inside his jacket, her palms outlining his chest and pulling upward on his shirt until her fingers touched flesh and she heard a deep intake of breath. Lionel fumbled to get the key right side up. Then, his mouth pressed against Luisa's, he stopped breathing as he reached behind and slid the key slowly into the lock. While his body focused on Luisa, his mind envisioned the curve of every cut in the metal. One turn and the door opened. It was all very precise. They stepped back, following the same arc as the door, never letting go of one another.

The room was dark. Luisa edged his hand away from the light switch. But Lionel wanted to see her. If it had been in his power, he would have operating room lights overhead as he made love to this woman who possessed the kind of beauty other women would gladly pay him to recreate. Unlike Ginny, his first wife, who everyone agreed was picture pretty, or Casey, who was all-American wholesome, Luisa had an elegance and intense sensuality that defied description. Or duplication. It was in her bones. Lionel held her shoulders in his hands as a sculptor holds a piece of marble and somehow feels a warmth within.

Luisa stepped back, leaning against the door. With one hand, she effortlessly unzipped her evening dress. It dropped to the floor, leaving her totally naked except for the large green emerald she wore around her neck. With her other hand, she undid the knot in her hair, shook her head once like an animal coming out of the water and then opened her arms to Lionel.

Dr. Lionel Stern was out of his league. Luisa Obregon was not the style to which he was or was ever likely to become accustomed. Standing before her, fully-clothed, Lionel felt bare and defenseless. The very fact that he was still dressed was more intimidating than her nudity. He stood perfectly still as Luisa began to undress him.

Not one word was said.

As soon as Lionel was undressed, Luisa slid to the floor in front of him. For the first time since high school he was embarrassed for having an erection. But it was not an issue that was within his control. He could not hide his desire for her. So many things were new. In the darkness that surrounded them there was no right, no wrong, no turning back. She reached for his hand, fell back weightlessly onto the carpet and guided him on top of her.

For the second time that evening, he lost all track of time.

His fingertips recorded every inch of her as though he had never seen a woman's body before. Nothing in his experience prepared Lionel for Luisa Obregon. And even Luisa had not prepared him for the surprise of finding surgical scars beneath each breast.

# 32

It HAD BEEN a terrible day and a very long night for Rochelle Whitaker. She was tired and angry by the time she landed after midnight in Los Angeles, having worked for three days, on her feet most of the time. She guessed that she had walked more than twenty miles up and down the two-hundred-and-twenty-foot length of the Boeing 747, serving coffee and cocktails and food to poorly mannered, demanding passengers who treated her like a waitress in a truck stop.

Then, the moment she stepped through the door of her apartment, she had a fight with Larry and threw him the hell out. In the two months since he had moved in, the only thing they had agreed upon was that they both liked her breasts big. It was Larry who helped convince her not to go back to Dr. Gold for that dumb second operation.

It was nearly dawn, but as tired as Rochelle was, she decided to clean out the fridge as her final kiss-off to Larry. He had said he was in sales but he never said what kind. As far as she could tell, Larry never worked at anything except polishing off six-packs and slamming her into the mattress whenever he felt like it. And whenever she felt like it. That was the trouble with bums like Larry. They were so damn dependable.

With the fridge clean, Rochelle felt in control of the apartment, and her life, again. She turned on the water for a long soak in the tub. Thinking she heard something, Rochelle walked back into the living room. She gasped.

"What the hell are you doing here?"

They were the last words Rochelle would speak. No sooner had she said them than she saw the dull metallic reflection of a knife held high, sweeping down at her.

Rochelle screamed.

At first, she was surprised when there was no sound. She screamed again, not a voluntary act but an unconscious reaction to horror. The only thing she heard was a gurgling that bubbled from her neck. Her chest became warm.

More screams were impossible. There was no air to fill her lungs. She grasped her throat and felt the strong pulsating flow of sticky fluid that erupted from her neck. There had been no pain until a deep searing sensation filled her stomach and totally consumed her. It was as if her body had been sucked into the vortex of a large whirlpool and submerged completely into blackness. The last thing she felt was an excruciating pain in her breast.

The last thing she thought was why . . .

# 33

L̲IONEL WOKE WITH a start. It took a moment to realize where he was. He had slept harder than he could remember and awoke as Luisa entered the bungalow dressed in a shiny red Fila jogging suit. Within minutes the room was filled with the aroma of freshly brewed coffee. He lay back, closed his eyes and stretched, feeling the same invigoration as if he had gone on a good run.

Luisa was suddenly nude, out of the jogging suit, into the shower, and then wrapped neatly in a towel, it seemed within minutes. Lionel needed time to think of what he was going to say, as if it were necessary that he say something specifically appropriate. But it was no use. There was nothing in his repertoire as a man or as a doctor that prepared him for what surrounded him. Luisa Obregon was not a woman, she was an event.

He sat up on the edge of the bed and brought a fistful of bed sheet to his nose. Inhaling what remained of Luisa's scent, he felt uncharacteristically smug. He also felt guilty. It was as though he had never made love before, and as though he had no right to have done it. Confused and satisfied, he went into the bathroom and showered.

Luisa now wore a short white silk robe that barely met her knees. She handed him a glass of juice as he finished wrapping a towel around his waist. "Good morning, Doctor."

He kissed her gently. "Pretty classy room service."

She smiled. "Obregon service. I hope you don't mind. I

borrowed your car. It took me a while to find a market open at this hour. I could not bear to have you wake up to hotel room service." Luisa took the glass from Lionel and put her arms around his neck. "If it were my house in Colombia, I would make you a splendid breakfast." She leaned her head against his chest. "I wonder if I shall ever see that house again."

It was the first personal remark Luisa had made. Not once during the entire evening had she asked Lionel about himself or said anything about herself. She was as much a stranger as the moment he first met her. Perhaps even more so when Lionel thought about her connection to Morrie Gold. As physically right as she felt in his arms, nothing else about Luisa fit into place.

Lionel followed her into the small kitchen. She had bought figs and raspberries and mangoes. There were sausages and beans bubbling together in a pan. Thick slices of dark bread were covered with jam. Ordinary things that somehow became exotic and mysterious in her presence. "Does Morrie like your breakfasts?"

There was a long pause. Luisa turned to face him. "Morrie has been very kind to me. I think of him as a wonderful man, a very helpful friend. But I don't make breakfast for him."

"Are you in some kind of trouble?"

"No, not unless I go back to Bogotá." She hesitated again. "I was married to a man . . . who deceived me. He was very powerful. Very rich. Antonio was known as the Coffee King. But neither his power nor his wealth came from coffee. He had nothing whatsoever to do with coffee. He was a clever, very clever man. Certainly enough to make a complete fool of me, but not clever enough to fool the men with whom he did business." Luisa pulled the silk robe tightly around her. "My husband was killed. Murdered actually. He was shot in the face twenty times." The tears were gone. There was nothing but desperation on her face.

"My God."

"I was in Florida when it happened. I heard it on the television in my hotel room. Before that morning I had no idea he was involved with people who were capable of doing something like that. But the Colombian government believes something else entirely." Her voice grew cold. "They . . . believe that I was involved in the business. They also believe that my husband gave me a great deal of money before he was—before he died. More than seven million dollars." Luisa sat down opposite Lionel and sighed. "So, they watch me twenty-four hours a day. They follow me wherever I go to be certain I don't get any of it out of Colombia. I can assure you that it is difficult to get even modest amounts of money out of that place, let alone a fortune like that." She put a hand to her forehead. "It has been such a nightmare."

"I'm sorry." Lionel sat on the carpeted floor in front of her.

"Please, don't think badly of me. I made a terrible mistake. I married a dishonest man. Perhaps I should have suspected, perhaps I was too concerned with myself." She forced a sad smile. "The career of a ballerina is not as long as the life God has given me. I thought, like many other women, that my husband would provide the security I never had. Instead, he has brought me to this. You must believe me, I only want to take out of Colombia what is mine. It is all I have in the world."

Lionel put his arms around her, considering how Morrie had managed to turn Luisa's situation to his own advantage. Luisa and Stephanie, undoubtedly both victims of different sorts. Both casualties of his own self-aggrandizement. "Of course, I believe you. Why are you afraid I would think badly of you?"

She faced him with tears in her eyes. "Because, my sweet, you hate Morrie Gold."

Lionel leaned back. "You know, of all the things I thought we might be saying to one another, I would have never thought the subject would be Morrie Gold."

"Neither did I, but we have to. There is nothing else for us to talk about ever . . . unless first we talk about Morris. I am afraid that you might think that last night . . .

you and I . . . was because of Morris, because of the hearing tomorrow."

"No," Lionel said with surprise. "As a matter of fact it never occurred to me." It had indeed not crossed his mind. But it suddenly made sense. It was his turn to sigh and he did so audibly. How accurate were his perceptions? He felt slightly cold.

A slight hesitation. "Of course, you're not that kind of man." Another pause. "Morrie came to Bogotá for a conference. I met him at a party. He told me about the work he did. I was interested because one of my servants had a child who had an abnormal lip since birth. I hired Morrie to do the surgery. When I told Antonio about it, he was very pleased. He suggested we open a clinic. I didn't understand why Antonio was being so generous. As it turned out he wanted to buy respectability. Morrie wanted the clinic as well. He, too, wanted to buy respectability."

"And you? What did you want to buy?"

"At first, nothing. I was giving. Charity balls, public appearances, as much as I could do to raise money for the clinic. After Antonio was killed, Morrie offered to help me."

"And last night you offered to pay him back." The muscles in Stern's jaw rippled.

She shook her head yes. "But it wasn't what you must be thinking. He pointed you out to me and said that if he lost his license he would no longer be in a position to be able to help me."

Lionel folded his arms across his chest, feeling more naked than ever. "And Morrie helps those who help themselves." Then he smiled angrily. "Christ, I feel like one of those dumb blondes in the movies who knows she's been had."

"Earlier last night, I would have used you. Lionel, that is true. I would have done anything to protect what little I have left. But then circumstance, whatever it may have been, changed that. You had an emergency and I had an argument with Morrie."

"And that's when I called."

"Dear God, I was so happy to hear from you. I needed you to want me. And it was so clear, that for whatever reason, you needed to be wanted also."

Lionel closed his eyes, shook his head in resignation and walked over to Luisa and opened her robe. He leaned over and kissed her nipples, feeling them grow hard in his mouth. She gasped for breath and pulled back as though needing time to catch up to her feelings. Staring into his eyes, her face expressionless, Luisa took a handful of raspberries and crushed them against her breasts. He watched in stunned fascination as the juice ran down her body. As Lionel bent forward to suck the juice from her breast, she reached out and took the towel from his waist. Lionel wondered if this was the way they always had breakfast in Colombia.

An hour later, Luisa and Lionel, their arms around each other, lay in bed. Lionel was exhausted, as much emotionally as physically. However he searched for the right words, there was nothing to say. It was perhaps the first time in his life when he felt explanations were simply not needed.

"You know everything about me. Tell me something about you," Luisa whispered.

"What do you want to know?"

"You are divorced?"

He smiled. "I guess so. We, Ginny and I, were together for two years. The truth is, I guess, I never felt married and because of that now I don't feel divorced. Ginny and I just started and then we stopped. Maybe we never even started." He paused. "I was dumbstruck when she asked for a divorce. I just couldn't believe it. There were no lovers, no affairs, no 'we grew apart.' We just never grew together. It took me a long time to understand how isolated Ginny felt and even longer to understand that I couldn't fix it up. My whole life is fixing things up. A patch. A repair. An entire reconstruction, rebuild the whole damn thing. Making things right. Making things right for other people. Can't say I've done such a good job with my own situation. My wife said I was married to my scalpel. And some . . . other people seem to agree." It was much easier to discuss

Ginny. Opening up about Casey would have at that moment been impossible for him.

"I have never understood American women," Luisa said softly. "Perhaps it is because we Latins are accustomed to our husbands' having mistresses. It makes me feel victorious when they come home."

Lionel stared at her. "I can't imagine why any man married to you would have a mistress."

She touched his cheek. "Do you think I would want a man who didn't?"

"I don't know what to think about you."

"Nor do I know what to think about you." She came back playfully. "So many things I would like to know." Luisa hesitated.

"Such as?"

"I feel embarrassed in front of you. I wonder what a plastic surgeon thinks when he sees and feels scars under a woman's . . . under my breasts."

He laughed. "Last night I wasn't a plastic surgeon. I didn't notice. I thought they were . . . quite beautiful." Lionel looked at her. They were in fact large and firm and fabulous. "Maybe larger than I would have made them," he said with a large grin. "But, if you're asking, I have no complaints. None whatsoever."

"Is that all?"

"What else is there?"

"Are you wondering why a woman would change her body just to please her husband?"

"Is that why you did it?"

"Flat-chested women make better ballerinas than wives. Particularly in South America."

Lionel held Luisa tightly. He kissed her gently, burying his face in the nape of her neck. He wanted to ask whether Morrie had done the surgery, but he already knew the answer. Morrie had been grateful to Antonio Obregon for funding his clinic. What better way to show his appreciation than by surgically improving his wife to suit him? The ultimate in thank-you notes.

His hands moved up and down her back as he tried to

comfort the exotic woman he held in his arms. Lionel realized that he had never met a more exciting woman. One moment, she was cool and elegant, projecting an indomitable will. The next, she was frail, as vulnerable to sighs as other people were to earthquakes.

It struck him odd and it struck him hard. At that moment he thought of Casey.

# 34

"THE BONE GRAFT feels pretty solid," Lionel said as John Maltry twisted the third steel wire that secured a narrow strut of bone from a piece of Stephanie's fifth rib into a trough chiseled between her nasal bones. "I'm ready to turn the forehead flap."

Lionel cut along blue ink lines he had drawn on Stephanie's forehead just after general anesthesia had been induced. Two vertical parallel lines, two inches apart, outlined the flap in the middle of her forehead that extended upward to the hairline. After cutting the flap of skin, Lionel rotated it downward 180 degrees to drape over the bone graft strut. To preserve the blood supply it remained attached in the area between the eyebrows. Stephanie's new nose was formed.

"It really looks like a nose!" Franklin Upton exclaimed. "A masterpiece, Dr. Stern."

Lionel ignored Upton. He thought instead of Stephanie, the night before, showing him magazine pages of fashion models—all with beautiful noses. She had pointed out her two favorites. It had been a potential conflict with reality that Lionel chose to sidestep. Instead, he discussed it with her father, unwilling to say what was the truth: Stephanie would never appear in a perfume ad. Under the best of circumstances, what he could achieve was a nose that looked like a nose. Not likely one that anyone would point to admiringly, but something that would dissolve into the rest of her face rather than glare as a deformity.

181

Upton continued. "What you've done, Dr. Stern, is more an art form than surgery."

Maltry shook his head and snarled, "Put a lid on it, Upton."

Flo the Flash was rearranging the shiny instruments on her surgical tray as if she were playing a shell game. "Funny, I thought this was surgery."

Lionel inset the ends of the pedicel of thick forehead skin into the nose with sutures. The tip of the flap formed the central columella and on either side, the folding of the forehead skin made a pleasantly curved nostril rim. The end of the bone graft formed the delicate tip of the nose. "Do you know, Dr. Upton, when this procedure was first described?"

"Well, since most reconstructive techniques were developed during the latter part of World War One and rediscovered during World War Two, I'd say somewhere between forty and seventy years."

Maltry smiled. "Wrong, Upton!" he sang out. "You missed it by about three thousand years. The very first written account of the procedure you are witnessing with your own baby blues appeared in Indian writings in Sanskrit about a thousand years before Christ. As I recall it was in Sanskrit, wasn't it, Flo?"

"Yes, that's what it was," she replied, rolling her eyes toward the ceiling and giving a wave to the circulating nurse to turn up the stereo, hoping to drown out or at least discourage Maltry.

"Used to be," Maltry said, slipping into his role, "there were a lot of people running around without noses because they were caught in the wrong bedroom or the wrong war. They used to cut your nose off if you were a prisoner or an adulterer. As a matter of fact, there were so many people running around without noses that a group of tile makers quit making tiles and began to make noses from foreheads." Maltry sutured the edge of Stephanie's forehead to her cheek. "Okay, Upton, how about telling me about the blood supply to this flap?"

Upton didn't hesitate. "Superficial temporary artery."

"You sure?"

"Yes."

"Sure you're sure?"

"Yes!"

Flo made a low buzzing sound. "Gets them every time."

"Wrong, Upton. It's the supraorbital and supratrochlear. And that really pisses me off." Maltry began seriously, "Dr. Stern, I think we'd get better at this operation if we had more practice. Why don't we start cutting the noses off first-year residents for being cocky smartasses?"

"That's enough, John." Lionel glanced up at the clock. "Let's finish this up." They had begun the procedure three hours earlier.

"You hear about the girl murdered in the Marina?" Maltry asked, changing the subject but still glaring over his mask at Upton. "Slashed to death."

"My mother always said it was dangerous being a stewardess."

"Can you believe she lived one block from my apartment?" Maltry asked with a whistle.

"That so," Lionel said absently.

"Some kind of pervert. Slashed her throat and just about everywhere else from what the paper says." Maltry narrowed his eyes. "Hey, Upton, where were you at the time of the murder?"

Upton quietly gave him the finger.

"The whole thing is pretty gruesome," Maltry continued. "Better be careful when you go home tonight, Flo."

"Thanks for the advice, doctor," Flo said nonchalantly, as she passed the last suture. "But I can take care of myself. You might want to warn that slasher to keep his distance or he'll end up with his name in the paper. Too many weirdos around here. One of them picks on me and I'll save the police some work."

As Lionel bent down to look at Stephanie's new profile, his back, stiff from the four hours of immobility, rebelled. He straightened up gingerly and slowly, glanced again at the clock and bent over again. The suture line of the forehead flap was intentionally hidden in the crease where the side of the nose normally meets the cheeks. The only conspicuous irregularity was the thickness between the eyebrows where the forehead was still attached. Stephanie's new nose blended into her face and made it whole. Lionel gave a short nod of approval and stretched his back again.

"Real nice, Lionel," Maltry said firmly.

"Yes, yes," Flo muttered softly beneath her mask. That was all the Flash ever offered in the way of approval. It made him feel very good. But Lionel's real satisfaction came from what the surgery said about his profession. The procedure he had just performed was what plastic surgery was all about—the repair of catastrophic damage over which people had no control—and it was this that had first drawn Lionel to plastic surgery. It was indeed the divine right of man to appear human. What he had trouble reconciling was that in this case, the catastrophe was Morrie Gold. And worse yet that Morrie Gold signified, for a much larger audience than Lionel could ever reach, the definition, the essence of plastic surgery.

Lionel turned into the corridor where Stephanie's father sat waiting. As he approached, Lionel gave a thumbs-up signal. "She's going to be fine."

Arthur Green sighed with relief. He put a hand to his face and shook his head. When he looked up at Lionel his eyes were filled with rage. "Okay. Now let's go get that bastard!"

Lionel patted Mr. Green on the back and nodded. "I'll meet you there." He had enough time to shower quickly before getting to the BMQA for Morrie's hearing. Green was right. It was time to get the bastard.

# 35

$P$ETER PACED BACK and forth in the confinement of the elevator as it ascended to the top floor of the Gold Institute. He examined himself in the reflective glass that surrounded him. His three-piece dark blue suit, shoulders sharply padded, was the picture of conservative elegance. If Lionel could only see him now. Peter shuddered at the reaction, no, the explosion he knew would occur.

No question about it, he looked substantially better than he felt. He removed the handkerchief he had arranged neatly in his lapel pocket only minutes before and patted his moist forehead and upper lip. The elevator moved slowly, and the perspiration increased as he approached his destination. It was not a question of nerves. It was a question of sheer panic.

When the door finally opened, Peter considered the possibility he was on the wrong floor. Nothing he saw resembled anything medical. Gray ultrasuede walls. Overstuffed sofas. Pictures of movie stars on every wall. Silk flowers in tall crystal vases illuminated by soft light from above. A Chinese cloisonné pot. It looked like a living room on the cover of *Architectural Digest*.

"Good morning. Dr. Dalway?" Elise Evans extended her hand. "It's so nice to have you here. May I get you a cup of coffee? You've got a busy morning of surgery scheduled."

At that moment, a bourbon would have been more to Peter's liking. "No, no thanks," Peter said, wondering what the hell she meant by a busy morning. He folded his arms to cover the fact that his hands were trembling. Peter's nerves were raw. Coffee would be out of the question. Morrie had mentioned only a simple procedure. What was he trying to pull?

Evans led Peter through a door to the inner office, where the formica desktops were immaculately clean. The stacks of charts and papers were so neat they appeared to be joined with glue.

"I know how much Dr. Gold appreciates your assistance," she said, respectfully. "Once surgery is scheduled, patients make their plans. You know how that sort of thing goes."

"Sure," Peter replied nervously. "Do they know—"

"You leave the patients to me, Dr. Dalway." She touched his forearm reassuringly. "I've already explained everything about Dr. Gold's temporary absence to our lovely women." Mrs. Evans proceeded happily on, as though Morrie were off to the White House to receive a medal rather than to a hearing at the BMQA. "Our young ladies have had previous surgery in our Institute in Colombia as part of the research Dr. Gold has been conducting over the past several months. It is truly magnificent work, and it concludes today as a matter of fact. I know how sorry Dr. Gold must be that he cannot be here to finish it himself. It would give him such a sense of completion. He is very proud and tidy about such things."

"What kind of research?" he asked. Mrs. Evans smiled back. It was a smile that could have burned a hole right through him, Peter thought.

"Oh, I'm not much of an expert on that. You'll have to ask Dr. Gold. He is the scientist. It has something to do with using two stages of implants to prevent that awful hardening of the breasts some women get after an enlargement. I know Dr. Gold believes his method will become the one preferred by surgeons across the country very soon now." Evans's face quickly flashed an artificial smile. "Well, our first patient is already here. Shall we begin? There is the operating room," she said as she swung open the door to an orderly room, with an empty operating table in the center.

Quite abruptly Peter felt his heart pounding in his chest. The pounding was so loud that he could hardly hear Evans. "Did you say something about coffee?" he managed.

Mrs. Evans opened another door just down the hallway. "I'll get the coffee while you change into scrubs in Dr. Gold's dressing room." The singsong voice was now a screech deep within his head.

Peter shut the door quickly, leaned against it and sighed heavily. He felt his clothes stick to him, his shirt heavy with moisture as he took it off. He stayed in the dressing room for several minutes, taking slow deep breaths as he tried to calm himself. He felt claustrophobic and wanted to run. The fear of stepping into an operating room again was a few hours ago manageable. It had suddenly expanded to the dimensions of an ugly demon capable of devouring the small child he had so quickly become. Peter tried to reason. He didn't owe Morrie anything. He didn't have to put himself through this. Not unless he wanted the Dalway Clinic. There was a knock at the door. Time was running out.

"Your coffee, Doctor?"

It wasn't Evans. Peter turned the knob and opened to Luisa. She wore an emerald green knit suit, her hair tight against her head in a very businesslike knot. She held out a cup. "I thought you'd like it black."

Suddenly Peter realized he had no shirt on. As he reached for it, Luisa took his hand and smiled. "It's quite all right. I was a ballerina. I also was in the body business."

Peter took the cup and sipped the coffee eagerly.

"Is everything satisfactory?"

He looked back at her with the eyes of an animal caught in the glare of headlights.

"You are perspiring."

"Oh . . . that. It happens when I get around beautiful women." Peter gulped the coffee. After a moment, he smiled. "Where did you disappear to Saturday night?"

"You must think me very rude."

"Actually, I think you very extraordinary." As Peter spoke, he inadvertently raised his hand and spilled coffee on his arm. Quickly, he put down the cup and began blowing cool air on his skin.

"Are you all right?"

"I'm fine."

"You're not fine," she said, helping dry his arm. "Should I call a doctor?"

"I *am* a doctor. And nothing is wrong," Peter said with a wave of his hand. "Just a little nervous."

Luisa's eyes focused hard on him. Her voice was strained. "You have nothing to be nervous about. You have an excellent physique."

He smiled. "I'm surprised to see you here today. I guess I've never understood the connection between you and Morrie and this whole Institute thing."

Luisa helped him on with his scrub shirt. Her hands smoothed it over his shoulders and down his chest. Slowly. "I am the kind of woman who draws her strength from powerful men. I used to need them when I danced and now I need them in my private life." The distraction was obviously soothing to Peter. She continued, now massaging. "The Institute is very important to me. By helping the Institute, you help me."

"Yes, and I'm very flattered by that. It's just that it has never been clear what it is I'm to do here and exactly what is going on." Peter made a circular motion with his hand, gesturing toward Gold's office. There was a bewilderment about him that was not lost on Luisa. "This whole thing, being here in this Institute, a urologist doing cosmetic surgery, the last six months, have been a blur to me . . ."

"Shhh." She put a finger to his lips. "Two simple implant procedures, Peter, to further Dr. Gold's research." Her other hand pressed into his hip and moved up and down. "He has placed a great deal of confidence in you. He believes you can do it. And so do I." As she studied his eyes, she could feel him begin to decompress.

Gently, he bit the tip of her finger. That was more like it, Luisa thought. Yes, ah yes, the "little boy" in them was so useful.

"Perhaps you can explain it all to me at dinner," Peter said, now apparently quite calm.

Luisa took both his hands and gently squeezed them together. "For me, Peter. Do it for me," she said very softly.

But the calm was all too transient. When Peter stepped into the operating room, his pulse began to race again and his heart felt as though it had migrated upward and filled his throat. The patient was on the operating table, her bare breasts surrounded by sterile linen. Thank God, he couldn't see her face. Thank God, she couldn't see him.

Mrs. Evans nodded and passed him the scalpel. In his gloved hand, it felt like a lead weight. The heat from the overhead lights invaded the skin on the back of his neck. He began to perspire heavily again. In a small explosion in his head, the face he couldn't see beneath the drapes in front of him became visible and belonged to the man. He saw himself tying off the renal artery just before he cut the kidney away. The wrong kidney. Peter's hand began to tremble. He felt the moisture accumulate inside the thin rubber gloves, making it even more difficult for him to feel the scalpel. Peter hesitated.

"How are we doing, young lady?" Mrs. Evans asked the patient. There was a slurred answer to which Evans didn't listen. Instead, she whispered to Peter, "Doctor, you can see Dr. Gold's previous incision."

There was a thin red incision line, about three inches long, in the fold of the skin beneath each breast.

"I've already injected the local anesthesia, Doctor."

Peter nodded. He looked down, checking to be certain he was holding the scalpel. He made the incision with his right hand, but it was necessary to steady it with his left. The heat of the operating lamp spread over his neck and expanded upward and over his head, again bringing with it a collage of visions that flashed in quick repetition—the incision in the flank of the old man, an X ray turned upside down on a view box. For a fraction of a second, Peter thought he heard the sound of a helicopter overhead. The sound seemed quite real. It was some time before it was replaced by another whisper from Evans.

"The patient is here, Doctor. Just a little deeper," she said, pointing her index finger to a shiny, blue convex membrane that bulged in the depth of the breast mound. Her voice had a hard edge now. No singing quality. Peter tried to use a pair of dissecting scissors, but his hands began to tremble so that the movements of the instrument accomplished nothing. Evans took them from him and deftly cut the thin membrane and retrieved the large breast implant and placed it carefully on her back table, quickly covering it with a towel. She then took a smaller hemispherical implant that had the consistency of glasslike transparent Jello and placed it into the large pocket lined by the membrane.

The procedure took only a few minutes but as Peter watched helplessly, the heat from overhead continued to expand somewhere deep inside his head. He felt a wave of nausea sweep over him, and the weakness that came with it made him sink down to one knee. The deeper and faster he breathed, the less oxygen seemed to be available to him. The operating room became an oven. The walls seemed to be squeezing in from every side.

"Doctor, what is the matter?" Mrs. Evans asked in horror.

"Not feeling well," was all Peter could manage to say. He stared at the floor, at Mrs. Evans's white oxfords, suddenly aware of another pair of shoes walking past him.

"What's going on here. What happened?"

It was Luisa. Peter wanted to look up, but his head was too heavy.

"I can handle it," Mrs. Evans replied.

"But what about the other one?"

"I said I can handle it! Just get him out of here."

Peter felt two hands under his arms. "Peter, can you get up?" Luisa asked.

He shook his head no. "In a minute."

"Let me help you."

Peter got up onto his knees. "I tried to tell you," he said.

"Can you walk?" Her voice was impatient. Luisa attempted to lift him up, but Peter pushed her away. He managed to stagger out of the room. She followed right behind him.

The minute he was outside, he said, "I'm going to be sick." More scuffling of shoes as Luisa led the way to the bathroom. "Please," he said, breathlessly. "Leave me alone."

Without a word, Luisa disappeared. Peter held onto the bathroom bowl like a man clutching a life preserver. He leaned his head over, starting to cry as he felt the retching from deep inside his stomach. He tried to sit up and glanced back into the other room. His eyes in soft focus, he thought he saw Luisa take the two breast implants and put them into her purse. But that didn't make any sense. Make sense or not, his head was clearing and he knew what he had seen.

When he had regained his composure a few minutes later, Peter walked into Morrie's private office and sat down heavily on the sofa. Luisa put a cold compress on his head. Mrs. Evans, stonefaced, looked down at him.

"I'm sorry," he said.

"No matter, Doctor," Evans responded with an artificial casualness that did not hide her disdain.

Peter turned to Luisa. "It was so hot in there."

Mrs. Evans continued while blotting his forehead. "You were unfamiliar with this kind of surgery. I'll get an operative report ready for you to sign. You know how Dr. Gold is a stickler for every little detail."

"I'm fine now," Peter said, standing up. He looked at Luisa. Her eyes were cold and level.

"There is one more patient," she said.

Peter nodded. "I'm okay."

Luisa motioned for Mrs. Evans to sit down. "There is a problem, Peter."

"Look, I'm really embarrassed about what happened." He looked over at Evans. "Lucky that Morrie has someone who handles a scalpel as well as you do." He was the only one smiling. "You want me to sign off on that one?" He took the report from Mrs. Evans and scribbled his signature. "Not that I did that much."

Luisa moved closer to him. "The next patient wishes to postpone her surgery. But she is already overdue for the second procedure. It is important to me, Peter, and all the work that I have done on behalf of the Institute, that all surgery proceeds on schedule. Delays threaten to invalidate the research results. Morrie and Mrs. Evans and I have all worked too hard for that to happen. Morris plans to present the results directly to the media. As soon as he does that, we will have more patients than we know what to do with. The expansion into a urology clinic will be a natural extension of the Institute's expansion."

Peter nodded affirmatively. "Sure."

"Now, how are you feeling? You look fine." It was true. The ashen color had vanished from Peter's face, the tan color returned.

"I'm a hundred percent," Peter asserted.

"Well then, there is not much more to do," Luisa announced with some finality.

Mrs. Evans jumped in. "I can take care of the other patients this afternoon since you're . . . not feeling well. I can show them an introductory video, talk about financing, that sort of thing, so that you can acclimate yourself a bit more gradually."

Peter looked at Luisa. "I really do want to help." The enthusiasm was sincere.

She smiled and took Peter's hand. "Of course you do. And you can be of great help. Help us with the next patient. Be charming. Convince her to have the surgery, as only a good doctor can. I'm sure once she talks with you, she'll feel much better and confident about it."

"Shall we go?" Mrs. Evans asked. "Here, put on a clean set of scrubs. Along with a nice, freshly starched laboratory coat it presents a fine image."

Peter nodded, putting his handkerchief on the desk as he made his way to the dressing room.

"Sharon! How good to see you!" Mrs. Evans opened the door. The tall, very attractive, thirtyish blonde was dabbing the corners of her eyes. "Let me introduce Dr. Peter Dalway, a new associate of Dr. Gold. We're rather lucky to have him join our staff."

Sharon took Peter's outstretched hand but looked at Mrs. Evans. "I need to see Dr. Gold," the woman said quite firmly.

"I know," Mrs. Evans said. "But he was called out of town on an emergency. You know how seriously he takes all his responsibilities. Don't worry, though. Dr. Dalway is eminently qualified to handle your surgery. Besides, as I've explained, it's such a minor procedure."

Sharon sat down. "Look, I don't have a whole lot of time. I'm very upset and I don't think I can handle any more today." She began to cry.

Peter glanced over at Mrs. Evans. Why the hell were they trying to convince her to have the surgery? She was clearly distraught. But Evans merely narrowed her eyes and glared back at Peter.

"We were all fond of Rochelle," Mrs. Evans said. "And what happened is a terrible tragedy."

"Who's Rochelle?" Peter asked.

"She's . . . she was my friend," Sharon sobbed.

Mrs. Evans took a deep breath. "Rochelle was the poor girl who was murdered at the Marina."

"That slasher business?" Peter asked.

"I cannot imagine who could do such a thing. What is this world coming to? None of us are safe anymore," Evans said as she filled out the surgical consent on her clipboard.

Peter stared at Evans. The old witch. He could see her with a scalpel in her hand. Most murderers had more warmth about them than this old bag. He had seen her type in every hospital he had ever worked. Burnt-out, ornery old women with a grudge against the world.

"There's a whole group of us," Sharon said. "We've worked the Bogotá run for nearly a year. We used to call ourselves the No-Tits Kids." She put a hand to her mouth. "It was Rochelle's name for us."

Peter looked at Sharon. No one would ever call her that again. An otherwise thin girl, her chest was massive.

"That was before we met Dr. Gold and Señora Obregon. Oh, it's not that I don't appreciate what you all have done. We all do, believe me. I wouldn't even have come over here if I didn't feel obligated to Dr. Gold. It's just that I don't care about the damn research right now. I've been up all night, I'm due at the airport in a couple of hours . . ." She turned away. "I'm supposed to fill in for Rochelle. Can you imagine they would ask me to do that?"

The situation seemed clear to Peter. The woman was obviously in no condition for surgery. He could understand that Morrie had brainwashed Luisa with the supposed importance of his work, but an experienced nurse like Evans had a responsibility to the patient.

"Sharon, I thought you understood the problem. We're trying to prevent that awful hardness," Evans said, holding her clipboard evenly with both hands.

"Well, it's not going to happen in a couple of lousy days! Is it, Doctor?"

Peter felt the weight of the stares of the women as they studied him. His forehead felt hot again. The perspiration returned. He could feel the blood drain away from his face. He was certain Evans could see it because of her expression as she turned away from him. He was incapable of an answer.

"Sharon, my dear, you've been through a lot, I know, but here you are. You're ready and we're ready," Evans said, arranging the surgical consent on her clipboard once again. "And it would save you another trip."

Sharon stood up abruptly. "Doctor, please tell Dr. Gold that I will be back. I'm really sorry, but I simply can't put myself through any more today."

Peter nodded agreeably. "I understand."

"Thank you, Mrs. Evans. I don't mean to be difficult." Sharon walked out the door, Mrs. Evans following behind, trying to change her mind.

Peter went directly to Morrie's office and lay down on the sofa. This plush office was no place for him, he thought. Especially not with that Evans windup doll running on fast forward. Maybe, he thought, medicine wasn't for him either.

The door swung open and Luisa glared at him. "What the hell happened?"

It was a Luisa he had never seen. Her eyes glazed with anger, her lithe body—usually graceful—was tense and angular.

"Nothing happened, I'm afraid," Peter replied wearily. "I guess you're going to have to tell Morrie's accountant there's one less entry on the books. Actually, two. I'm out of here as well." Peter smiled bitterly. "No charge for my services."

"But I told you how important it was to me that both procedures be completed."

Peter wondered why it was so important to her. What difference should it make to her? Why the hell would Luisa care whether the implants were removed? Suddenly he remembered seeing her put the implants into her purse. But why? "The girl was near hysteria," he added. "She was mourning the death of her friend. She had to leave in a couple of hours. Those are hardly ideal conditions for surgery."

"The world is less than ideal, Peter, in many ways. I put my trust in you. As did Morrie."

"Is that why you stuffed the implants in your purse? To prove to him that I had really done the work?" He watched as every muscle in Luisa's face tightened as if it had suddenly turned to stone. Something, although he had no idea what, was not right. And it did not involve him. "What's the big deal?" He shrugged. "She said she'd be back in a couple of days."

"It *had* to be today." Luisa held tight to her purse. "You have no idea what you've done."

Peter shrugged. "I guess not." But before he got any more involved in whatever it was that was happening, he sure as hell was going to find out.

# 36

Aₛ Lɪᴏɴᴇʟ ᴅʀᴏᴠᴇ to the BMQA, he felt his emotions tug at him from all sides. Fresh from the operating room, he was ecstatic with the results of Stephanie's surgery and was eager to tell Casey all about it. But fresh from Luisa's bed, the last person he wanted to see was Casey Crawford.

He stood in the open doorway to her office and smiled at Janet, her assistant, a plump, very plain, fortyish woman who probably looked forty when she was in kindergarten.

"Morning, Doctor. She's in the conference room."

"Thanks." With any luck at all, someone else would be there. Lionel needed time to sort out his feelings about Luisa before he could begin to deal with Casey. Not that for a moment he thought he was in love with Luisa, but at least for a moment, he enjoyed being able to give a woman what she wanted from him. Unlike Casey, who demanded equality, Luisa sought virility. As part of her elegant packaging, Luisa wore vulnerability as though it had been designed for her. She brought out the masculine hero within him, and he enjoyed the feeling.

Lionel opened the door to the conference room. He needn't have worried about being alone with Casey. As chief investigator for the BMQA, Casey sat on one side of a large table next to Frank Soltano, BMQA's chief legal counsel. Mr. Green and his attorney were on the other side, and Morrie—by himself—opposite them all. Lionel nodded to Casey, and she motioned for him to sit down at the end. They had not spoken since Casey had left Peter's party.

The moment he saw Lionel, Morrie rose and extended his hand. Lionel smiled to himself. The son of a bitch was really playing the part. Dark blue suit, silk tie, even glasses. Stern looked carefully. Most likely the glasses had no optical correction, but it was a nice touch. "Good to see you again, Lionel. How is my patient Stephanie progressing?"

Smart. Now everyone thought Morrie knew Lionel well enough to be on a first-name basis. Lionel shook hands uneasily with Morrie. "She's doing fine."

Morrie smiled and looked directly at Arthur Green. "Wonderful!"

Casey's assistant, Janet, came in carrying a load of files and sat next to her. Directly in front of Casey was the thick folder containing the letters of complaint against Gold. Another woman brought a briefcase containing a transcribing machine that resembled a narrow typewriter. Casey looked at her watch and cleared her throat. They were ready to begin. It was precisely 11:00 A.M.

"I'd like to thank all of you for being here so promptly," Casey said. She looked over at Lionel, her eyes saying a thousand other things to him. "The board would particularly like to thank Dr. Stern for his willingness to testify and serve as a medical expert in plastic surgery. Let the record show that Dr. Stern is a board-certified plastic surgeon and a professor of plastic surgery at University Hospital. His curriculum vitae is submitted for the record."

Lionel stared at Casey, suddenly thought about Luisa and looked away.

"As you may know, this agency operates under the State Department of Consumer Affairs. That means we're here to protect the people of the state of California, potential patients all. Our purpose in each case we review is to make an assessment of the standard of care received. However, simply because a patient develops a complication, no matter how serious, does not mean the care was inadequate or incomplete."

Arthur Green stood up and pointed across the table at

Morrie. "What the hell are you talking about? She went to this quack to have a bump taken off her nose and ended up losing her entire nose. She'll never be the same again!"

"Mr. Green, please sit down!" Casey said. "I understand this is an emotional issue for you, but you are entirely out of order."

Morrie raised his hand. "Perhaps not. I'm sure we're all aware of the great stress that Mr. Green has been under."

Casey ignored the remark. "The question we address this morning is whether what took place in Dr. Gold's office at his institute met the standard of care available in Los Angeles. Not the highest surgical standard, please understand, but the average—the standard of care available in this community. And that is all. We are not addressing the issue of malpractice. That's for the respective lawyers to sort out in court if that should transpire. We are all aware that this case appeared serious enough to the board that we obtained a temporary restraining order that prompted this hearing. Our job this morning is not to determine guilt but to document the reasons for our concern in this case and hear from Dr. Gold."

Morrie smiled. "Rather like trying the accused man after he's been hung."

Casey glanced quickly at her attorney. "You have not been hung, Dr. Gold. A restraining order has been issued and has been in effect for only one week. Should this hearing prove our actions unwarranted, I personally assure you that none of this will appear on your record and you will receive a formal apology."

Morrie nodded. "And, I would think, a rather large settlement if I chose to pursue legal restitution." He raised his eyebrows in response to Casey's look of annoyance, then pointed to Soltano. "Well, isn't that why you have counsel present? Certainly, he's not here to protect me."

Soltano leaned forward. "Dr. Gold, if I may, I'm surprised to see you here alone. Our office advised you that you should be properly represented by counsel, and encouraged you in that regard."

"For what reason would I need counsel? I have nothing to

hide. I have done nothing wrong. My actions do not require defense."

It occurred to Lionel that Morrie could always try to have whatever decision resulted from the hearing thrown out of court because he was not properly represented at the hearing. Morrie never missed a trick. But Lionel also knew Soltano. He was looking at Morrie as though he were breakfast. Although Lionel had never been sued, it was almost a statistical certainty that it would happen someday. In the high-risk specialties—orthopedics, neurosurgery, anesthesia, obstetrics and plastic surgery—doctors could expect to see one case filed against them every five years. According to the statistics, he was long overdue. And if it happened, more than anything, Lionel would not want Frank Soltano on the opposite side of the bench.

"We have over two hundred complaints each month," Casey began. "With just two full-time physicians and eight investigators, we can act only on the more urgent and serious cases—"

"In your opinion," Morrie interjected. Stern had to marvel at Morrie Gold's demeanor. He didn't seem to be angry, just lightly annoyed. And ultimately confident.

"In my opinion," Casey added.

"What the hell are you talking about now?" Arthur Green stood up. "Is it only somebody's *opinion* that my daughter's nose fell off?"

Casey's voice was sharp. "Mr. Green, if you cannot restrain yourself, I'm going to have to ask you to leave."

"Nonsense," Morrie said. "The man is distraught. For God's sake, let's show some compassion. Besides, I want him here. He has every right to understand just what happened."

Lionel glanced up at Casey. She raised an eyebrow, giving him a "you'd-better-have-the-goods" look. He couldn't help thinking that Luisa's eyes would have said "please help me."

"What I am trying to say," Casey continued, "is that due to Dr. Gold's high visibility in the print and media advertising in the Los Angeles area, we felt this case should be determined as expeditiously as possible."

Morrie said, "Thank you." It was said as if he had interpreted Casey's comment as a compliment.

"I'd like now to turn this over to Mr. Soltano," Casey said.

Soltano, a swarthy man with moist lips, cleared his throat. "Dr. Gold, it is the purpose of this hearing to ascertain the events surrounding the surgery you performed on Miss Stephanie Green in your office on the morning of May fifteenth. However, before we begin I should like to ask once more whether you wish to appear at this hearing without benefit of legal counsel."

"It is my decision to appear *pro persona*."

"May I assume, Dr. Gold, from your use of legal terminology that you are aware this is a formal legal proceeding? You will be under oath in giving your testimony, although rules of the courtroom do not necessarily apply."

"I am aware of precisely what this hearing is. You see, I'm rather familiar with lawyers and their tricks."

"Dr. Gold, I should like to make clear at the outset that I don't need tricks."

"What do you need, Mr. Sotero?"

"Soltano. I need answers."

Morrie looked at his watch. "Well, as soon as you start to ask questions, I'll be happy to supply answers."

"Thank you, Doctor. I assume you're experienced in these matters." Soltano leaned over as Janet handed him a paper.

"Meaning?"

"I was wondering, Doctor," he began, looking at the paper, "how many malpractice suits have been brought against you?"

"I'm not sure that has anything to do with this case, Mr. Santana."

"Soltano. More than ten?"

"Perhaps."

"More than fifteen?"

"I don't know."

"More than twenty?"

"I do not put notches on my stethoscope."

"How long have you been practicing medicine?"

"Nearly fifteen years."

"And more than twenty suits?"

"What kind of suit, Mr. Serano? I have a rather extensive wardrobe. Yes, I would think I have more than twenty suits."

Soltano frowned and shook his head. "Are you currently licensed to practice medicine by the state of California?"

"Yes."

"At any time has that license been revoked or suspended?"

"No. Never. I am fully licensed by the state."

"Are you certified by any medical specialty board?"

"I am founding member of the American Board of Surgery for Rejuvenation."

"Can you describe this organization and its qualifications for membership?" Soltano held out his hand toward Janet, waiting for a piece of paper.

"It is an organization of physicians interested in surgery designed to beautify. The American Board of Surgery for Rejuvenation. Our standards are high. Our qualifications are that the physician be in practice for at least five years and devote more than fifty percent of his time to cosmetic surgery."

"Is this organization recognized by the AMA?"

"No."

"The American College of Surgeons?"

"No."

"The American Board of Medical Specialists?"

"No. These are all highly political groups, Mr. Solero. They lobby for the benefit of their members. My organization is devoted to the concerns of our patients."

"Soltano."

"As you wish."

"Does this board have annual meetings or publications?"

"No."

"Do you issue certificates?"

"Yes. Actually, they're quite nice."

"I'm sure they are. Is this certificate, Doctor, the extent of your certification to practice in your specialty?"

"I *am* board certified."

"By the board you created yourself."

"For protection of patients . . ."

"Who do you think you're kidding, Dr. Gold?"

"I am licensed by the state to practice as a physician and a surgeon. For the record."

"For the record, my concern is your competence to practice in the area of plastic surgery." Janet handed Soltano a series of pages clipped together. He looked at them and nodded. "Tell me, Doctor, do you teach at any medical schools?"

"No."

"Are you currently on the plastic surgery staff of any hospitals in Los Angeles?"

Morrie looked squarely at Janet. "I have quite large enough a practice with my private patients."

"Isn't it true, Doctor, that you are not a member of the medical staff of any hospital in Los Angeles?"

"I have been on the staff of four hospitals in Los Angeles."

"But you no longer have privileges to use the facilities in any hospital in the greater Los Angeles area."

"I no longer require such facilities. I do all surgical procedures in my office."

"But suppose you have an emergency?"

"Isn't that what emergency rooms are for?"

"For the record, Doctor, you do not have admitting privileges at any hospital in the Los Angeles area."

"I do not require them."

"Do you have them? Yes or no?"

"No—" Morrie paused. "—because I do not require them."

"Dr. Gold, have you had any specialized residency training in plastic surgery?"

"I have taken a number of courses—"

"The question was—"

"Are we here to listen to your questions or to my answers?"

Soltano motioned for Morrie to go ahead.

"I have taken a number of courses in all areas of plastic surgery, particularly cosmetic surgery."

"How many courses?"

"Entirely too many to recall."

"Can you recall the most recent?"

"I believe it was a three-day course given by several well-known plastic surgeons in New York."

"Are you aware, Doctor, that plastic surgery residency training requires at least six to eight years *after* medical school?"

"I am, but I don't see—"

"In your opinion, do you believe that occasional seminars are adequate substitutes for years of supervised training?"

"In my opinion, I do not understand where this line of questioning is leading. I am licensed by the state to practice medicine and surgery. There are no restrictions or definitions on my license, on anyone's medical license. Quite wisely, the state leaves it up to the individual physician to determine whether he is capable of handling cases in any specific field."

"It is precisely that determination that brings us here today, Doctor. To evaluate whether you were capable of handling the procedure you performed on Miss Green."

"That is not the problem at hand. I believe the question is more accurately why the patient did not heal as anticipated."

"Am I to understand that you consider the loss of a patient's nose, the entire nose, the result of a problem in the manner in which the patient heals?"

"Absolutely."

"Isn't it true that most rhinoplasties are performed by using incisions inside the nostrils?"

"Yes. But patients differ. This was not a usual case. I did not select the usual solution."

"To what do you attribute the loss of Miss Green's nose?"

"Some abnormality in the anatomy of the nose, some aberrant blood supply. There was no way of predicting this prior to surgery."

"You have performed this procedure successfully on other patients?"

"That is beside the point."

"For the record, how many times have you performed this procedure?"

"That is irrelevant."

Soltano's face grew red. "Doctor, at the time you performed surgery on Stephanie Green, isn't it true that you had absolutely no specialty training in plastic surgery—"

"I have years of experience!" Morrie interrupted.

"And isn't it also true that your major credential as a plastic surgeon is membership in an organization that you yourself founded and the principal function of which is to give out certificates that imply expertise in an area in which you have had no formal training?"

"I do not intend to answer any more of your questions."

Soltano smiled. "I don't think I have to ask you any more." He looked over at Janet, and she handed him another sheet. "I'd like to call on Dr. Lionel Stern."

Lionel took a deep breath. Gold was so pathetic he almost felt sorry for him. Almost.

"Dr. Stern, I want to thank you for being here. For the record, reading from your c.v., I see that you graduated medical school from Johns Hopkins, where you took your general surgery and plastic and reconstructive surgery residency training for, let me see," Soltano said, drawing it out as long as he could, "for *eight* years. And you are currently on staff at University Hospital as well as in private practice. You have been certified by the American Board of Plastic Surgery. Is that correct?"

"Yes."

"Can you tell us something about the operative procedure used by Dr. Gold in the treatment of Stephanie Green?"

"Dr. Gold made incisions along the base of each nostril and the columella. The entire end of the nose had been separated from the normal attachments to the cheek and upper lip."

"Is this the normal procedure for a rhinoplasty?"

"No."

"Have you ever used or seen anyone use such a procedure?"

"No. I have read about it in some early texts on rhinoplasty, but I have never heard of its being used."

Soltano leaned forward to make his point. "Never?"

"No." Lionel kept his eyes directly on the lawyer.

"In your opinion, Dr. Stern, why would this particular technique have been used by any reputable plastic surgeon in Los Angeles?"

Morrie banged his fist on the table. "This is not a courtroom, Mr. Sobiano, and however frustrated you may be as a civil servant rather than having a private practice as most *good* attorneys do—"

Soltano smiled. "I'll be happy to rephrase my question. Let the record show that to clarify matters, instead of 'reputable plastic surgeon' we say simply 'surgeon.' "

Arthur Green sat back and laughed. Lionel didn't find it amusing and started talking over Green's laughter. "I can't say what Dr. Gold was thinking when he made the decision to use that technique. It could be a simple question of poor judgment. He may have been supremely confident of his abilities and simply unaware of how dangerous it is."

Morrie smiled directly at him. It was, at best, a patronizing smile. "I have nothing but the highest respect for Lionel, and given the unfortunate outcome of Stephanie's surgery, he is precisely the right man to have come in and cleaned things up."

There was stunned silence in the room.

Soltano sat back. "I take it, Dr. Gold, that you neither feel accountable for what happened nor responsible for solving the problem that arose in your patient?"

"A problem arose. They happen don't they? I'm sure, Dr. Stern, you have problems?"

"Of course I have. But there's a difference. You see, Dr. Gold, I am a surgeon. I was trained to know when to operate and what procedure to perform when I do. It took me nine years."

"Perhaps you're a slow learner."

"Perhaps I am." Lionel fought to keep himself under control. "But what I learned, I learned well. The surgery I do is based on principles. I know just how far I can push tissue, how close I can cut the blood supply, what I can get away with and how to stay out of trouble. And if I do get into trouble, I know how to get out of it."

"In your opinion, Dr. Stern, is it likely that the procedure that Dr. Gold performed would be successful? Is it likely that it would succeed?" Soltano queried.

"No. An incision was made in both nostrils and in the middle, the columella. The entire nose, all the soft tissue and cartilage of the tip, was separated, based only on the blood supply of the skin of the bridge." Stern loosened his collar. The skin of his neck was wet.

"I can show you the appropriate reference describing the procedure!" Gold interjected, still with an air of confidence. The professor would show the student how it was done. He had gone over the line.

"You've never performed that procedure before, never even seen it done. Maybe that procedure worked once for someone who decided to write it up, but you're going to lose one nose for every time it works. In my business, Dr. Gold, those are very bad odds!"

Soltano interrupted the exchange. "Dr. Stern, you have reviewed the documents in Dr. Gold's file. In your professional opinion would the care exhibited by Dr. Gold for Stephanie Green constitute gross negligence, that is, disregard for the patient's welfare and general well-being?"

"It would."

"In your opinion, would the evidence support the conclusion that his care constituted gross incompetence, that is, possessing inadequate knowledge to practice such surgery in the community?"

"It would."

No one in the room said anything for several moments. Then Lionel turned to the stenographer. "You have underlines on that machine?"

"Yes."

"Then underline 'gross.'"

# 37

LIONEL AND CASEY sat in their chairs long after everyone else had left. For a long time they said nothing. Lionel stared at the wall. Then he turned to her and smiled. "I don't know. Maybe we should get them all back in here and let them decide about you and me."

"I don't need them to decide."

He raised his eyebrows. "And the winner is?"

"No winners."

"A tie?"

"No, Lion. No win, no tie. Just two losers."

"Uh, oh. Now that doesn't sound like the Casey I know. Something must have happened. You've been dazzled by my performance this morning. Young Dr. Kildare against the evil Dr. Frankenstein. Who could resist?"

"Lion, I'm sorry about everything."

"Thank you. I'm sorry about it, too."

"I know. Everything is so clear to me, except my own feelings. I guess I've been taking it out on you."

"No argument here."

"Oh, Lion, once upon a time it was all so simple. I had my whole future mapped out. Only I hadn't figured on you gumming up the works."

"Casey, can't we ever have a normal conversation?"

"Yes, we can. Let's have a big reconciliation dinner. My treat."

"When?"

"Tonight."

"You want the truth or you want a lie?" he asked.

"I think I want a lie."

Lionel nodded. "I already have a date."

Casey got up from her chair. She walked toward him. "Thanks."

He stood up. "Some other time?"

She leaned over and put a hand to his cheek. "I came to a major decision yesterday. It's only fair to let you know."

"Yes?"

"I love you."

Lionel wasn't sure what to say. A week ago, he would have put his arms around Casey, and they would have gone off together into the sunset. But now he felt guilty, as immoral as Morrie, brainless for thinking there was any future with Luisa and reckless for endangering his relationship with Casey. Like some pimply-faced adolescent who couldn't think beyond the next erection.

The worst part was that everything had gone so far he didn't even give a damn.

# 38

As Luisa drove along Sunset Boulevard toward Chinatown, she knew Peter was following her, but pretended not to notice. He had run after her, rushed down the stairs while she was in the elevator. Peter wanted some answers that Luisa was not about to give him. She ignored him and drove quickly away, confident that he would follow. Her years of being constantly followed in Bogotá had taught her there were many ways to play that game. At the moment, she didn't want Peter to know that she had seen him in her rearview mirror. She also didn't want him to know that she was making it easy for him to follow her.

With her attention fully directed toward Peter, Luisa never noticed the man in the mirrored sunglasses who was three cars behind.

Luisa pulled alongside the Chinese restaurant and motioned to the three men who appeared to be valet parkers. Then she glanced in her rearview mirror. Perfect. Peter was three blocks behind, just slowing down. She hurried out of the car and walked quickly along Gin Ling Way. The string of bright paper lanterns hung motionless from red awnings in this windless afternoon. The street would be quiet and empty until evening.

As soon as Luisa entered the restaurant, she was met by two young Oriental men dressed in gray Hong Kong–tailored business suits. They escorted her past tables filled with Oriental families having lunch and into a small banquet room where a distinguished, elderly Chinese man with

210

manicured fingernails rose from his seat to bow slightly. He was impeccably dressed in a dark gray suit, white shirt and white silk tie. His face was almost completely flat and his lips barely moved as he spoke.

"Mrs. Obregon, more beautiful than ever."

"Mr. Lu," she said, "more charming than ever."

"Charming," he repeated. "I have never understood why Westerners think it is charming to be truthful." He smiled. "I am up to the letter C in my reading, and another word that puzzles me is *candor*. I keep wondering why you require so many words to define truth." He put up a hand as though to stop himself. "I am honored to have you join me. Please sit down. I am grateful we have this opportunity to discuss our mutual business interests."

The waiter promptly poured an aromatic jasmine tea. As he left the room, Luisa handed Mr. Lu the keys to her car. He nodded and gave them to one of the young men. Both men bowed slightly and left. For several minutes, Mr. Lu sipped from his small teacup. Then he spoke in a very soft voice, carefully articulating each word. "As you know, I grew up in my father's humble laundry shop. It was there I learned the basic principle of all business. A shirt promised for Monday must be ready on Monday."

. "Mr. Lu, please let me explain." Luisa leaned across the table. "Our quality is the highest possible. We give you the very best from the Muzo area. It has no equal in today's market. I can assure you that I have taken great care, not to mention considerable personal risk, in the selection process. You will receive only the finest."

Lu shook his head. "Unfortunately, quality is a subjective word. However, based upon the first four shipments, I would agree. But our initial arrangement promised seven shipments in total to be provided at regular delivery dates. I am afraid that my associates are less flexible and trusting than I." Another sip of tea. "The problem, Mrs. Obregon, is that we agreed to base the price on the value of the entire shipment. With only slightly more than fifty percent in our hands, it is impossible to project profits. Therefore, they are becoming impatient. They are beginning to question whether the profit is worth the risk."

"Mr. Lu, assuming that the quality of the remaining shipments is comparable to what you've already seen . . ."

He smiled. "You wish an estimate of your share?"

"Yes. The risk has become increasingly great for me as well."

"I can offer only a rough estimate. May I ask the amount of the capital investment you transferred out of Colombia in this recent shipment?"

"The equivalent of eight hundred thousand U.S. dollars."

Lu looked down at his fingers. They moved up and down the rows of an invisible abacus. "Assuming the quality remains high, well over three million dollars." A silence came over them both, each comfortable with it. Lu smiled. "A great deal of money for a woman."

"A woman alone, Mr. Lu, has many problems," Luisa said gravely.

"I don't wish to burden you further, but it is extremely important that once we have arranged buyers, the entire transaction move forward quickly. But, alas, that does not seem to be the case. Despite the fact that everything has been arranged, I have nothing to sell. It is difficult to make a profit in that uncomfortable position. I am a tolerant man, Mrs. Obregon, but some of my associates are not. They have asked me to tell you that shipments must be made more frequently in the future. In the very *near* future."

"I understand." She spoke with a finality that seemed to satisfy him. Then Luisa took a deep breath. "Now I am afraid I must burden you."

"What is it?"

"Someone followed me here."

Lu sat back. He pushed away his teacup. "That was very careless of you, Mrs. Obregon."

"Mr. Lu, it is one of the hazards of being a woman alone. It is often impossible to control men."

He reached beneath the table and pressed a button. "The second rule of business my father taught me was never to show dirty laundry in public." One of the gray-suited men, his hand inside the lapel of his jacket, swung open the door, ready to protect the old man. Lu spoke in rapid Cantonese and the man relaxed. Lu turned to Luisa. "You understand—"

Luisa nodded. "Of course, I understand," she said knowingly.

A few words from Lu, and the man, after glancing once at Luisa, offered Lu the keys to her car. He motioned that they be given to Luisa, who took them and sighed with relief. The delivery had been made, the shipment accepted. Luisa picked up her teacup and took a sip. That left just Melissa and Sharon. She wouldn't have to worry about Peter anymore.

# 39

FLIGHT 652 TO BOGOTÁ was scheduled to leave LAX on time. No thanks to Melissa Eckhart, who had a crying fit the moment she got on board. After embracing Sharon White and exchanging whatever sketchy information they had about the slasher who had killed Rochelle, Melissa became inconsolable and locked herself in one of the First Class lavatories. Sharon had to threaten to call the captain in order to get her out.

Melissa borrowed Sharon's makeup and, before the flight began to board, put some rouge onto her cheeks, which everyone had noticed were quite pale. "I've been up all night. Not a minute's sleep. From the moment I heard. Maybe even before I heard. The past couple of days I have been you-want-to-talk hyper. It was like I knew something was going to happen. You ever get those feelings? Oh, shit, will you look at what I did?" Melissa had put too much rouge on one cheek. She screamed at Sharon. "Will you look, you bitch? Oh, God, did I say that? Why would I say that? Why would I talk to you that way?"

Sharon sat down next to Melissa. "Hey, it's okay. Calm down. We're all upset. I just had a scene at Dr. Gold's office that you wouldn't believe."

Melissa grabbed hold of Sharon's arm. "Why don't they put the air on in here? What's wrong with those bastards?"

Sharon tried pulling her arm away. "Melissa, let go. You're hurting me."

She looked down at her hand, releasing it from Sharon's

arm as though it had been on a hot coal. "I barely touched you."

"Melissa, are you all right? Did you take some pills or something?"

Her eyes filled with tears. "Thanks for all your help," she said bitterly. "I just wanted you to fix my rouge so that I don't look like a clown. Is that so fucking much to ask? But it's all right. I can do it myself."

Sharon watched as Melissa, instead of taking rouge off her cheek, put more on the other side in order to make it even. Her first thought was to tell the captain that something was wrong with Melissa, but she was afraid of what they might find. Instead, she took the trembling woman into the bathroom, washed her face clean and put on fresh makeup. "I'm worried about you," Sharon said.

Melissa smiled brightly. "I'm okay. It's the no-sleep and Rochelle."

The two women hugged each other. Sharon noticed Melissa's entire body was trembling and that the back of her uniform was wet with perspiration. "You promise to let me know if this is too much for you?"

"I promise. But I'll be fine." Melissa stood back and tugged smartly at her jacket. She raised her forefinger and winked. "The flight must go on!"

Sharon eyed Melissa as the passengers boarded. Aside from appearing as though she'd taken too many perky pills, everything seemed to be going fine. There was an old lady and her young grandson for Melissa to chat with while Sharon settled in the rest of the cabin. It wasn't a full flight, and although Melissa would usually have carried the tray with champagne and juice, Sharon poured and served— grateful that Melissa had perched next to the old lady and was chattering on.

There was some turbulence after takeoff that kept them strapped in their seats, looking at each other. Sharon was tired. She closed her eyes for a moment, opening them to see Melissa drumming her fingers on her knee and fidgeting with her seat belt. "You okay?" she asked.

Melissa stared straight ahead at the bulkhead wall.

"Look, I've already got one mother, thank you very much."
Her voice was tight, almost a growl. It was then that Sharon
smelled the liquor on Melissa's breath. For the first time,
she was frightened. Melissa never drank.

They were an hour into the flight, doing last rounds on
bar service before lunch. Melissa was in the galley while
Sharon took orders in the cabin. Suddenly, from the corner
of her eye, Sharon saw something that wasn't right. Melissa
wobbled out of the cabin, holding a tray of glasses filled
with champagne, far more glasses than there were passengers. She was barely able to maintain her balance and had
a puzzled expression on her face. Once she got to the front
of the cabin, Melissa turned around slowly, some inner
force spinning her. After a look of shock, as though having
seen or felt something she couldn't explain, she raised her
hands, still holding the tray. Glasses toppled over. Melissa
threw the tray upward, hurtling champagne and broken
glass over the first four rows. As the passengers shouted and
jumped up from their seats, Melissa screamed, then fell to
the floor.

# 40

MORRIE WAITED IN silence for Luisa. He sat in a well-padded chair, facing the door. In the darkness. He had not loosened his tie. Or opened the mail. Or listened to his phone messages. At the moment, an area deep within him, far deeper than his stomach, was more demanding than his brain. It was a process. Morrie was reacquainting himself with a very old feeling: fear.

Not that fear didn't have a positive side. It had provoked some of his best career decisions and given him a business that awarded him in excess of a million dollars each and every year. More than most of those goddamn nose-to-the-grindstone, do-it-by-the-book plodders. It was that catalyst that had projected Morrie into the position he enjoyed.

For the first time in his life, Morrie didn't know what to do. He was now, temporarily at least, unable to practice medicine. And it was more than a possibility that he would never return to the profession he took such delight in practicing. The loss of the respect, of the admiration from his parents and staff—it was hard if not impossible to fully comprehend, let alone accept. He had been so careful to always do his best. What would he do without that? Perhaps he could buy the house in Bogotá from Luisa. At a distress price, of course. After all, she was willing to walk away from it and get nothing. How much could she ask? He'd keep his penthouse and donate the downstairs to some struggling medical charity that couldn't afford to say no. A five- or ten-year lease, if necessary. That would keep his name on the party lists and give him a place to stay while collecting prospective patients for his Colombian surgery boutique. While it wouldn't be easy to find a doctor in L.A. to buy his practice, he was sure he could come up with someone. He would shift his practice to Bogotá while he fought the legal battle to get his license back. Far from ideal, but not impossible. The thought also occurred to him that this was probably a good time for him to get married. One of those Bogotá debutantes whose stinking-rich family would turn cartwheels if their daughter married a famous Yankee doctor. An interesting idea. Morrie thought for a moment about his ideal woman. She would have to be the richest—and the ugliest—girl in Bogotá. He would transform her with his own hands into an object of incredible beauty. Someone who would worship him for her entire life. The face he imagined creating was Luisa's.

Deep in thought, he reached automatically for the phone before the answering machine intercepted it. "Hello."

"Morrie?"

It was a woman's voice. Someone he couldn't recognize. "This is Dr. Gold," he said.

"Morrie, I'm so glad I got you. I thought I'd have to go through fifty people."

"Who is this?"

"I've been thumbing through your file, Morrie."

"What file? Who is this?"

"What file?" She laughed. "What-the-hell file do you think? The file at BMQA. Morrie, this file could choke a horse."

"If you don't give me your name, I'm going to hang up."

"Morrie, you remember me, Janet Wallace, the dumpy blonde who sat next to Soltano? By the way, the way you kept calling him the wrong name? Saltine? Sultana? I loved it. It was a great touch."

Morrie thought back to the hearing. Casey Crawford's assistant. "What do you want?"

"Kiddo, it's not what I want. It's what *you* want."

"Very well, then, what do I want?"

"You want what I have. Your file, your only file here at

the BMQA. Morrie, you ever watch Joan Rivers? You know what she says? She says 'Can we talk?' Well, Morrie, can we talk?"

"I have nothing but the highest regard for the BMQA."

"Morrie, you're not talking, you're shoveling shit. You want to really talk?"

"Suppose I listen?"

"Okay. Listen to this. Alice Morgan. Deidre Chambers. Sue Ann Baxley. Shirley Phillips."

Morrie listened hard. All names of women on whom he had performed cosmetic surgery. All dissatisfied malcontents who had threatened to make complaints.

"Or how about, Nola French, Sylvia Kalish, Nancy Makon, to name a few? You handled those gals brilliantly. The settlements never exceeded thirty thousand dollars. So they weren't reported to us. You can imagine, I had to really dig for those."

Morrie was well aware that unless the judge awarded the plaintiff in a malpractice case more than $30,000, the BMQA was not automatically notified. "I don't know what you're talking about."

"Let me spell it out for you. I've got handwritten complaints from former patients of yours. I've got medical records. I've got statements from medical experts whose comments make Dr. Stern's remarks look like something left by the Tooth Fairy. So, the bad news is that between your file and the testimony on poor Stephanie Green, you're about to have quite a midlife crisis. In other words, you'll be lucky to end your days giving steroid shots to race horses in return for a little nonreportable income. The good news is that without this file I now hold in my hand, a nose is a nose is a nose. Nobody's going to remember who made the complaints against you, and certainly you're not going to tell them. They'd never revoke your license on just one case."

She was absolutely right about that. Despite Morrie's doomsday plan, everything this woman was saying was true. There was almost no price he wouldn't pay for what she had. Without it the BMQA had no real case and he had a license. "I still don't know what you're talking about."

"Then maybe I should hang up."

"I think that's a good idea. Frankly, I have nothing to talk to you about. I regard this phone call as an invasion of my privacy as well as a thinly veiled attempt at blackmail."

"What do you mean 'thinly veiled'? Morrie, get real. This is the best crank call you're going to get in your whole life. But I got to go. My car is in for a tune-up, and I have to pick it up in half an hour. Morrie, you should see my car. It belongs in the Smithsonian. Anyway, I have to get myself over to the Farmer's Market. I have this craving for Frank's French Fries."

"I have no interest in your whereabouts," Morrie said, writing it down. "Do not ever call here again."

"See ya."

Morrie put down the receiver and looked at his watch. Yes, he could make it in time.

# 41

LIONEL PULLED UP in front of the dazzling lights outside L'Orangerie and jumped out of his car as though he were on his first date. Lionel wasn't one to enjoy dressing up, but tonight he wouldn't have balked at wearing a top hat and tails. He was in the mood for a celebration. Things had gone right with Stephanie's surgery, things had gone right at the hearing, and the final step in the exorcism of Morrie Gold, the ultimate blow to that bastard, was to celebrate with Luisa. There was a wonderfully vindictive part of Lionel that relished the symmetry of it all.

Girard greeted him as he walked into the room filled with plants, the sound of classical music in the background. "Dr. Stern, how good to see you. The lady is already here."

From Lionel's point of view, as he walked onto the open patio toward the table, Luisa was more than merely there: she was the only one there. Black hair falling gently onto bare white shoulders, her body sheathed in white silk, and that incredible emerald her only piece of jewelry, Luisa created her own ballet simply by raising her eyelids as she saw him and by bringing her cheek close as he leaned over to kiss her.

"I'd kill to see you dance," he whispered.

Luisa smiled, bringing her hands from her lap, palms up on the table. "You dance with your arms. The feet are for movement, the torso gives motion, but dance is in the fingers." Her fingers beckoned Lionel to take her hands.

He reached out with his forefinger and outlined the palm of her hand, then around each finger as though tracing a pattern. As he touched the curve beneath her thumb, she tightened her grip on him. Lionel looked up. "Are we still dancing?"

She began to laugh. "Not if you have to ask."

"I have to ask," he said intently. "Half the time I don't know what the hell I'm doing when I'm with you."

"But half the time you do."

"Not very good odds for a surgeon."

"I'm not looking for a surgeon."

Girard stood at the table. "Would you like an aperitif?" Luisa declined, as did Lionel. Girard smiled and stepped back.

"What are you looking for?" Lionel asked Luisa.

"The fatal flaw. The chink in your armor that will convince me I should never have become involved with you."

"And have you found it yet?"

She held tight to his hand and spoke lovingly. "I can't even find the armor."

"Am I that transparent?"

Luisa nodded. "It's one of your most endearing qualities."

"How endearing?"

Another smile. "So that's it," she said.

"What's it?"

"The secret of your success. Chinks without armor. How clever of you."

Lionel leaned close. "There's nothing clever about me."

She leaned even closer. "No, there isn't. And that's the cleverest part of all."

Girard came back with menus. He offered one to Luisa. She looked at Lionel and shook her head no.

Lionel said, "Actually, Girard, we're not very hungry."

He got up and put a $20 bill on the table. "It was terrific. As usual."

A flustered Girard pulled the table back for Luisa, who got up saying, "Everything was lovely."

As they walked toward the door, Lionel whispered to Luisa, "Where are we going?"

She stopped in the middle of the aisle and put her arms around his neck. "You're right," she said, leaning close to kiss him. "You're not very clever."

Lionel and Luisa had just made love. They lay back on the bed in her bungalow at the Beverly Hills Hotel. Exhausted. Quiet. She was nestled in his arms, and Lionel thought he had never been at such peace with the world.

His beeper went off. Lionel muttered, "Shit," and turned it off. Then he dialed and waited impatiently for someone to pick up. "Dr. Stern."

"Doctor, I have a message for you from Dr. Crawford. Please call her at home immediately."

Lionel glanced over at Luisa. She looked up and caught the expression on his face. "What is it?" she asked.

"Nothing." Lionel dialed Casey's number. She picked up on the first ring. "Hi."

"Lion, where are you?"

"I just got your message."

"Have you been listening to the news?"

"No. Why?"

"Oh, Lion, I am so sorry. Peter's dead."

"What?"

"His body was found in an alley downtown." Her voice broke. "He was mugged and then stabbed. He must have tried to fight the guy off."

"Oh, my God."

"Lion, where are you? Let me come and get you."

"No."

"Are you all right?"

"No. I'll call you later." He hung up the phone and sat staring into space.

Luisa sat next to him. "What is it? Tell me."

After a moment, Lionel sat up feeling totally numb. "It's Peter Dalway. He's been killed."

Luisa gasped. She put a hand to her mouth. "Oh, my God! No!" Tears began to stream down her cheeks. "How could such a thing have happened?"

# 42

$F$OR THE FIRST time in his career, Lionel thought seriously about postponing surgery. Mrs. Chandler's face-lift and Mrs. Horowitz's abdominoplasty were clearly not life threatening. He considered saying that he had an emergency. But he had no idea of what he would do with the time, and doubted that he could find something to do that would or could make him feel any better.

Unlike the neurosurgeons and oncologists who dealt with death almost as often as they made rounds, Lionel was involved in the quality of life rather than life itself. His patient profiles ranged from the vain to the valiant; rarely did they include the dying. However, as a member of a profession dedicated to saving lives, there was little tolerance for wasting one.

Each of these factors made it all the more difficult for him to accept Peter's death. And the senseless manner in which he died. It had always seemed to Lionel that although doctors understood the clinical process of dying in order to better help the patient, they were often less able to withstand the trauma of personal loss. Perhaps it had to do with a false sense of security in thinking they were the professionals in matters of death when, in fact, the only people who were accomplished in that arena were the dead themselves.

Lionel's thoughts were drawn involuntarily, as they had been all too often in the previous hours, to Peter's death. What really happened? Had he suffered? Lionel would never know the answers. Probably just as well. Borrowing as much medical pragmatism as his conscience would allow, he accepted the reality that Peter Dalway was gone. What he could not accept was his own loss. And his own sense of guilt.

Lionel had called the police immediately and went down to see the detective in charge of the case. It made as little sense to Lionel that Peter would have been in Chinatown as it did his winding up stabbed to death in an alley. The police held out as much hope of finding the criminal as of retrieving the cash taken from Peter's wallet. A random robbery, no doubt.

Although Homer had already identified the body, Lionel felt a strange compulsion to go to the morgue to see Peter. It was a mistake. There was no sudden catharsis, no outpouring of grief that flushed his emotions clean. Instead, Lionel's grief made him feel responsible. Luisa told him of the episode at Morrie's office, and he began to convince himself that it might not have been such a humiliation for Peter if Lionel hadn't caused such a scene over Morrie. And then perhaps Peter wouldn't have, as the police put it, "been in the wrong place at the wrong time." Lionel felt that of all people, he should have been able to find "the right place" for Peter. It was the least he could have done.

By the time Lionel finished both surgeries, it was nearly two in the afternoon. He walked into his office to find Casey waiting for him. He wasn't surprised. She had called twice the night before and each time he begged off.

"Hi," he said, sitting down.

"Hi." There was a pause. "I was surprised you hadn't canceled surgery."

He smiled. "Mrs. Horowitz's tummy would never have forgiven me. And if I did, I wouldn't know what else to do except sit around and mope."

"Lion, I want to help."

"Thanks. I wish you could."

She walked over to him. "Give me something to do. Ask me to make you dinner or pick up your laundry. Just sit here with you maybe. I don't know what. I don't care what. Just don't shut me out."

He stared at Casey for a long time, trying to understand why he didn't want to share his feelings with her. In part, because he had Luisa tucked away in the back of his mind. And what kind of bastard did that make him? How could he ask for or take anything from Casey while Luisa was swirling around in his head? It was a tug-of-war that was going nowhere. It would have been unfair to involve her. Lionel tried avoiding the issue. He picked up a handful of phone messages. "Casey, believe me, I would give anything to be able to share this with you."

She didn't smile. "I don't understand. Is it that I've pushed you too far?" The phone rang. "Now you're the one shutting *me* out." Another ring.

"I'd better answer that. Gloria's out to lunch."

Casey nodded. "Yes, you'd better answer. It might be important."

Lionel reached for the phone. "Can I call you later?"

She walked to the door. "Don't make it too late."

He picked up the phone and covered the receiver. "Thanks for stopping by." Even before she left, he turned back to the phone, wondering whether it wasn't already too late. Then, all-business as he spoke into the receiver, "Dr. Stern."

"Oh, thank God." The woman's voice was high-pitched and she spoke quite rapidly. "I've been trying you all morning."

Lionel looked down at the phone messages. There were five from Melissa Eckhart. The name was familiar, but he couldn't place it. "Miss Eckhart?"

"Dr. Stern, do you remember me? I'm the flight attendant who was in for a second opinion on breast enlargement?"

"Yes." She sounded terrible. "What's wrong?"

Melissa's voice was unsteady. "I'm sick. I don't know what it is, but I seem to be getting worse. They had to turn the plane around and take me off the flight to Bogotá yesterday. Nothing like this has ever happened to me before. I'm so nervous. I think I'm going to die." She began to sob. "I need help, Doctor."

The word *Bogotá* ricocheted in his head. "Can you come right over to the hospital?"

"Yes. One of the other girls on the flight got off with me. She's been taking care of me. She'll drive me over."

Lionel was not prepared for what he saw when he walked into the examining room thirty minutes later. Had he not known who it was, he would never have recognized Melissa. Her skin was drawn tightly against her face, giving her cheek bones a prominence that assumed grotesque proportions. Her skin was devoid of color, as if it had been bleached away, and her eyes were sunken and dull but in constant motion, darting around the room like the tongue of a snake.

"I told you I was in bad shape," Melissa said apologetically.

Lionel held her head and felt her body tremble. Her skin was cool and covered with a light film of perspiration. "When did all this begin?"

"Shortly after I had the surgery."

"Surgery?"

"I went ahead with the breast enlargement. It wasn't that I didn't want you as my doctor. But Dr. Gold's surgery didn't cost anything. It was part of a research project and my best friend had the same operation." She began to cry. "Poor Rochelle. It was terrible. You heard about the slasher?"

It was all coming too fast for Lionel. His first priority was Melissa, but he couldn't get Morrie out of his head. "How long have you felt like this?"

"A few days. I think. I don't know. I'm not sure of time. I can't remember." As she spoke, Melissa shifted her weight on the examining table as if she were unable to restrain her body from moving. "It's hard to keep things straight in my mind. God knows how I showed up for the flight. Before that, I was okay. Oh, I had so much energy. Can you believe I started scrubbing floors in my apartment? I've never scrubbed floors in my life!" Her words followed each other rapidly, like the staccato of a typewriter. Then, more tears. "I'm so nervous. I haven't been able to sleep."

"For how long?"

She shook her head. "I don't know. What's wrong with me, Doctor?"

"Have you been taking any medication?"

"No. I never take pills. Last night, after the flight was the first time I took anything. A Valium. My next-door neighbor gave me one."

"Do you know how many milligrams it was?"

"No. It was blue."

"Ten milligrams. Did it help calm you down?"

"Not at all. I was still Little Miss Perpetual Motion. I don't know. Maybe I took two."

"And you didn't feel anything?"

"No, I didn't! I told you I didn't feel anything! Aren't you listening to me?!!"

Melissa's forehead was wet. Perspiration streaked down her temples in thin trails. Lionel took one of her cold hands and felt her pulse. It was well over one hundred beats each minute.

"I am listening to you, Melissa," Stern said as soothingly as he could. Something was very wrong with the young woman. "Do you have any other symptoms? Anything other than nervousness?"

"Please don't talk to me that way."

"What way?"

"That tone in your voice." She massaged her hands together. "It's very condescending."

Lionel knew he had no "tone" in his voice. But he did know that Melissa had some kind of legitimate medical problem. Fidgeting, perspiring and pale, rapid pulse. The question was what and how serious. "Melissa, I would like to examine your breasts."

She stared at him, her eyes widening. "Not you too!" She folded her arms across her chest. "I'm tired of everybody looking at my breasts."

"Melissa, I'm trying to find a clue as to why you feel the way you do."

"Then take a blood test like a real doctor. Or give me a pill." She shouted, "Give me something to let me sleep!"

Lionel spoke very calmly. "I'm a plastic surgeon, Melissa. I can help you if something went wrong with your surgery. Otherwise, I'm not the right person for you to see."

"Well, nothing went wrong with the surgery." She put her arms down and pushed out her chest. "See? Aren't they big? Gigantic. Enormous." Then she began to cry.

Lionel picked up the phone. "Melissa, I want to make an appointment for you to see another doctor, an internist. Bill Adams is the best one I know."

"Dr. Adams's office," answered the voice on the other end.

"This is Dr. Stern. I have a patient here in extreme distress. I'd appreciate it if Bill could do me a favor and see her right away."

"He's with a patient, Dr. Stern, and he's booked solid. But if you want to send her down, I'll do my best."

"Her name is Melissa Eckhart. She'll be right there. I'll call Bill. Thanks." Lionel put down the receiver. He spoke slowly. "Dr. Adams will find out what's wrong. He'll give you something that will make you feel more comfortable."

"Will I have to get undressed?"

"I don't know. But he will help you."

She put a hand to her forehead as though suddenly in great pain. "I can't remember your name."

Lionel took a prescription pad and wrote down ADAMS–406. "My name is here. Lionel Stern. And this is where you're going. To Dr. Adams on the fourth floor."

She took the paper and nodded. "Can I ask you something?"

"Of course."

"Do you think they're too big?"

# 43

LUISA OPENED THE door to her bungalow. It was Morrie. "I thought I asked you to call first."

"Luisa—"

"Come in, Doctor," she said impatiently. "Or don't I call you Doctor anymore?"

"Good afternoon, Luisa. What puts you in such a foul mood? It couldn't be your birthday again."

She closed the door behind him. "All right. What is so important?"

Morrie nodded sadly. "My dear, I did not want to tell you this on the phone. Peter Dalway has been murdered."

Luisa sat down. Suddenly, her movements were very feline. "I know. Lionel told me."

"Lionel?"

"Lionel Stern? You know him, don't you?" She smiled, playing with him, enjoying the sight of Morrie's rage.

His voice was flat. "Why were you talking to Lionel Stern?"

"Darling, how else would I know where to meet him tonight?"

"Luisa, be reasonable. This is hardly the time to turn against one another."

"How dare you accuse me of that after I've done nothing but sing your praises?" She mimicked her own performance. "Dr. Gold is such a genius. I'm so proud to play a part, no matter how small, in his brilliant new research. I am so grateful that he is helping my people." She took a deep breath and let out an exasperated groan. "I am so sick of it all. I want to be free of you." She walked to the bar, made two brandy and sodas, and handed one to Morrie. He hesitated. "Go ahead," she said. "Surely you don't have to worry about drinking before surgery."

"How dare you have dinner with Stern. What about your commitment to me and to my work. You, of all people, being seen in public with the very man who's trying to destroy my career. Don't you realize what that makes me look like?"

"Yes. It makes you look a fool to those who think you and I have more than a business relationship. Not that I don't look a fool to those who think we just have a business relationship. I've been to see my associates. They are tired of waiting. Your delays have made them nervous. I had to guarantee that everything would be completed within forty-eight hours."

"That's impossible. You should have made them under-stand." Morrie sipped his drink. "Things happen."

"Antonio always told me that things do not simply happen. Someone makes them happen. Or not happen." She paused, emptying her glass in a single gulp. "So I assured them that we'd be finished by tomorrow."

"But that's not possible. First of all, I don't know where Sharon and Melissa are—"

"I do. We've had a stroke of good luck. Melissa took ill on the way to Bogotá. The plane turned back, and Sharon got off to take care of her. They're both in town. All you have to do is get them in and replace the implants."

"But I can't perform surgery. That's why I needed Peter."

"Peter was useless. You should have hired someone and not asked for a favor. Aside from being stupid, you're miserly and small. You should have paid a doctor, and you shouldn't have taken Stephanie Green as a patient. The only thing big about you, Morris, is your ego. You put every-thing we've worked for at risk."

"As it happens, my license may not be at risk for much longer. There's been a rather interesting turn of events."

"It's no longer interesting to me, Morris. There's only

one thing I care about: the implants. Find a doctor to get them for me."

"It's not that simple."

"Then do it yourself!" she shouted. "I don't care how you get it done, but get it done! You have less than forty-eight hours. Or else, I swear, you're out! You'll never see a penny."

There was a long pause. Her angry words hung in the air between them. Morrie spoke without emotion. "Did you go to bed with him?"

"Yes." Luisa watched as Morrie nodded slowly. It was obvious that it upset him. She had finally been able to wound that incredible ego of his.

Morrie stared into his drink. "Did he notice the implants?"

"Yes."

Then, very softly, "Did he think it was good work?"

# 44

LIONEL WAS ON the phone with Bill Adams's nurse. Her voice was testy. "Yes, Dr. Stern, of course I'm sure. She never showed up."

He apologized and put down the receiver, wondering what the hell could have happened to Melissa. He dialed her at home. No answer. He took the phone number with him as he left to make rounds.

Arthur Green stood up the moment Lionel entered Stephanie's room. "Any word yet?"

Lionel nodded first to Stephanie. She smiled back warmly. "Word on what?" he said absently as he opened her chart to check the nurse's report on temperature and pulse.

"On the bastard's license! I want him nailed. Permanently."

Smiling at Stephanie in order to change the subject, Lionel asked, "How are you doing?" Maltry had taken out the sutures early that morning, and the flap had already begun to blend nicely into the rest of Stephanie's face. Now in the fourth day following surgery, the swelling was subsiding, and with the exception of the fullness in the eyebrow area she was beginning to look almost normal. The evidence of the catastrophe that had struck had, for the most part, been erased. Externally at least.

"I don't know. There are so many thoughts going through my head."

"Tell me."

She paused. "I'm grateful I won't have to go through life like a freak. But I feel so cheated, Dr. Stern. It's not that I don't think you're a great doctor, because I do, but I always thought the only thing stopping me from being an actress was my nose. Now, I'll never find out. It's like I'm back where I started. I'll never know if I could have made it."

Lionel had given her back sanity and he had made her whole again. But he realized that Morrie had taken something from her spirit and Stephanie would never be the same. "There will be scars, but they can be covered with makeup."

Arthur Green waved a finger at Stephanie. "No makeup at the trial!"

"You've decided to sue?" Lionel said, feeling the weariness that had come from all the events. For the moment at least he had heard too much about Morrie Gold.

"I can't talk him out of it," Stephanie said with some sadness.

"You bet I'm going to sue," Green exclaimed. "I don't just want the bastard to lose his license. I want every penny he's got." Then, a sudden worried look crossed Green's face. "Why? You don't think we'll win?"

"Oh, I think you'll get a judgment against him, and I'm the last person to do anything to protect Morrie, but are you sure you want Stephanie to go through all that again? We were just talking about covering up scars and you're going to have to bare them all. For everyone. The media's going to play this one for all it's worth."

Arthur banged his fist on the chair. "Good. I want everyone to know the truth about Morrie Gold!"

Lionel shook his head. "But that's not all they'll want to know. You'll be putting Stephanie under a microscope. They're going to have a field day with her. Her face is going to be plastered on the front pages of newspapers throughout the country. On television. She'll be hounded by the press for interviews and will have to relive the horror over and over again for millions of people."

Stephanie looked at Lionel. Her eyes sparkled. She lay back slowly on her pillows and smiled triumphantly. "Wow. You couldn't buy publicity like that."

# 45

Melissa Eckhart got onto the elevator, holding the piece of paper on which Lionel had written ADAMS—406. But the elevator was full, and for some reason she was unable to get close enough to the panel to press number four. Melissa thought there must have been hundreds of people in that elevator, most of them so very tall. Where did they get all those tall people from? Angry too. They all seemed angry. They wouldn't let her near the panel. They wouldn't let her press the button. They wanted her to miss her floor.

She waited until they got to one, hoping that after all those tall, mean people left she would be able to press number four. But as soon as they got off, another hundred people, even more frightening looking, got on the elevator and pushed her to the back. They pushed so hard she could barely breathe. She thought her bones would break as they crumpled her into a little ball and turned her around until she faced the back wall of the elevator where she could see nothing and couldn't tell what floor she was on. Suppose it was four?

When she thought it was safe, she turned slowly around to face the front of the elevator, her eyes narrow, her shoulders hunched over for protection. This time she would make it to the panel. This time she would press the button no matter how they tried to stop her.

Oh, God. They had taken the panel out of the elevator. She searched the wall for it with her hands, but it was gone.

There was no way to press the button. There was no door to get out. They had taken everything with them. She was alone, riding up and down, and there was no way to stop or to call for help or to get out. Worst of all, her head hurt as if it were being split in two.

When Melissa Eckhart was wheeled through the double doors of the emergency room, the third-year medical resident assumed she had either a head injury or some kind of drug overdose. She had been found screaming in the elevator, beating the floor, incoherent, jabbering about someone taking the buttons. He had little time for lengthy differential diagnosis.

Within moments, Melissa was unconscious. And then the seizures began. There was no sign of any injury. No medications in her purse. No syringes to signal that she was a diabetic or a drug addict. The resident slipped a green plastic airway into Melissa's mouth, which pushed the relaxed tongue forward, allowing her to breathe and preventing her from biting her tongue. Despite Melissa's uncontrollable shaking, a needle was inserted into one of the veins of her arm and blood was removed to be sent to the lab for an assay of the body's salt balance, sugar, and for the presence of any drugs. The blood workup was standard operating procedure; it was also useless, since it would take about two hours, which in the clinical circumstance he faced, might as well have been an eternity.

Judiciously, he played the odds. The resident's first therapeutic move was standard. He administered intravenously a small but concentrated dose of sugar, on the possibility that Melissa might be hypoglycemic. It was an outside shot, but maybe she was a diabetic who had made a mistake and had taken too much insulin. It was a harmless probe.

The sugar did nothing. Melissa's convulsions continued and within minutes became worse. During that same period, the nurse had removed all of Melissa's clothes. No bruises. No needle marks. No information.

While a muscular paramedic held her head, the resident

managed a glimpse of the right retina. Nothing there. Neck clean. No blood in the hair. Why the convulsions?

He began to arrange some diagnostic priorities in his mind. Unlikely that she was a diabetic who had taken too much insulin. No needle marks, probably not a junkie. No blood anywhere, no bruises. Not certain, but unlikely that there was head trauma. At that point, he assumed she had been taking some kind of drug by mouth. No better than a guess.

The convulsions continued. Although the blood chemistry came back and showed nothing conclusive, he couldn't wait the two hours required for a more complicated analysis for the presence of drugs. First, he gave Valium, then phenobarbital intravenously. Melissa's spastic, uncontrolled movements worsened, and her blood pressure continued to rise, now 200/110. He increased the dosage of the two drugs to extraordinary limits, without response. He was helpless. Nothing worked.

He began administering antihypertensive medications, but her pressure continued gradually but irreversibly to climb until it reached 260/130. No one in the ER had ever seen a pressure that high. But then it began to fall. Quickly. Within just a few minutes it was 90/40 and then it could not be heard. Melissa's EKG, quite normal until that point, began to show random, irregular beats that soon combined to show only a bizarre pattern of electrical excitation that came from several different areas within her heart. In less than a minute, there was no electrical activity at all.

# 46

MORRIE PARKED HIS car in the lot at the Farmers' Market. He put on his sunglasses and walked inside, looking for Frank's French Fries. And Janet Wallace.

The conglomeration of individual food stalls that made up the market was abhorrent to him. It was, in Morrie's mind, the personification of gluttony. Even worse, it was gluttony without style. He hated the people he found there, the busloads of tourists, the overweight women giggling as greasy pieces of fried chicken or egg roll stained their polyester blouses; old people with milk mustaches, young kids with whipped cream on their cheeks.

And Janet Wallace. She waved to him from a table in front of Frank's French Fries. As he approached, she patted the seat next to her with one hand and held up a potato with the other. "I just can't believe you've never eaten here before." He waved away the potato. She shrugged, dipped it into a large pool of ketchup on her plate and pushed it into her mouth. "Ask me what I'm going to miss about L.A. and I'll tell you Frank's. Now I know it's not as romantic as sunset on the beach, but the truth is I'm not a very romantic person, Morrie. I mean, with a puss like this, what chance did I ever have?" Janet put down her potato and pinched the flap on her upper arm. "Morrie, look at this. Isn't this disgusting? And my thighs. A national disgrace."

"If you don't mind," Morrie said impatiently, "I'd like to complete our business."

"Morrie, this *is* our business. My arms, my thighs, my face. I also want my melons turned into grapes, my tummy tucked and cute buns at last. You think I ought to dye my hair or would that be too artificial-looking?"

Morrie Gold sat at a table in front of Frank's French Fries with $500,000 in cash stuffed into a small nylon duffle. "I cannot imagine why you wished to meet at this indiscreet and god-forsaken place."

"Morrie," she began, eating another french fry, "where did Greta Garbo go when she wanted to be alone?" Janet waited for an answer, then shrugged as he looked stone-faced at her. "She found herself a crowd. Where better can you be alone than in a crowd? Hundreds of people walking by. You think they know I'm blackmailing you and you're sitting here with all that money? Come on. Grow up." Janet leaned over to the woman sitting at the next table. "Excuse me, miss, may I borrow the salt?"

On the plus side, Morrie took perverse pleasure in being able to come up with a half million dollars on short notice. Doing so made him feel richer than anything he'd ever bought. But as much as he enjoyed that, he was loath to hand the money over. "How do I know, after I pay, that you won't come back for more or bother me at some later date?"

"Morrie, do I look like some kind of crook? Or am I some middle-aged frump making a last-chance daring attempt to find happiness in a size-six dress, never mind I should only be lucky enough to be ogled by some horny young delivery boy? You know, you New Yorkers are all the same. You don't trust anyone."

"I do not trust you."

"That's because you don't trust yourself. But I'm not you, thank God. After reading your file, and even after what I'm doing right now, they could give me the Congressional Medal of Honor in comparison to you. You know, Morrie, you're really garbage. And if you're looking for a reason to trust me, it's this: I'd sooner die a virgin than have anyone who knew Janet Wallace before she mysteriously disappeared find out that she did business with a scumbag like you." Janet reached into her shopping bag and took out a large manila envelope. "Here." She held it up with two fingers as though it were a package of smelly fish. He took it and handed her the duffle. "And in case your arithmetic is off by as little as one dollar, honk if you're surprised, I have another copy. Also my lawyer will have a copy in the event of any attempt on my life or property or threats to my well-being."

Morrie stood up. "I shall never try to find you. However, if you ever contact me again, or use any information against me, I will have you killed."

Janet stood up and waved a potato in his face. "You better pray I have a healthy and a happy life. Because I'm telling you something, Dr. Frankenstein, the day they tell me I'm terminal, I'm going to come back and expose you for the fraud you are."

Janet stamped her foot. "Now get out of here!" She sat down. "I want to enjoy the rest of my fries in peace!"

# 47

A<small>T SIX O'CLOCK</small>, the beeper, a permanent
fixture on his belt, woke Lionel Stern up. He had fallen
asleep on the papers atop his desk. The digital readout on
the beeper showed an unfamiliar number, and for a moment
he hoped it was Melissa returning one of the many calls he
had made all afternoon. But then he realized the call had
come from within the hospital. He dialed quickly. The call
was answered on the first ring.

"Pathology."

"Pathology?"

"Loomis," the voice said impatiently. Paul Loomis was
chairman of the department of pathology.

"Sorry, Paul. This is Lionel Stern."

"I'm glad I caught you." Loomis's voice had a prissy
quality, lips tightly pursed against the tongue to articulate
words precisely.

"What's up?"

"My chief resident called me on a difficult case."

Lionel looked at his watch. It sure as hell must have been
a difficult case. The chief resident would have to be
completely stumped to call his boss after 5:00 P.M. And
secondly, Paul Loomis didn't ask advice from anyone. He
extracted a dignified pride from the fact that unlike other
physicians who were forced to contend with the burdens of
unknowns, he dealt mostly with information that was well
understood. There was no particular hurry so far as his

patients were concerned. Loomis could study them quite thoroughly. No appointments needed. All of Loomis's patients were dead. None by his own doing, however, a fact he frequently joked about. It was the only joke he ever made.

"What can I do for you, Paul?"

"I have a young girl down here who was brought into the emergency room two hours ago. Apparently . . . ," Loomis continued slowly, obviously reading from the chart, "she was having a series of grand mal seizures. From what I can figure out she was unconscious and having constant convulsions. The neuro people saw her in the ER but couldn't figure out what the fuck was going on."

Two things struck Lionel. He wondered what this had to do with him, and he realized he'd never before heard Loomis use profanity.

"There were no signs of trauma," Loomis continued. "No head wounds, nothing. Her blood pressure went up to two-sixty over one-thirty and then she dies. An apparently healthy twenty-five-year-old woman."

"How can I help you, Paul?"

The answer came like a blow from a hammer.

"The patient's name is Melissa Eckhart. We went through her purse for some clues that might tell us something, medications, that sort of thing. She had a sheet from your prescription pad. It had written on it Adams, four-zero-six. Frankly, I called Adams first, but apparently he keeps internist's hours."

"Jesus Christ."

"Was she a patient of yours?"

Vertigo swirled around Lionel and went down into a bottomless spiral. His body felt as though there was too much blood in it. Simultaneously, as Lionel realized it was an unusual reaction for him to have, he realized it was the same reaction he'd had in response to Peter's death. He felt guilty.

Loomis methodically continued with his objective curi-

PRACTICE TO DECEIVE 245

osity, oblivious to Lionel. "I noticed surgical scars under both breasts. I assumed she'd had a relatively recent augmentation mammoplasty, so presumably she was your patient."

"She came to me for help," Lionel said, as though confessing.

"When did you last see her?"

"Today. Early this afternoon."

"This afternoon?" Loomis's surprise intensified Lionel's guilt. "How did she look when you saw her?"

"My God, I can't believe it . . ."

"Lionel, you there?"

"Yes. She looked lousy, but there was nothing I could put my finger on. She was nervous, pale, anxious. Her pulse was fast, about one hundred, but there were no cardiac irregularities. It was just the way she looked and acted. I could see there was definitely a problem, but I had no idea it was *that* serious."

"Perhaps she was taking drugs."

"I doubt it. I asked her and she denied it. She seemed worried enough that I'm sure she was telling me the truth." Lionel felt like a third-year medical student presenting his first case to a faculty physician.

"Anything else? Anything that might be helpful? You know, nothing makes sense in this case. A healthy young girl has seizures and dies. No previous history. Nothing to go on."

"Oh, my God," Lionel groaned. "Of course there's something else. Paul, I'm sorry. She was a patient of Morrie Gold. He's the one who did the mammoplasty."

"That quack who advertises? Jesus. Well, let me get in touch with this Gold character. I was only calling to get some information before we begin the autopsy."

Lionel was surprised. He knew that in all deaths surrounded by questionable circumstances it was mandated by law that an autopsy be performed. But it was usually handled by the county coroner. "I wish I could have done something . . ."

"I'm sure you did what was appropriate. We've notified

the coroner and he gave us the go-ahead. Must be over-loaded down there."

"Yeah." Lionel hung up the phone. He wondered if Peter was part of the overload.

# 48

"PLEASE, MRS. OBREGON, I can't think straight." Sharon White's voice quivered on the other end of the phone. "First Rochelle, and now Melissa is sick. I don't know whether I'm coming or going."

Luisa took a deep breath, eager to sound as calm as possible. "I'm sure Dr. Gold can give you something so you'll have a good night's sleep."

"All I can focus on right now is Melissa. You don't think anything's happened to her?"

"Of course not. Melissa has a good head on her shoulders and besides, if I remember, she has some family in Los Angeles."

"Yes, but I don't want to call them in case she's not there. I don't want to worry them."

"Of course not. Are you sure you wouldn't just like to stop by and let Dr. Gold give you something to relax you? I understand completely about not wanting the surgery today. But I am so eager to help. I know it sounds odd, but I feel very protective of my little brood."

"I appreciate that. Actually, I'm glad you called. I was sitting here by myself going crazy."

Luisa tapped her pencil. "Sharon, perhaps you'd like me to stop by. We could chat a little—"

"Oh, no. I'd never impose that way. Besides, I'm going to soak in the tub for a while and that should make me sleepy."

"But it's no imposition. It would make me so happy. Poor darling, you're so far away from your mother . . ."

"Mrs. Obregon, you've really been a great help. But honestly, I think I just want to be by myself."

"All right. But promise you'll call as soon as you hear from Melissa. I want to be sure she's all right."

"I promise."

Luisa put down the receiver. Before she had a moment to think, the phone rang. Perhaps it was Morrie. He had left hours ago, saying he'd be back shortly. She put a hand to her forehead and answered it. "Dr. Gold's office."

"Hello. This is Dr. Loomis, chairman of the pathology department at University Hospital. I'd like to speak to Dr. Gold."

"I'm sorry," she began impatiently, "but Dr. Gold isn't here right now."

"I was afraid of that. Nothing seems to be going right on this one. Perhaps you can help. I'm about to perform an autopsy on someone I was told was a patient of Dr. Gold."

Luisa instantly assumed it was a question about Peter. "I expect to hear from Dr. Gold shortly."

"Have him call me as soon as possible."

After taking down the number, Luisa asked, "May I tell him who it's in reference to?"

"A patient named Melissa Eckhart."

It seemed that Luisa's heart stopped beating. She was afraid to say anything.

"Hello?"

"Yes, Doctor," Luisa managed.

"You got the name? You want me to spell it?"

"No." Then fearfully, "What happened to her?" Luisa asked.

"That's what we're trying to find out. All we know is she started to convulse shortly after leaving Dr. Stern."

Now Luisa's heart was racing. "Lionel Stern?"

"Yes."

"I'll be sure that Dr. Gold gets the message."

"Thanks."

Luisa hung up the phone, her fist clutching the receiver.

She didn't know which she was more afraid of: what would happen to Melissa's body or the fact that Lionel might already know too much. Only one thing was certain as Luisa crumpled the sheet with Loomis's phone number. Like it or not, Sharon White was going to have some company.

# 49

THE PATHOLOGY DEPARTMENT, like the operating rooms, was located in the basement of the hospital. Lionel walked along the narrow tiled corridor that led to the very chilly room where three large stainless steel autopsy tables tilted downward, each equipped with running water to wash away the blood.

"This is a pleasant surprise, Lionel," Loomis said, looking up over rimless glasses. "Good of you to come." A diligent and completely colorless man, he looked as though he should have been a bank teller. While most physicians believed that medicine was a delicate blend of science and art, as far as Loomis was concerned "art" was applicable only to sculpture, painting and music. "I, of course, began with the head."

The routine autopsy practice of removing the brain for examination had always, since his second year in medical school, been a mild shock to Lionel. Melissa's scalp had already been cut and peeled away from the skull so that her forehead rested inside out, completely covering her face— the identical technique he had used for Felix's surgery. It was impossible to recognize Melissa, her nude body so impersonal on the shiny steel table bathed in a constant stream of water. Her breasts were beautiful.

Loomis took Melissa's brain in both hands as if it were the morning paper and tilted his head to bring his glasses into focus. He spoke into the small microphone hanging from the overhead light. "The brain is of normal size and configuration without any evidence of trauma or hemorrhage." There was a hint of exasperation in his voice. "We'll go ahead and look inside the chest and abdomen, Lionel, but something tells me we're not going to come up with anything."

"Did you call Morrie Gold?" Lionel asked.

"He'd gone. Doesn't matter one way or the other. I don't believe that quack knows which end of a scalpel to use in the first place."

Lionel sat at an old oak institutional desk in the corner of the room and turned the pages of Melissa's hospital chart. Most patients who die in a hospital leave behind thick charts, notebooks of paper that document the final series of events in their lives. Melissa's chart held only four sheets of paper.

"I can't find anything in the heart," Loomis complained. "I wish my lungs looked as good as this young lady's." He spoke as though she were still alive. "Beats me. I can't find a thing. Nothing in the stomach, either." Loomis tapped his scalpel on the metal table as he tried to think of what to do next. "The only thing I can do is go by the book and remove all artificial material."

Lionel closed the chart, and although anxious to leave the cold, oppressive room, he wanted to see Morrie's handiwork up close. As he approached Loomis, the older man was completing an incision beneath Melissa's left breast.

Unlike surgical incisions, the fatty tissue merely separated, unaccompanied by normal bleeding. Lionel stared in fascination, not at Loomis's almost clumsy surgical efforts as he removed the first soft, glistening sack from behind her breast, but at the silicone implant itself. It was opaque and white. It should have been clear, glassy, colorless.

The pathologist methodically continued his work, completing an identical incision beneath the right breast, while Lionel studied the white jellylike mound resting on the steel table as if it were a hypnotic crystal ball. Another white sack was delivered from incisions under her right breast.

Lionel did his best to sound as casual as possible. "Paul, would you mind if I took these implants? We've been doing some research on silicone prostheses. I could use these in our study. We're trying to determine if the silicone shell changes while it's in the body." Lionel was surprised at how easily the lie came.

"Sure," Loomis answered absently while beginning to sew up the breast wounds. "God knows we haven't done this poor girl much good. We don't know any more than we did when we started. Maybe she can help someone else."

Paul Loomis had obviously never seen a silicone breast implant. Lionel was grateful for that. He wanted time.

In the privacy of his office, Lionel took a syringe and needle from the cabinet and carefully punctured the shell of the silicone bag. He was surprised to find that even through the wide bore of the largest needle, the thick white contents could not be withdrawn into the barrel of the syringe. Lionel used a scalpel and cut through the silicone bag. He whistled softly as he examined the contents and then lunged for the phone. "This is Doctor Stern. Can I speak to the medical resident in charge of ER, please?"

The resident's voice came on quickly, but uncertain. "This is Doctor Elliot."

"Sorry to bother you, but I wanted some information about a patient you treated down there. Melissa Eckhart. Do you know who I'm talking about?"

"Even if I tried, it would be a long time before I forget that one. We did everything but shake rattles and call for an exorcist. Believe me, we gave that girl the best we have. Nothing, I mean *nothing*, worked."

Lionel heard the agony in the young resident's voice. "I know. I read the chart. You did everything that could have been done. The good guys lost." He began to choose his words carefully. "I just got back from the autopsy. Paul Loomis went over everything and—"

"She had a brain tumor!" he interrupted hopefully. "Either that or some kind of intracranial bleed, right?"

"No. Loomis didn't find a thing anywhere." That part was true. "Did you send a blood sample for drug levels?"

"Yes, as soon as she came in. But those tests take a

couple of hours. I was sure she had taken something. An OD, I'd bet."

"And?"

"And the tests aren't back. But it's really strange. She didn't have any needle marks, so it wasn't heroin, and she couldn't have sniffed that much cocaine." Elliot sighed. "I've gone over it so many times I've lost count. That's why I thought she had some kind of brain tumor."

"Thanks anyway. Dr. Elliot, what's the name of the technician in the toxicology lab?"

"Maggie."

"Thanks again."

Lionel put both implants on the table. He touched the one that was cut, his fingertips gliding across the surface as though it were still a breast. He shook his head and dialed Toxicology. "Maggie, this is Dr. Stern. If I give you a small sample of a drug, can you tell me what it is?" As he listened, he quickly checked off the top three entries on the list on the yellow pad.

He used a wooden tongue blade and dug deep within the implant to remove a sample of the thick paste. The blade hit something. Lionel coaxed out two irregularly shaped dark pebbles. Then he cleaned away the white paste and held one of the stones against the light, revealing the most intense green color he had ever seen.

# 50

A<small>FTER HIS MEETING</small> with Janet, Morrie drove out to his beach house in Malibu. The maid had been there earlier in the day to clean and see what needed to be replaced in the refrigerator as she did every other day. It was a getaway house built on the Playboy philosophy for a man who had wanted to be a playboy before there was a Playboy. The house was designer casual, a sybaritic palace to which the hardworking playboy physician could come to get away from it all.

Instead, Morrie sat on the glass-paneled deck holding "it all" in his lap. The file. His catalog of $500,000 worth of failures. Morrie Gold sat bolt upright in his suit and vest and tie and shoes with black grosgrain shoelaces. He stared out at the beach. The ocean breeze, kept at a respectable distance by open-topped L-shaped glass-paneling, was brisk and cool. Morrie was sweating as he leaned over and turned on the propane gas jet in the barbecue. After adjusting the flame, he opened the file for the first time.

Carol Anderson. Abdominal liposuction. She had developed an infection. Her lawyer charged that Morrie had taken too much fat and had not replaced enough fluid and hadn't put her on the appropriate antibiotics. She had to be admitted to a hospital by her family physician, but all that happened was some scarring. It could happen to anyone. He crumpled the paper and threw it into the fire. Laura Blixen. Blepharoplasty and brow-lift. She was obnoxious, fat and pushy. And she looked like a basset hound. He had recognized that just removing the excess skin of the upper lids would not be enough. He had developed a brow-lift procedure that had tightened the skin of the forehead. But following the surgery one side of her forehead was paralyzed. Obviously a variant of the normal anatomy that could not have been anticipated. He had paid for her to have corrective surgery in New York. Burn it. Shelley Rubino. Breast reduction. That bitch had the most enormous breasts in the world. Should have entered her into the Guinness Book of Records. She knew there would be scars. The nipples were at different levels after the surgery, but the breasts were smaller—and that was what she wanted. Goddamn her. He tore the pages into small pieces and threw them into the fire. Goddamn them all. Bloodsuckers! Malcontents!

Morrie stopped reading. At first he just glanced at the names on each complaint before tossing the files into the fire, but then he stopped looking. What was the point? What could he prove by looking at each one? Nothing. It didn't make sense. How could a doctor who was as incompetent as the file would make him appear have a house in Malibu? A whole goddamn building on Sunset Boulevard? Cars. Hand-tailored suits. Enough money to pay that bitch $500,000 and not even feel it. He didn't feel it. A mosquito-bite on an elephant. It meant nothing to him. Nothing!

# 51

L<small>IONEL</small> S<small>AT</small> I<small>N</small> his office, drinking coffee, looking at his watch and wondering how the hell long it would take Maggie to get back to him with her chemical analysis, when the phone rang. "Yes?"

"Lion, it's me." Casey sounded subdued, almost depressed.

"Casey, thanks for calling, but I told you I'd speak to you soon. There's really nothing you can do for me." Lionel hated the impatience he heard in his voice.

"Then what about doing something for me? Something's happened. My assistant, Janet, is missing and so is the file on Morrie."

"Jesus. You don't think she's trying to pull something?"

"I've been with Soltano all afternoon. He says without the documentation in the file we have no case."

"But you must have copies of all those complaints."

"Lion, this isn't the FBI. We don't even have a computer system. We have manila folder files and big metal cabinets. Sometimes they are in alphabetical order, and sometimes they aren't."

"And Janet?"

"I'd have trusted her with anything. I just don't understand."

Lionel took a deep breath. Even more than he wanted to comfort Casey at that moment, he wanted to get her off the phone. "Listen to me, stop worrying. Forget about the file

256

for now. If I'm right, we've got something a hell of a lot better, maybe even dangerous."

There was a long pause. "What are you talking about?"

He didn't want to explain. "I'm being paged," he said. "I've got to go."

She knew he was lying. "I'll see you in the morning."

"In the morning?"

"Lion, check your messages. It's Peter's funeral."

# 52

"MRS. OBREGON!" Sharon stood in the open doorway, wearing a robe. Her eyes were red and swollen.

Luisa smiled warmly. "I could lie and tell you I was just in the neighborhood, but the truth is I've been worried sick about you. Forgive me."

Sharon reached out for Luisa's arm. "And I could lie and tell you that you shouldn't have come." She closed the door and turned to Luisa, her eyes brimming with tears. "But I've never been so glad to see anyone in my whole life." Sharon put her arms around Luisa and began to sob. "I'm so worried about Melissa that I don't know what to do. I have such terrible thoughts. I keep thinking about what happened to Rochelle, and I'm so afraid that the same thing will happen to Melissa. I should never have left her alone."

Luisa held onto Sharon, rocking slowly back and forth. "Trust me, my darling. What happened to Rochelle did not happen to Melissa."

As Sharon sobbed in her arms, Luisa positioned herself as a dancer prepares to take a great leap. She inhaled deeply and in a single sweeping arc slashed Sharon's throat from ear to ear with a scalpel.

There was a muffled cry from Sharon, her face expressing the horror that she had no voice to scream. Instead, she held tight to Luisa. In a final act she reached toward Luisa. After a moment, unable to stand any longer, her eyes open but unseeing, Sharon lurched forward and knocked Luisa to the ground, her fingernails digging into her cheek. Luisa hit the side of her face on a table as she went down, but the only thing she felt was the flow of Sharon's warm blood on her chest. Luisa struggled to free herself from the dead girl's grip, and finally crawled out from beneath her, Sharon's blood covering her face and hair.

The blood didn't matter. The pain on her cheek didn't matter, although she could already feel her flesh beginning to swell. There was only one thing Luisa cared about. She rolled Sharon onto her back, pulled open her robe and, leaning over closely, began slashing at her breasts. Luisa wielded the knife with such ferocity that it took a moment for her to realize that someone was knocking on the door.

"Sharon?" a voice called out. "You okay in there?"

# 53

IT WASN'T UNUSUAL for Lionel to spend late nights at the hospital. Normally, it wasn't even unpleasant. There was a comforting hum to the hospital at night: all the visitors and workmen had gone home. There were no rounds to be made, no students to be watched as carefully as patients. There was time to think. That was the problem.

It would be another four hours before the toxicology lab could identify the white paste. He had been calling Luisa to say he'd be very late, but there was no answer. Next he dialed the toxicology lab.

"Maggie, got anything?"

"Sorry, Dr. Stern, nothing yet. The sample is still in the first set of reactions. It's all automated, and I can't do anything right now."

"Yes, I understand."

"It'll be at least three hours, maybe longer."

"I know. Thanks, Maggie." Lionel hung up, thinking that if he were on the other end he'd ask, "Then why did you call?" He knew what was going on. The white powder had been mixed with ethanol and introduced to a series of small capillary columns where it would evaporate into a gas with the help of a pressurized flow of another inert gas like nitrogen. Once in a gaseous state, the drug would be bombarded with electrons, breaking up the unknown chemical into several of its components and presenting the computer with a characteristic molecular signature. That chemical fingerprint would then be compared to a library of known pharmaceutical and street drugs until an identification was made.

Lionel stood up to stretch. He dialed Luisa again. Still no answer. He glanced at his chair and decided not to sit down. He would go to the cafeteria and wait. Perhaps there would be some fresh coffee.

He walked along the corridor, passing a staff lounge where he stopped at the sight of two young residents asleep in front of the television set. Lionel listened to their snoring rather than the news brief on TV, but his attention was caught by the phrase, ". . . has police convinced there is a connection between the slashing death last week of flight attendant Rochelle Whitaker and that of Sharon White found earlier this evening. Both women died of deep lacerations, including a brutal slashing of their breasts."

The effect on Lionel was startling. He struck his forehead with the heel of his hand and then broke into a run back to his office, slamming open the partially closed door and grabbing for the phone. He called the L.A. coroner's office.

"Good evening, this is Dr. Stern at University Hospital. There was a young woman brought in this evening, they think she's a victim of the slasher—"

"Was she a patient of yours, Doctor?"

Without hesitating, Lionel said, "Yes."

"Just a moment, Doctor. I'll put you through to Dr. Anaya."

While waiting, Lionel tried to figure out what to say. His mind went blank.

"Dr. Stern? This is Dr. Anaya. Can I help you?"

"Doctor, I'm not sure, but I think you may have a patient of mine down there. A young woman named Sharon White."

"You're not the first call I've had." There was something in Anaya's voice. "Dr. Stern, do you mind if I call you back?"

"Of course not."

"We've had reporters calling with all kinds of aliases, and it wouldn't be appropriate for me to be quoted at this time."

"Sure. I'm here at my office at University Hospital. I'll hang up and you can call me back through the switchboard."

"I'd feel better about that. No offense."

Lionel hung up the phone, keeping his hand on the receiver. After more than a minute had gone by, he wondered what was taking Anaya so long. Perhaps he had another call. It was an endless three minutes before the phone rang.

"Dr. Anaya?"

"Thank you, Dr. Stern. Can't be too careful these days. All this publicity only makes things harder as far as I'm concerned. Two lousy cases and the media dreams up some kind of psychopathic killer drooling at the mouth."

"You think it was the same person?"

"I don't particularly care one way or the other. But both victims had the same very regular, very precise cuts, almost like surgical incisions. Christ, I see a lot of gruesome stuff down here." There was a pause, then a distinct change in Anaya's voice. "Well, Doctor Stern, suppose you tell me about your patient, and I'll let you know if it's the same girl."

Lionel suddenly realized that he was in over his head. As much as he wanted to see Sharon's body, he had no idea how to identify her. Taking a chance, he thought about Melissa. "Well, without getting the file—"

Anaya's voice was sharp. "Why don't you get the file?"

Lionel ignored him. "She was twenty-one, twenty-two, about five-eight, and—" He paused. "—she was a flight attendant."

"Looks like you dialed the right number, Doctor. How about taking a ride over here and giving me an ID?"

"I'll be right down."

As Lionel hurried to the parking lot, he was convinced that Anaya was right. There was no drooling psychopath. The scattered pieces of the puzzle were beginning to come together, and Lionel saw the outline of Morrie Gold.

The bureaucracy of the morgue was not the obstacle Lionel had expected. Anaya appeared at the front desk shortly after Lionel arrived. He was an obese, jowly man with a thin, neatly trimmed mustache that formed a perfectly straight line across his upper lip. His eyelids were more than half-closed from the column of smoke that rose from the short cigar precariously balanced between his lips. In his hand, he waved the report on Sharon White.

"We're short of typists, like a lot of things around here," he said, motioning around him as he led Stern to a room lined with drawers labeled with pieces of white adhesive tape with names written on them. "Hope you can read my writing. There wasn't a great deal I could say about this one. You can look for yourself." Anaya casually pulled out a drawer and raised a plastic sheet away from the absolutely white body of a young woman whose blonde hair was matted together with dried blood.

Lionel was shocked by what he saw. The wound that cut across Sharon White's neck had almost severed her head from the body. There was another cut just under her left breast. The wound had been inflicted so deeply that two edges of the skin spread widely apart, distorting the surrounding anatomy of the chest.

"Seen enough?" Anaya asked.

"I think this woman and the other you've examined were killed by the same person," Stern said quietly.

"That so?" Anaya replied in mock belief.

"The killer was not crazy, he was after something. These girls were carrying drugs and precious gems on them. The killer wanted to retrieve them."

Anaya stood frozen for a moment, and then took the cigar from his mouth. "Do you watch a lot of television, Doctor Stern? Quincy? Mystery thrillers? Maybe detective novels?"

"They were both stewardesses and both of them lived in the Marina," Stern said firmly.

"Do you know how many stewardesses live in the Marina?"

"And both of them worked for the *same* airline. Pan American. And Pan American flies to Colombia, every day. They are in and out of that country all the time."

"Interesting coincidence, Doctor Stern. Maybe it means something and maybe it doesn't. I always thought that in our business, as doctors, we deal in facts." Anaya walked to his desk in the corner of the high-ceilinged white room and took out a stack of eight-by-ten glossy photographs. "This is the other woman. Look for yourself, the wounds are much different." The body in the glossies was mutilated almost beyond recognition.

"What if the killer was interrupted?"

"What do you mean?"

"What . . . if the killer didn't get everything he wanted? Maybe somebody knocked on the door. Something like that. Was there any evidence of a struggle?"

"Now I *know* you watch too much television. Too much *bad* television." Anaya's heavy face was completely sober, a fraction away from anger.

"We can find out. Can we see what's behind the right breast?" Stern's eyes narrowed.

"Doctor Stern, forgive me, but I've heard just about enough. Maybe this girl was your patient and maybe she wasn't. I don't know what kind of half-assed idea you got in your head, but I have a lot of work to do and I draw the line when some doctor I don't know from Adam wants to operate on a corpse."

"But you have to remove the artificial material anyway."

"What artificial material?" Anaya asked.

Lionel pointed to Sharon's right breast. "There."

"Okay," Anaya agreed slowly. "But only because I have to do it. That's regulation."

The task was accomplished quickly. Behind Sharon White's right breast was a thin sack of silicone filled with a creamy white paste. When Anaya opened it, he scraped away twenty-nine green stones of varying size, the largest slightly smaller than a marble. Anaya took one and held it to the light. His eyes opened wide, and he pursed his lips and whistled two notes. He looked squarely at Stern in disbelief for a moment, and, without saying a word, walked over to the microscope on a table next to his desk. Anaya placed the stone under the scope and studied it for several minutes.

"Okay, Doctor Stern." Anaya shook his head slowly, his eyes narrowed. "Do you have any idea what these stones are?"

"I'm not sure, but I'd bet they're emeralds."

"You're right. Uncut emeralds, and very high quality. Gems and rocks used to be a hobby of mine a few years ago before I gained so damn much weight and had to take up golf. I'd guess they're Colombian," he said, holding it up to the overhead light. "You can tell by the color. The greenest green in the world. 'Green fire' some call them. These have no yellow in them like the stones from Zambia or Brazil, which are just about the only other places in the world you can get them. The Colombian emeralds have no competition really. Look at that color. Even uncut and unpolished all you see is pure green. That's one hell of a lot of money." Anaya picked up one of the larger stones. "Each one of these is at least twenty carats. Even if you lose thirty percent in cutting, which you do, in this rock alone you've got about twelve to fifteen carats." Anaya whistled again as he sifted through the stones. "With this kind of color, and that's what people buy them for, you're looking at the most expensive gem in the world. They can go for ten, maybe twenty thousand dollars a carat. The arithmetic in this implant adds up very fast."

But arithmetic was not of great interest to Stern at that moment. He looked back at Sharon's body. There were other cuts beneath both breasts. Intuitively, he reached out to touch the scar that was still visible beneath her breast. It was too long. It was the same scar he had seen on Melissa. And Luisa.

"You like doing that, Doctor?" said an unfamiliar voice.

Lionel pulled his hand back as though he had been touching fire. Anaya had been joined by a young, oval-faced man, with a police badge hanging from his shirt pocket. A shoulder holster neatly held a short-nosed .38 pistol.

"I think this woman and Rochelle Whitaker were killed by the same person," Lionel announced.

"What person?" the young man asked. "Is it possible you could be that person, Doctor?"

"Listen, my name is Lionel Stern. I am a plastic surgeon."

"I know. Dr. Anaya called me. I'm Lieutenant Perrino. We checked through the hospital switchboard. You seem, in my opinion, Doctor, to have all the right credentials."

"For what?"

Perrino lit a cigarette casually. "Murder."

"What the hell are you talking about?"

"I think the question is more accurately, what the hell are you talking about? For one thing you're not this woman's doctor like you said."

"How do you know?"

"We found a bottle of prescription drugs. Her doctor was Morrie Gold."

"I think you'll find he's more than her doctor."

"And what does that make you?"

Lionel was sweating profusely. "I want to talk to the police."

"That, Doctor, is exactly what we had in mind." Without any ceremony, Perrino slipped a pair of handcuffs on Lionel.

Sitting opposite him in a small room in police headquarters two floors above, Perrino read Lionel his rights and allowed the obligatory phone call. Instead of phoning his lawyer, Lionel had a call put through to Ellsworth Crawford.

"While you were on your way to the morgue," Perrino explained, "we did a priors on you." He shrugged. "Nothing came up."

"What were you expecting?" Lionel replied, clearly shaken.

Perrino smiled. "It would have been easier if you'd had a string of priors and were wanted for murder in six or seven states." A weak laugh.

"This isn't funny, and I don't appreciate being hand-cuffed and brought in here for questioning."

Perrino nodded. Lionel half expected an apology. He was unprepared for what followed. "That's tough. I've got another dead woman downstairs and some swank plastic surgeon says he's her doctor but isn't."

"There was no need for handcuffs."

"Doctor, in case you didn't notice, this is not the Bel Air Country Club. Now maybe you'll tell us what you were looking for and why you decided to spend your evening at the morgue instead of one of those fancy restaurants where they serve spaghetti without tomato sauce."

Lionel leaned forward across the table. "I don't have to tell you anything."

The detective leaned close to Lionel and spoke softly. "Strictly off the record, Doctor, what have you guys got against a little friendly tomato sauce?"

There was no reason not to tell Perrino what he knew, but the detective's next question was "Doctor, have you ever heard of a woman named Luisa Obregon?"

Suddenly Lionel was glad he hadn't said anything. He would have to be careful not to implicate Luisa in any way. But after years of dealing with patients who often asked questions just to hear *how* he answered rather than *what* he answered, Lionel sensed that Perrino already had consider-able information. "Yes. I met her at a party."

There was a pause. "That it?" Perrino said. "Where else did you meet her? L'Orangerie? The Beverly Hills Hotel?"

Lionel was stunned to realize that he had been followed. "Why the hell don't you question Dr. Gold instead of me?"

Perrino slammed his fist on the table. "Because I have no reason to suspect Dr. Gold of anything. He didn't lie to us. He didn't show up at the morgue, looking for something. But I sure as hell would like to know why you wanted us to think that Sharon White was your patient. What were you looking for tonight, Doctor?"

Perrino sat down on the edge of the table. "And I want to know what you've been looking for with Luisa Obregon."

Very slowly, Lionel told them all about Melissa Eckhart.

As he explained what he saw when he cut open the implants, Perrino pushed his foot against a chair and sent it across the room.

"That's how she did it!" Perrino whispered. "Emeralds!"

"Not *she!*" Lionel said. "*He!* It was Morrie Gold. The son of a bitch is smuggling emeralds and cocaine—"

"Coke?" Perrino asked. "C'mon, Doc, there isn't much room inside one of those implants, is there?"

"You've got to know Morrie Gold," Lionel said with resignation, "with that greedy son of a bitch every little bit counts. There was extra space between the stones. It was cocaine paste and he used it like a packing material. It comes from Colombia like the emeralds. And it was worth a lot of money. He just didn't plan on it leaking out of the implant."

"Is that what you think happened to the girl at the hospital? That—what's her name—Melissa?"

"I'm certain of it. She had no idea what was happening to her. No one did. I sure as hell didn't," Stern said quite slowly. "There was a slow leak of the cocaine into her body. The smallest of holes would have been enough to give her an overdose. There was most likely a tear in the implant, caused by the stones rubbing together. The implants with the cocaine and emeralds were supposed to be removed and replaced by real implants after three weeks. If everything had gone according to Morrie Gold's plan, none of this would have happened. No one would have died . . . or been killed." Stern sat back. "None of the people involved knew what was going on. The women thought they were participating in medical research and getting free surgery in return."

The detectives looked at him, weighing what he was saying. "Don't you understand?" Lionel continued. "He's been using Luisa Obregon as a front. She's a devoted person, a fund-raiser for his clinic down there, and Gold has taken advantage of her," Lionel pleaded. "On top of that, there are people in Bogotá who follow her every move because she's involved with him. Her life has been a living hell."

Perrino nodded his head slowly. "Very interesting observations, Doctor. Are you absolutely certain about the cocaine?"

"I took the implants out of the pathology department and took them apart. The white paste is being checked out at the hospital toxicology lab right now."

"You have both implants there?"

"Yes. Locked up in my office."

"We will need the stones as evidence."

"To hell with the emeralds!" Lionel shouted. "Why don't you get Morrie Gold?"

# 54

Oɴ ʜɪs ᴡᴀʏ back from the beach house, Morrie stopped in at a car showroom on Wilshire. It was time to trade up from the Mercedes. After all, considering how much he had paid Janet for something that went up in smoke, he shouldn't think twice about spending a few dollars on something more permanent.

On the spot, Morrie bought a white Bentley that had once belonged to Clark Gable. The salesman who recognized Morrie from his ads never knew what hit him. Morrie named his own price, saying he'd be back in the morning with cash, and even got them to put in a full tank of gas. Premium. Which was what it was all about. Getting a little extra out of life. Enjoying yourself. Treating yourself well.

It was while estimating how many face-lifts and eyelid surgeries it would take to pay off the Bentley that Morrie began thinking of ways to increase business, create new markets. He had decided to give up rhinoplasty as being too unpredictable. His first thought was family discounts on facial surgery—all those women who complained they had inherited ugly features must have sisters and daughters with the same problem. As he thought about the formulation of a "mother-daughter special," it occurred to him that Stephanie probably wouldn't have turned into such a neurotic mess if she'd had the surgery when she was much younger. Her entire personality might have been different if she hadn't been so unattractive during the formative years. And then it came to Morrie: his next series of ads would go after the teen market. Why should all those kids have to go through high school feeling rejected?

Morrie couldn't wait to call his ad rep. He parked the car in front of the Institute and went into the office. The answering machine was blinking. Before even turning on the lights, he pressed PLAY.

"This is Dr. Loomis again at University Hospital. I was calling to see if Dr. Gold is back yet. I'm trying to finish up the autopsy report on Melissa Eckhart and would appreciate his getting back to me. The number is . . ."

Morrie stopped the tape, pressed rewind and, his heart beating rapidly, replayed the tape. "This is Dr. Loomis again at University Hospital . . ." An autopsy on Melissa spelled potential disaster. He switched on the light and sat down, staring into space, wondering whether Luisa knew what he now knew.

"I called Dr. Loomis back."

Morrie jumped. Mrs. Evans was sitting in the dark. "Elise? What the hell are you doing here?"

She didn't move or acknowledge his question. Her voice was flat. "He told me that Melissa had gone to see a Doctor Stern—"

"Lionel Stern?" Morrie had that feeling in the pit of his stomach, the little boy being caught doing something naughty.

"No one seems to know why poor Melissa died."

"Did he say anything about the implants?"

Mrs. Evans ignored Morrie's questions. "Dr. Loomis said he had spoken to your nurse—but I wasn't here. I had, as you instructed, canceled all appointments and had gone to the lab. I assume he spoke to Señora Obregon."

Morrie thought about Luisa and Lionel together, wondering whether Luisa had been responsible for Melissa seeing Lionel, wondering whether the news of Melissa's death had driven Luisa closer to Lionel. The permutations and combinations on how it happened seemed endless, but he was more concerned with the only conclusion he could reach: they had decided to cut him out.

"On the way to the lab I had the radio on in my car."

Mrs. Evans spoke as though in a trance. "They announced there had been another 'slasher' killing. Another flight attendant. I expected they were talking about Melissa. Thank God I had stopped the car. I was waiting to make a turn when they said her name was Sharon White."

"Sharon?" He put a hand to his head.

"Dr. Gold," she said without a trace of emotion, "I demand to know what is going on."

Morrie stood up with such force that he overturned his chair. "Shut up!" he shouted. "Shut up! Shut up! Shut up!" He was yelling as much at his own thoughts as he was at Evans. He had to find Luisa. What the hell was that bitch doing? Had she gone mad?

Morrie rushed to the door, then stopped abruptly, turned and ran up the stairs to his bedroom. He opened the top drawer of his dresser where there were neat stacks of sweaters. He reached into the depths, pulled out a .9-mm Beretta and placed it into his belt. He buttoned his coat, ran down the stairs and slammed the door behind him. The motor started hard. Those bastards! He'd kill them if they forgot to put in a full tank!

# 55

"Y OU'RE FREE TO go, Doctor." Detective Perrino unlocked the door to the holding cell. "But not too far."

After only half an hour behind bars, Lionel was itching to run. But instead of imagining himself in the stadium, he was running down the path at the Beverly Hills Hotel toward Luisa's bungalow. He was convinced she had to know what was going on. As Lionel walked into the day room, Ellsworth grabbed hold of him.

"Who the hell is Luisa Obregon?" he asked.

Ignoring the question, Lionel shook Ellsworth's hand. "Thanks for getting me out of here."

"Don't thank me. Casey did it. You don't think I want the hospital lawyers knowing about this if they don't have to."

"I didn't do anything."

"Who is Luisa Obregon?"

"It doesn't matter. Ellsworth, I've got to go."

But Ellsworth hung on to him. "It mattered to Casey. You should have seen her. She marched in here with Soltano to get you out of this, and I'm telling you she had a look in her eyes that could have saved Marie Antoinette from the guillotine. Until—until she heard what you were up to with this woman."

"Why would any of that be discussed?"

"Because Soltano wanted to know what they had on you. The poor son of a bitch wanted to protect his case against Morrie Gold, but you took care of that all right. After your

273

playing footsie with this woman of his, you can take your 'unbiased' testimony against Gold and flush it!"

"What did they tell Casey?"

"Enough."

Lionel felt as though he had run right into himself. He had chased and chased for miles only to run out of track. Now, more than ever, he had to find Luisa. But there was one thing he had to do first.

"Where is Casey?"

"She's waiting for me in the car. She didn't particularly want to see you."

Lionel clasped Ellsworth's hand again. "Give me a minute with her."

"It's your funeral, Lionel . . ."

When he got to the parking lot, Lionel saw Casey sitting in the passenger seat of Ellsworth's car. She was staring into space and didn't notice as he came alongside her.

"I'm sorry," he said, leaning down to the open window.

She didn't bat an eye. Or even turn toward him. "How could you do that to me? I trusted you."

"Casey, it has nothing to do with trust. You rejected me, you kept pushing me away. What was I supposed to do?"

She turned to him for the first time. "I really thought we had a chance, Lion. I thought the good guys were finally going to win. And now I feel like such a fool."

"If it's any consolation, I do too. I can't even pretend to understand what happened, but I never meant to hurt you."

"Oh, Lion, how in hell am I going to get Morrie now?"

He wasn't certain he'd heard right. "Morrie? You're talking about Morrie? I thought you were talking about us!"

Casey narrowed her eyes and hesitated before she spoke, as though stifling a cry. "Us? Is there no limit to that goddamn ego of yours? I suppose you think I'm sitting here like a wounded prom queen whose boyfriend made a pass at some overripe femme fatale?"

"Jesus."

Casey opened the door, enraged, and got out of the car. "This Luisa Obregon of yours must be some piece of work. I guess she's the kind of woman you've always wanted."

Lionel shook his head and turned away. There was no way to deal with Casey now. He headed for his car. She followed.

"Tell me all about it, Lion. Tell me how she makes you feel like the sun rises and sets around you. How she doesn't have a career that competes with yours. How she's going to make you her whole life." As Lionel opened his car door and got in, Casey bent down to the window. She was yelling now. "Tell me how she's all woman. Tell me how she's better than I am. I want to hear it. Goddamn it, you bastard, tell me!"

Lionel started the motor. He looked at Casey through the closed window. He wanted to get out of the car, take her in his arms and erase Luisa from both their minds. But he couldn't. Instead, he shifted into gear, then stopped to open the window. "Casey, I'm sorry. What do you want me to say?"

Her face covered with tears, Casey leaned over and spoke softly. "I want you to say you missed me. Lion, . . . Will you marry me?"

The moment she said it, Casey put a hand to her mouth, stepped away, then covered her face as she began to sob. Lionel saw Ellsworth hurrying toward Casey. He put the car in reverse and pulled back slowly. There was no time to lose, he had to find Luisa. There was too much going on, too much unfinished business, too much danger and entirely too much he didn't understand.

# 56

LIONEL STERN PULLED into the driveway of the
Beverly Hills Hotel much too fast, the brakes bringing his
car to a squealing halt. He opened the car door and was on
his feet before the motor had stopped completely. He
shouted to the valet in a commanding voice, "Leave it
there. This is an emergency. I'll be right out."

The lobby was quiet, emptying out for the night. He
passed the Polo Lounge, a sudden blast of noise when
someone turned on a radio, then out the exit and along the
cement path through the dense foliage of the courtyard to
Bungalow 5. He rapped sharply on the door. "Luisa! Luisa!
Are you in there?"

"Go away." Her voice was flat, with a harsh quality he
had never heard before.

"Are you all right? Open up."

"I'm not feeling well. Please go away."

"Luisa, I must see you. Open the door. Are you alone?"

"Tomorrow. I'll call you tomorrow."

Lionel stepped back, then buried his shoulder into the
door. Reluctantly, the door gave way, and the momentum
carried him stumbling into the room.

Luisa was standing completely composed and erect.
Dressed in a gray suit, her hair knotted at the back of her
head, she was a caricature of executive poise. There was an
open valise on the bed.

"Call me? From where?" Lionel asked as he appraised

the room. The lights in the room were dim, but he noticed she kept one side of her face away from him.

"Get out! Damn you! Leave me alone!"

Lionel reached for her and pushed her toward the light. She put a hand to her face, and he saw the bruises and four red parallel lines that coursed obliquely across her left cheek. "My God! What happened to you?"

"Please go away!"

"Morrie!" The name came out as a growl. "It . . . was . . . Morrie, wasn't it?"

Luisa hesitated, then dropped her head away from him wearily. She looked back at him. "Of course. Yes, it was Morrie." She spoke rapidly, suddenly dramatic, as though performing. "He wanted me to have dinner with him. I told him I couldn't. He flew into a rage when I mentioned your name."

"Bastard." The word was recognizable only from the force of inflection.

"I've never seen him that way. He threw me to the floor, calling me obscene names. I wanted to call you, but I didn't want you to see me this way." She put her arms around him. "It was horrible. He was a madman. I thought he was going to kill me."

"It's lucky he didn't. Do you know what's happened? Do you know about Melissa and Sharon?"

"Who?"

"Two more flight attendants are dead. Both Morrie's patients. He has been using them to smuggle emeralds out of Bogotá."

"What?"

"I opened the implants. I saw them."

Luisa stepped back and stared at Lionel. Unbelieving.

He had to convince her. "I have the emeralds locked up in my office."

She stood for the briefest moment immobile, then stepped toward him, wrapping her arms around him tightly. "Oh, Lionel, the things Morrie has done. You must help me get away . . . from him."

"Come with me to the hospital. I'm afraid for you.

You're a walking time bomb. There have been too many deaths. I don't want you to be next."

"Whatever you say. Yes, your office, I'll be safe at the hospital."

Lionel drove well within the speed limit, not wanting to risk being stopped. It was nearly midnight when they reached the hospital. They went directly to his office. He opened the door and switched on the lights.

"Good evening." Morrie was sitting in a chair, waiting.

"What the hell are you doing here?"

Gold ignored Lionel. "Well, Luisa, my dear, it seems our girl has had a busy, busy day."

Lionel walked to the phone. "I'm going to call Security—"

"No!" Luisa's voice was a command.

As Lionel turned to her, she reached into her purse and pulled out a gun, the silencer already in place.

Morrie sat up straight, the smile instantly disappearing from his lips. "Don't be stupid, Luisa," he said, calmly reaching into his jacket.

"That is one word, Morris, that you of all people should never use." She took a single step forward, aiming the gun at him. Morrie froze. Her movements were so fluid and balanced that they appeared to be taking place in slow motion. As soon as he saw the gun, Lionel, acting out of reflex, struck her arm. He did so just as she pulled the trigger. There was an unusual, very loud hissing noise and Morrie Gold's left cheek exploded into a mass of red flesh. But he too was in motion. He fell forward, and as Lionel struggled with Luisa for control of the gun, Gold stumbled to his feet and ran out of the office.

The struggle was over quickly: agility triumphed easily over strength. In a motion much like an Olympic diver, Luisa twisted and rolled and gracefully stood up, the gun pointed directly at Lionel. His face was pale and gaunt, filled with a look of horror and disbelief. For him, out of confusion, chaos had suddenly emerged. "Lionel, please, where are the emeralds?" Her voice was now calm and sweet, and in contrast to Lionel's rapid breathing she appeared relaxed. "I don't want to shoot you, but too many people have already died. Even people who should never have."

It suddenly occurred to Lionel that Peter had been killed immediately after filling in for Morrie at his clinic.

"Oh my god. Peter . . ."

"Perhaps. Please, the emeralds. I only want what is rightfully mine."

Lionel's heart was pounding from fear that this beautiful woman would shoot him any moment and aching with the knowledge that she was responsible for Peter's death. Nothing surprised him any longer. It all seemed so real, and he now seemed so numb to it all. Even Luisa, gun in hand—and shooting Morrie, the emeralds—all seemed perfectly logical, as if he had come in on the middle of a movie and was able to follow the plot perfectly.

He walked over to the desk, unlocked the drawer and placed the envelope filled with emeralds on the desk.

"You are an attractive man, Lionel, physically at least. But you are no doubt the most naive person I have ever met. It is a weakness, and it makes me sick." Once again he heard the strange explosion and then felt a sharp pain in his right chest. His entire body, as though pushed by someone, turned around, and he was suddenly very cold. He heard the crinkle of paper as Luisa took the envelope from his hand. And then it was very dark.

Luisa walked quickly out of the office, trying to look as inconspicuous as possible. It was after midnight and the hospital was almost deserted. She paced herself, careful not to rush down the corridor and draw attention. Rather than walk through the main entrance, she would take the elevator down to the parking level. The problem was finding a car to get out of there. At worst, she would walk into Westwood and call a taxi.

She took each step as though counterpointing the beat of her own heart. For a moment, she thought she heard it beating. But what she heard were footsteps behind her. It took all her dancer's discipline not to quicken her pace. There was no telling who it might be. Step. Step. Step.

Suddenly she felt something sharp in her back. And then the voice of Morrie Gold. "The stairs, Luisa, my dear." He jabbed his gun into her back, leading her past the elevator to the stairwell. "Now it's my turn." As Luisa opened the door, she glanced over her shoulder. The left side of Morrie's cheek looked like raw hamburger, and blood was streaming down his neck.

Her mouth grew dry; her mind tried to process the information. How could she get away? He grabbed hold of her arm and she gasped. He walked behind her as they went down the steps. Intuitively, she absorbed the cadence of their moves, translating each step into an inner rhythm, a rhythm she could anticipate and subtly control with each step she took. Once Luisa felt the beat each time she raised and lowered her foot, and knew that he was keeping time with her, she waited until they reached the top of the next landing. Down one step, down two steps, and then—never moving her body to alert him—she raised her left foot higher and slid it momentarily around his leg, throwing him off balance. In the split second she had while he fell, she jumped over the railing to the next set of steps and out the door into a basement corridor. Two laboratory technicians, their backs to her, walked down the corridor toward the elevator.

"They probably have macaroni again today," the short one groaned.

"The macaroni isn't as bad as the Spanish rice. I hear they make the stuff upstairs in one of the chemistry labs."

While they waited for the elevator, Luisa walked softly in the other direction and turned into the room they had just left. She closed the door behind her, leaning back for a moment to catch her breath. And then Luisa saw the body.

On an aluminum table directly in front of her was the naked blue-white body of a handless, footless man who had been sawed in half vertically—from the groin to the top of his head. The halves lay open like a split lobster. Bloodless. There were splinters of bone and shreds of skin on the buzzsaw between his legs. She put both hands to her mouth, turning away to find that the room had rows of large open metal shelves on which cross sections of body parts had been encased in plastic cubes like monstrous paperweights. Heads. Hands. Feet. A shoulder. An eye.

In the corner was a large tub filled with hot clear liquid styrene, circulated by a pump so that it would not solidify. Clouds of steam gusted off the surface of the liquid as it swirled in a circular pattern. Various-size molds—cubes and rectangles—were piled up against one wall. The metal shelves were marked, like a library index, by subject: Comparative Anatomy, Skeletal, Neuro, Pediatric.

Footsteps. Luisa slipped behind one of the shelves as the door opened slowly. It was Morrie, a trickle of blood still coming down his cheek. He stepped into the room, pistol in his hand raised to fire. Luisa reached into her purse for her gun. She waited for him to catch sight of the man on the table, waiting for him to be distracted. At that precise moment, Luisa stood erect and fired.

Morrie dropped to the floor behind one of the tables. But then he called out, "I told you we were a perfect match. We are both fighters. But it still remains to be seen which one of us is the tougher."

Luisa couldn't tell whether she had hit him or not. She waited for a sound. But there was nothing. Quietly, she took off her shoes and began to walk in his direction. A bullet hit a sectioned skull imbedded in styrene on the shelf just above her and shattered it into a shower of glasslike pieces. She stopped.

"Give me the emeralds, you leave. We can both be winners in the game," Morrie said.

She tried following the voice but it was no use.

Luisa looked out from behind the shelves, staring into lifeless heads without eyes, trying to find a hint of movement that would lead her to the prey.

"You made the transformation from smuggler to killer so quickly and so easily." His voice came from behind her. Luisa turned, but still she couldn't see him.

Luisa eased herself around to the other side of the metal

shelving, careful not to make a sound. She held onto the edges of the shelves as her eyes searched through the open spaces. As her fingers moved along the metal, she suddenly felt something and looked down. It was a man's hand. From the corpse on the table. She made a gasping sound.

Morrie was suddenly standing at the end of the aisle. Smiling. His gun raised. "It is a simple matter, my dear. In the long run, I don't lose."

Luisa reached slowly into her bag and held out the envelope with the emeralds. Morrie motioned her to come closer. She advanced toward him, shaking the envelope so that he could hear the stones.

"Put the gun down, Luisa," he warned.

Luisa held out the envelope, just barely out of reach. She nodded but, instead of putting the gun down, fired directly at his chest. Morrie staggered back but then lunged forward toward Luisa, grabbing the envelope from her. Infuriated, she fired again, this time directly into his groin. He stumbled backward, both hands between his legs, and screamed as he fell into the tub of hot styrene. Luisa ran to him, watching in horror as the emeralds floated out of the envelope and down into the thick viscous liquid.

Morrie Gold's last breath formed a round bubble that could not escape the plastic.

# 57

LIONEL REACHED FOR the black cord, tugging at it until the phone fell to the floor, grazing his head. He held his lower chest tightly, breathing rapidly. Hearing the tone, he used his other hand to dial the emergency code. "Yes, Doctor?"

"Six . . . oh . . . eight," he whispered.

"Can you speak up, Doctor?"

"Six . . . oh . . . eight," he grunted. "Gunshot . . ."

"Dr. Stern, I can't hear you. Is everything all right?"

Lionel dropped the phone and collapsed on the floor. Moments later the door to the office burst open and an ER team was kneeling down beside him, administering a mask of oxygen while checking the extent of his wound.

"Casey," he whispered.

"You'll be fine, Doctor. Doesn't look as though it hit any organs. Just lie back and stop trying to talk."

Lionel shook his head. "Call . . . Casey."

"Call Casey," one of the nurses repeated. "Casey who?"

"Tell . . . her . . ."

"Doctor, try not to talk." They lifted Lionel onto a stretcher. He waved his hand to get their attention. "Casey . . ."

"Yes, Doctor," she said humoring him, "we'll call Casey."

"Tell . . . her . . ."

"I'll tell her," the nurse repeated as she tried to put the oxygen mask over his face.

With as much strength as he could muster, Lionel pushed the mask aside. "Tell . . . her . . . yes."

Perrino and another detective talked to Lionel in his room at University Hospital. They allowed Casey to stay. She sat at his bedside, next to two water-filled bottles connected to a red rubber tube that went into Lionel's right chest. The water bubbled each time he took a deep breath, but, as Casey noticed, in the three hours since he had come back from the operating room the bubbling had progressively diminished, indicating that the hole caused by the bullet tearing through the right lung was beginning to seal nicely.

Lionel spoke in short words and only occasional phrases, limited by the pain caused by the lung rubbing against the tube as it inflated with each breath.

Everyone stopped to watch when the evening news came on the television mounted on the wall opposite Lionel's bed. The death of Morrie Gold was the lead story, coupled with Lionel's having been shot. The announcer mentioned that Gold had experienced difficulty with the BMQA and that his license had been suspended, but constantly referred to him as the "prominent and well-known plastic surgeon"— the kind of notoriety Morrie had always sought.

The connection with the smuggling of cocaine and emeralds was mentioned, but only briefly. Police informants had uncovered that a large transfer of emeralds was about to take place and represented a means to convert cash earned from drug sales into a small, valuable commodity that could easily be transported and, once cut into smaller stones, impossible to trace.

It was the second time in his life that Lionel had been shot. It was the second time that his chest had been perforated by a bullet. This time, there was no mud. No dust. No jungle. But despite the infinitely more secure environment, the second injury was far more painful because Peter Dalway wasn't there to fix it.

There was a gentle knock on the door as it opened. "Doctor Stern? Hi! It's me, Stephanie. I wanted to deliver these personally." She tiptoed into the room as if someone would wake at the sounds made by her feet. In her hand was a small flower bouquet. She pointed to her nose and lifted her chin. Then she turned to show him her profile. It was a proud maneuver, accompanied by a small dance step.

Lionel laughed and then coughed, making the bottles bubble like a fountain.

"I'm sorry. My father said not to stay long. I just wanted to make rounds on my doctor."

As Stephanie backed out of the room, she almost knocked over a young boy about nine years old who was waiting outside.

"Is Doctor Stern inside?" Felix whispered.

"Yes," Stephanie replied, "but I think he's very tired."

"Yeah, I know. Chest wounds are usually like that," Felix explained, his face serious and professional. "He'll be a lot better in the morning. I'll come back then. You a friend of his?"

"No. Not exactly. I'm his patient."

"Oh, yeah? What for? You're so pretty already," the wide-eyed boy said, scrutinizing her.

"Oh, thank you," Stephanie replied, after a momentary pause. "Thank you very much. When you see Doctor Stern in the morning, be sure to tell him what you said," Stephanie said with a beaming smile.

# 58

"I DON'T WISH to be impolite, Señora Obregon, but we had made detailed arrangements for a much larger transaction." Lu's usually polite voice had a hard edge. "I needn't remind you that it is no easy matter to gather the amounts of cash we previously discussed. In order to obtain this sum, I am now in the debt of several other businessmen, not to mention the plans that were already made to move the merchandise you promised when we first established our mutual arrangement. I am disappointed."

"I appreciate that, but in such situations we don't always have complete control, do we?" Luisa replied as firmly as she could.

"What is your wish?"

"To exchange some selected stones for cash."

"Señora Obregon, I am . . . aware of the recent events that have been reported on the news. You have stones available?"

"Yes," she replied.

"I am surprised, but then again, happy of course for your good fortune. May I inquire as to the estimated amount of the transaction?"

"No less than five hundred thousand dollars," Luisa replied quickly.

"That, unfortunately, is but a fraction of the amount we had planned."

"I am aware of that. This represents all I own in the world

286

and has taken a great deal of effort, not to mention risk, to obtain," Luisa said. "I have encountered some difficulties."

"Yes, as I said, I listen to the news. It is fortunate that you have some . . . reserve assets."

"I consider all contingencies."

"Will you be returning to Colombia?"

"Never."

"Then we can set an appointment sometime next week?"

"That is impossible. You know very well that I must proceed immediately."

"But that may pose some logistical problems. It will be necessary to confirm the value of the stones. They must be examined."

"They are a bargain at that price."

"However . . . considering the hasty circumstances . . ."

"That is something that can be discussed when they are examined. The circumstances may be hasty. Nevertheless, the value is there."

"Under usual circumstances, Señora, negotiations between buyer and seller are a matter of course. But as I have already explained, we have already gone to extraordinary lengths and some expense. There must be some compensation for the unorthodox nature of this transaction," Lu said, as if any further discussion would be superfluous. "I suggest we meet at the same restaurant."

"I would prefer somewhere else."

"Señora Obregon, from my perspective this appears to be a buyer's market. Yet, the seller—"

"Any airport hotel of your choice," Luisa interjected quickly.

"As you wish. The Sheraton Hotel in two hours. The room will be reserved under the name of Mr. Lester Ching."

Luisa hung up the phone, examined her new passport and adjusted the position of her .9-mm automatic pistol in the corner of her purse, releasing the safety. She then called a cab.

"Señora! My apologies!" Lu exclaimed with as much emotion as he had ever displayed. "The difficulty at the door was simply due to the fact that neither I nor my security staff recognized you at first. A new look indeed. Short hair becomes you and the light color only enhances the beauty of your face. Yes," Lu said in final appraisal, "it all becomes you. And I'm sure it will turn out to be very . . . convenient. Even after working with you for so many years, you never cease to amaze me."

"Yes, it has been a long, and I hope mutually beneficial, relationship," Luisa said cheerfully, as she sat down on a chair, trying to establish an atmosphere as friendly as possible. She was careful to choose a chair whose back faced a wall. "I have always provided you with the finest of merchandise."

"This is true," Lu replied, still studying her. "And I hope we, on the other hand, have provided the very best in service. You were correct, I am sure, that when we established our association, your husband was taking unfair advantage. His unfortunate death was managed with great care and dispatch."

"And you were paid with dispatch and . . . great care," Luisa added politely, with a hint of sarcasm.

"And the man who followed you last week—"

"Mr. Lu, let us get down to business." Luisa took a small leather change bag from her purse, turned it upside down, and twenty irregular-shaped green stones tumbled onto a small square of black felt that already lay on the table in front of her. Five in the group were the size of walnuts. The remainder were the size of children's marbles. Most were roughly rectangular and appeared to be merely common rock on some sides. However, all of the stones had several surfaces that sparkled with a deep and brilliant green color.

Lu sat down at the table and picked up the stones one at a time, examining each against the light from the open window with a small eyepiece lens. The process was quickly done. As he went, he separated the stones into two piles, one much larger than the other. One of his staff examined the larger pile as he set them down. They exchanged comments in Chinese as they worked.

"You had promised twenty large stones of exceptional quality. Only five of these fit that description."

"You are correct." Luisa hesitated before continuing. "I will be able to deliver the rest at a later date. They're . . . not immediately available."

"It seems our agreement means little to you," he said, as though delivering a harsh reprimand. Then a practiced smile cracked through his hard facade as he pointed to the gems on the table. "Out of respect for our long relationship, I will not bargain with you as one haggles in a market. Our offer is quite firm, Señora. Three hundred thousand."

"That is a fraction of the price we used in our exchange last week!" Luisa looked at the passive man with a cold gaze.

"That was last week. An eternity in our business. Moreover, we have only a fraction of what was promised. Unlike you, I cannot conduct business in a vacuum. I must have something to sell. My work is just now beginning." Lu motioned to one of the other men. "We have the money in new bills. Three hundred thousand dollars. Two hundred thousand is in one-thousand-dollar denominations. I would suggest redeeming them in a foreign country. We have found the Cayman Islands convenient for such matters. The other one hundred thousand is in small denominations that can be negotiated anywhere and will cover your travel expenses." Lu handed her a small canvas bag. "You can inspect each strap. We have made every effort to consider all contingencies on your behalf."

"How about the contingency of paying me what these stones are worth? You know very well that at least eight of these roughs are more than fifteen carats."

"In the cutting we will lose at least thirty percent of the original rough."

"That's basic. You knew that from the beginning."

"Perhaps . . . if we had more time to examine them, we could adjust our offer upward. Slightly. But considering the—"

Luisa smiled in resignation, then stood up and extended her hand. "Very well."

"We have arranged for a car to take you wherever you wish," Lu said with a slight bow.

"You are too kind, but I have made arrangements. And, if I am not there in"—she looked at her watch—"a few minutes, they will come here. So I must leave." Luisa reached into the canvas bag, took out three rectangular packages and wrapped them in a red-and-blue-patterned scarf that she put in the depths of her purse. Her hand remained within the purse, her fingers fitting comfortably around the handle of the pistol. "I have only a short way to go. Thank you." Luisa bowed ever so slightly, sidestepping across the room, always facing the three men.

In front of the hotel the traffic on Century Boulevard moving toward the airport was not heavy at two o'clock in the afternoon. The sound of the approaching jets, just overhead, one hundred and fifty yards from touchdown, was loud. There were no taxis waiting, as they usually were at the entrance. A hotel van was unloading passengers, their suitcases and bags stacked in large piles. Suddenly a bright yellow cab knifed through the line of cars and pulled up in front of Luisa.

"Airport?" Luisa asked. The driver nodded.

As soon as she got in, the taxi exploded away, throwing Luisa back against the seat. The driver navigated wildly, veering away just inches from the first car he encountered. The taxi lunged to the right, now speeding along Sepulveda Boulevard, turning away from the main entrance to the airport. Two blocks flashed by Luisa's window as the driver wound through a series of short streets and entered a large open area adjacent to the far reaches of the runways.

Reacting to the havoc that had so abruptly surrounded her, Luisa reached for the pistol. But the taxi's lurching movements had thrown her purse to the floor. Luisa reached for the door handle, but it was firmly locked.

The brakes screeched loudly. Just before the car stopped, the driver suddenly turned to face Luisa, pointing a shotgun directly at her. She noticed for the first time that he was Asian.

"Your purse, Mrs. Obregon. And don't open it," the driver commanded.

Luisa did as she was told.

The driver removed the scarf-covered money and then the pistol. He ejected the full clip of ammunition and hurled it out the window. He then returned the purse to Luisa, tucking the money inside his shirt.

"Considering the manner in which you conduct business, we are being more than generous allowing you to keep your life. Your ticket is in the purse." The driver unlocked the door and motioned for Luisa to get out.

# 59

LUISA SANK BACK into the plush upholstery of her First Class seat and ran her fingers through her new blond hair, wondering how much time it would take before she would be comfortable with the look. Oddly enough, with all that had gone on in the last twenty-four hours, it was just about the only thing she felt *uncomfortable* about. For a woman who had just been robbed of $300,000 she was surprisingly secure and optimistic. By the time she landed in Geneva, she would feel even better.

Part of her satisfaction was derived from a vision of Morrie Gold imbedded in plastic. She had battled with that pompous mass of ego for what seemed an eternity. And now there he was, appropriately displayed to the world, a grotesque art form.

She looked out her window at the billowy clouds below, imagining her flight to Geneva as more than a passage. It was a rebirth. A journey to the heavens and then a new life.

She folded her arms against her chest, discreetly feeling the borders of her own breast implants. Pressing harder, she felt a rush of pleasure and her nipples became hard as she imagined identifying the irregular outlines of the large stones. She rubbed even harder and thought she felt the click of raw emeralds against each other. She closed her eyes, continuing the satisfying motion until she felt a momentary flash of pain. But it passed in an instant. Given Lu's recent betrayal, she was glad she had the foresight to keep the finest stones hidden safely inside her. How she had argued with Morrie about having that special insurance. But as always, she had won. It was now her security.

Luisa drifted off to sleep, but within a few moments abruptly returned to an alert state of magnificent clarity. She hadn't slept in two days, but Luisa felt no sense of fatigue. Instead, within the minutes that followed, her nerves became painfully raw. She asked the stewardess for some champagne, taking deep breaths to calm herself. She consumed the small glass in a single gulp and asked for another. And then another. Her hands began to shake with a fine tremor. Nerves, she told herself. So much had gone on. But she had triumphed.

Luisa looked out the window and surveyed the clouds once again, realizing as she did that she was beginning to have double vision. Then there was a slight numbness in her hand that made it difficult to grasp the glass.

"Are you feeling all right, miss?"

Luisa smiled at the flight attendant. "Thank you. Yes," she said, suddenly aware that her skin was covered with a heavy layer of perspiration. She reached for her mirror, but her hands were now trembling. It took several minutes to open the zipper on her handbag. She was horrified by what she saw. The skin on her face was bloodless, gaunt. Her eyes hollow and dark.

Luisa breathed deeply, trying to relax, but every muscle in her body began to ache. She spilled the champagne. Her arms started to shake uncontrollably, and she felt a chill penetrate into the deepest part of her body and then ricochet randomly outward. The involuntary spasms extended to her legs. Try as she might, it was impossible to control the contortions of her limbs. This loss of control made her sense of desperation all the more menacing. Every muscle in her body began to contract in agonizing spasms.

"Oh, my god, miss . . ."

Luisa didn't hear the attendant. Her head felt as though a knife had been thrust between her temples. Everything around her began to spin as a series of convulsions enveloped her body.

As she lost consciousness, she thought of Morrie Gold. That stupid, greedy bastard! She had considered all of the contingencies except one.